KATE WATSON

STRAWBERRY FIELDS FOR NEVER

To my sissy poos, without whom I barely could get through a day, let alone life.

(I mean, I could, but it would suck.)

I love you more than sour keys.

CHAPTER ONE

JANE

*W*hen the conference room door finally closes, I've chipped my manicure from rapping my finger-nails. I should have sprung for gels, but manicures in the West Loop area of Chicago are criminally expensive. I can hardly justify high-end nails when worry that we can't pay rent on the Jane & Co. offices keeps me up at night.

But today, all of that changes.

Ash gives me her patented apologetic smile as she drops to her chair. "Sorry, Jane!" she says in a voice so naturally sing-songy, mine sounds like a smoker's in comparison.

"No problem," I say brightly.

"No problem?" Parker, who's running today's meeting, arches an immaculately groomed eyebrow, a look that nearly makes me forget that, at five feet even, she's a full eight inches shorter than I am. After years of friendship, I can read Parker like a coupon book, and right now, her eyebrow is screaming, *Who are you and what did you do with Jane?*

1

Right. My best friends are in this room. They know me better than my family. When I didn't comment on Ash's perpetual tardiness, they knew something was up. Still, my bright response isn't the lie it would have been even last week.

Because after two years in business together—two years of clawing and struggling and scraping for every job—I have enormous news. News I apparently need to wait on, because Parker has recovered from my uncharacteristic display of chill and is already starting the meeting.

I'm almost annoyed by her efficiency.

"Ash, where are we with the McLadyPants account?" Parker asks.

I purposefully don't pick at my newly chipped nail. It's cool. I can totally sit here with my hands crossed on my lap and watch my friend present her finished ad while I pretend I don't have the hugest news ever. It's a testament to how good Ash is at her job that I laugh when we watch the ad on her tablet.

McLadyPants is an underwear company that doesn't take itself too seriously, as you can imagine from the name. They sell lingerie that neither look nor feel like torture devices, but what really sets them apart is their "Blanche Knows Best" line: granny underwear as comfortable as it is cute and with a decent cult following on social media. Unfortunately, their previous male-led marketing firm focused on the lingerie over the underwear, showing a fundamental misunderstanding of what women actually care about.

Comfort > sexiness for those keeping track at home.

We've been working on this account for months, and the efforts have paid off. Parker took one look at their revenue streams and identified marketing opportunities that the previous firm hadn't even considered. Millie used her history in buyer psychology to identify what McLadyPants's customers were really looking for (see: comfort over sexiness). Lou, well, Lou hung out with us and occasionally pulled her law degree off the shelf to help us with contracts … when she wasn't writing hit YouTube songs or going on caffeine and cookie runs. Meanwhile, Ash used her quirky marketing genius to craft an ad campaign as authentically female as it is funny, complete with a montage of women with inferior underwear trying to shift wedgies out during a board meeting/on a date/in front of a classroom/sitting on the bus, etc.

A calm, regal, Kate Winslet-inspired voiceover says things like, "Do you know the only thing worse than chasing a toddler with poop stuck to his shoe? Chasing a toddler with poop stuck to his shoe … while having a wedgie."

The ad is relatable and hilarious and perfect. We had to temper some of Ash's wilder ideas at first, but this one hit all the right notes. After we all clap, I'm practically bursting out of my granny undies with the need to tell them, but then they give their updates by department.

Ash explains about the McLadyPants launch, twirling a giant spiral of cinnamon brown hair around her finger and letting it bounce around her heart-shaped face as she speaks. She used to dye bright streaks in her hair but hasn't for the last few months. The natural look suits her just as well, but I can't help worrying that she stopped because of how much it costs.

Millie talks about her latest client meeting, and all I can think of are the threads pulling around her gray tweed heels. She hasn't bought a pair of new shoes in ages because she's still paying hospital bills, and she's wearing the shoes she has into the ground. She left private practice to start the firm with us two years ago, but I know she's started taking telehealth clients on the side.

Lou's recent YouTube fame means that she's the only person in this room not relying on me for her next meal. But I worry that I'm failing her by pulling her into our sphere at all. Watching her friends struggle hasn't been easy on her or her anxiety. She's offered a cash infusion more than once, but I would rather go bankrupt than take a penny from her.

And Parker. I ache just thinking about how much she's sacrificed to be here when she could be at one of a dozen Fortune 100 companies that were chomping at the bit to hire her after what happened with her last employer. The pain is even worse when I remember the payout she could have had but gave up.

And it's my fault. If I hadn't suggested we start the agency …

"Jane?" Parker looks at me. "What about you? Any updates?"

My earlier eagerness has dulled into something steadier and more determined. Yes, I'm excited, but more than that, I have a burning desire to fix things for my friends.

"Just a small one," I say. My friends all look at me curiously while our (thankfully unpaid) intern blinks her big eyes at me, waiting to take notes. My heart hammers in my chest and, in spite of myself, a grin spreads across my face. "We got the Sugar Maple Farms account."

You know that GIF that shows up when you search for "Happy Dance"? The one where Elaine from Seinfeld comes into Jerry's apartment and they all dance and scream with their hands in the air?

That.

It's the most gratifying thing I can imagine. Even Parker, who is the Queen of Composure, lets Ash pull her up and laughs as the rest of us scream and squeal together.

We've had some successes in our short two years, but all of our accounts have been small—a couple hundred thousand at the most. Each account attracts the next one, but we've needed a big company to take a chance on us. We've needed a break.

Sugar Maple Farms is that break. It's more than "that break." It's six times bigger than we ever dreamed "that break" could be. Ash jumps over and hugs me tight. Her curls get all up in my face, but I just laugh and squeeze her back. "Janie Jane! That's awesome! Hot Grandpa Carville knows a good thing when he sees it!"

"Are you talking about Jane or Jane & Co.?" our intern asks with a saucy wink. My grin falters as an ache forms in my throat. She can't know how much that joke stings.

Ash throws herself down in her conference chair and does a full spin, limbs splayed. "Both," she says.

"Mr. Carville is an almost eighty-year-old sweet Southern gentleman. And he was just as sweet with each of you when you all met him," I counter, hoping to head off the deep flush working its way across my cheeks. Millie catches my eye as I sit.

"He really is a sweetheart," she says in her ever-peacemaking way. "He told me he has a grandson he'd gladly marry off to any one of us, if we're interested."

"Wait up. You're telling me there's a *young* version of that man somewhere in the world? He looks like he stepped out of a Spaghetti Western, and I am here for it," Ash says, fanning herself. My friends had never even heard the term when we all met in our Intro to Marketing class freshman year. We were partnered together for a project and hit it off immediately. By sophomore year, we found a place together off campus, and we've all been roommates ever since.

"And if he does exist, I call dibs," I joke, trying to match their lightness.

"Girl, we all got that memo sophomore year when you put up that life-sized cutout of Clint Eastwood," Parker says, not exaggerating. I'm the resident movie buff, and I've taken my duties to educate them seriously. "Jane, this is *huge*. What does the job entail? Mr. Carville wasn't too big on details when he was out here last month. I thought for sure he'd pick some Good Ol' Boy firm down in South Carolina."

I'd wanted a little more time to let them scream in excitement before getting to the details. Because, honestly, the details make my stomach feel like it's dropping somewhere down around my left knee. "Well, first, I should let you know he didn't like our fees."

Ash rolls her eyes so hard, they take her head with them. "Ugh, what is it with dudes and trying to negotiate our rates?"

"I know, but in this case, it's working in our favor. He's agreed to pay us an additional 20 percent of the total fee. Upfront."

Screams.

Literal screams.

After her initial gasp, Millie squeezes her eyes closed in what looks like a prayer. Ash pounds her hands on the table, giggling like a maniac. And Parker ...

Crap. Parker's eyebrows are warring. Their lift reads excitement, but the tiny tremor in her left eye tells me that she senses a *but*. "Jane, why would he willingly pay us extra on a three-million-dollar account? Lou, have you looked at the contract yet?" Lou shakes her head. "What happens if we don't meet his measurables?"

I run a hand down my navy blazer and hold it over my stomach. "Funny enough, he didn't outline specific measurables. He said that we'd know it when we saw it, and he offered the upfront bonus as added incentive because it's such a big job. Amazing, right?"

"Dang skippy!" Ash says, pounding a fist on the conference table. But Millie's face is joining Parker's now. The two glance at each other before their eyes drill holes into my brain.

"Jane, what exactly does the job entail?" Millie talks as if I'm a rabbit she doesn't want to spook.

"Like I said, it's a full rebrand of Sugar Maple Farms. Even though they're one of the most recognizable names in the industry, they haven't updated their marketing in decades, not since they attempted to market fruit like it was nature's Doritos." They all wrinkle their noses like they smell something rotten. "It's essential that we keep the nostalgia of the brand while moving them into the twenty-first century."

"And?" Parker asks. I pretend I don't know what she's getting at, but my insides don't get the memo. "Jane. I have just as much of an MBA as you, in case you've forgotten. A rebrand of this magnitude is going to take all of our bandwidth. This isn't just a new website and logo with some social media outreach. He wants the entire label overhauled and the farm itself restored to its former hometown glory. We're talking events and multiple new revenue streams. This job is big enough that he's crazy to be throwing extra money at us. And to have zero measurables? What's the catch?"

My lips pull tightly into something that feels more grimace than grin. "No catch, exactly. More of an opportunity." My heart goes thu-da-thu-da-thu-da-thu-da-thu-da, and I'm suddenly afraid my friends may not consider this job to be the boon I think it is.

"And?" Parker repeats.

"And the job is going to be on site for an all-expenses paid stay on their farm just outside of the sleepy but beautiful town of Sugar Maple, South Carolina!"

The excitement in the room dies faster than a henchman in a Western.

"Jane Harrington, please tell me you didn't already sign that contract." I'm technically the CEO, but no one can put the fear in me like Parker can.

"I had to. He called me last night and made the offer, and he said that he needed our commitment immediately. He said his current caretaker would sabotage the deal if he found out, and he doesn't want that to happen. The 20 percent upfront was on condition that I sign it last night."

Parker's face is stone. "Why would he say that?"

"I don't know," I admit. "I should have asked, but he sounded so urgent and ..." I trail off, not saying the quiet part aloud. *We need the money. I was scared that if I didn't say yes, the jobs you were all talking about would be the last we'd ever get, and I would have failed every one of you. We wouldn't be able to afford the rent on this place, let alone on our loft. We would be dead broke, and I'm the only one in here who knows what that actually feels like. I can't do that to you guys.*

As always, Millie jumps in as mediator, her deep red hair casting a glow on her angelic face. "It's a huge opportunity. Career making, even. I can see why you took it."

"Millie's right. It makes sense." Parker says, though her support is dampened by her pinching the bridge of her nose. "Okay, so let's whiteboard this. With the McLadyPants launch next weekend and the accounts we're still on, we can do some backend work now and then go full bore on Sugar Maple Farms in the fall."

"So, there's kind of one more thing about the account," I say. Parker slams her eyes shut. "Mr. Carville wants us down there in two weeks or there's no deal."

In my head, when I was telling my friends about how I'd single-handedly saved the company and, by extension, all of them, I imagined very different reactions. Jumps for joy, tears of gratitude, hugs of relief.

What I'm met with instead is mouths wide open in hurt, heads cocked in bewilderment, eyebrows knitted together in anger.

And that's how I come to be sitting in the Columbia, South Carolina airport two weeks later, waiting for a car from Sugar Maple Farms to pick me up.

All alone.

CHAPTER TWO

JANE

*T*hirty minutes later, I'm still waiting. The airport isn't big. I've walked the whole thing twice now, inside and out, and no one is there. No driver stands around with a sign for "Jane & Co." or "Jane Harrington" or even just "Jane." No truck with "Sugar Maple Farms" emblazoned on the side has circled the terminal.

Nothing.

I try Mr. Carville's number again and go straight to voice-mail. I left a message already, so I hang up and, instead, look through the email his assistant sent the night we formalized the deal. Mr. Carville clearly said to email his assistant my itinerary so he could have a driver waiting for me. I call the assistant's number—again—but it goes to voicemail, too. I hung up and texted last time, but maybe the assistant prefers voicemail?

I listen to the voicemail recording, crossing one hand against my body and drumming my fingers across the opposite arm, and then I stop.

"For all things related to Sugar Maple Farms, please contact Anita Farnsworth."

Huh?

I try the number the assistant left, and a woman who sounds as sweet as she does Southern answers. "This is Anita."

"Hi, Anita. My name is Jane Harrington. I'm the CEO of the firm that Mr. Carville hired to rebrand Sugar Maple Farms."

"O-kay," she drawls slowly.

"I'm here at the Columbia airport. I sent my itinerary to Mr. Carville's assistant, who was supposed to have someone pick me up and take me to the farm. Only, no one is here, and the assistant's voicemail instructed me to call you."

There's a long pause. "When did you make these arrangements with Mr. Carville?"

"About two weeks ago."

"Two weeks ago? Well, that sounds about right," Anita says, a bit of vinegar in her molasses voice. Mr. Carville must be a poor communicator. "My apologies, Miss Harrington." She says *miss* like *miz.* "If you tell me what door you're waitin' at, I'll send one of the boys to pick you up. Rusty's over in Irmo for the Farmer's Market today, anyway."

We say our goodbyes, and I debate running back inside the terminal to escape the seven billion percent humidity and surprising heat. I thought the February weather would be mild, but it's 78 degrees, and I've heard more than one person complain about record-breaking heat. I'm getting swampy in my wool blazer, but I don't want to risk missing the car when it comes. So I stay on the bench and sweat.

I don't dare take off my blazer for fear of pit stains, but I twirl my long, sandy blonde hair into a topknot. I'm about to check my appearance in my phone's camera when I see notifications.

I have a text from my sister asking for money, a reminder to pay my credit card bill, and a handful of missed texts from my friends. I can't deal with my sister right now. I'm not sure if I'd prefer the credit card bill or talking to my friends, though. We work and live together, but things have been different. Ash keeps teasing me about my "next big reveal," while Millie is in meddling-mode, hinting that there's something more to this whole job than just good financial sense. Parker is still visibly frustrated with me, though I don't fully understand why. I'm here by myself, and she gets to work on the account remotely, for heaven's sake.

Mr. Carville is as dear as I told my friends he was. We talked on the phone four or five times before he flew out last month, and each time, he was warmer than the last. I kept something from my friends, though, because I'm not sure how to share something so … personal.

In our final conversation, Mr. Carville did, in fact, give me one measurable. But it wasn't something that fits on a ledger or a profits and loss report.

It was more of a promise.

"My wife and I started Sugar Maple Farms with nothing but an idea and an acre of land," he said that night, "and with a lot of love and work, it grew into what it's become today. Farm work changes a person. Humbles you. It's hard to feel powerful when a little frost can drop you to your knees. We loved it more for the struggle, though, and we taught our children to love it, too. At least we tried." He stopped, his voice swelling with emotion. "All of our grandkids have an appreciation for it, all but one. My namesake."

He sounded too choked up to talk, so I filled the space. "That must be hard. I'm sorry, Mr. Carville. I hope he comes around."

"That's where you come in," he said, his words sweet and shaky with feeling. "We have a lot of brains on the farm, but we need more heart. Your past campaigns haven't only been smart, they've been filled with light. That's why I'm hiring your firm." He sounded tired but urgent. "You have to promise that you will turn this farm into the sort of place where my grandson wants to grow old. Help him rediscover the love he had for it in his youth."

What? How could he ask something like that? "Mr. Carville, I don't know how to do that. I can't make that promise."

"But you can, Miss Harrington. You can, because you're *you*, and you'll know it when you see it."

"Mr. Carville—"

"There's something about you that we need at the farm. Promise me, please."

"Mr. Carville—"

"Please." The urgency in his tone made his voice crack. "Nothing matters more to me, Miss Harrington." He paused, and when he spoke again, I had an image of him on his knees. "Please."

This was more than a contract. It felt like an oath. Something solemn, sacred, even. This grandson had no idea how lucky he was to be loved so much, to have someone make plans with him in mind, but I did. I couldn't let this sweet man down.

"I promise."

He sighed, and when he next spoke, he sounded content. "Thank you." He breathed. "You're what the farm has been missing."

It was such a strange way to end the call, but it felt important. Binding. It makes me both nervous and eager to see him again. And while he hasn't responded to my calls since finalizing the contract, and while it's definitely odd that his visits were so well coordinated and the contract was so timely, yet there's no word from him or his representatives now that I'm here, well ...

It doesn't matter.

I'm optimistic and excited.

Also, I'll admit: he reminds me a little of my grandpa. Sometimes I miss my grandpa so badly, I feel like my heart has been hollowed out.

So yes, maybe there is something more to this job than money.

My phone buzzes, and I answer a call from Millie.

"Hey MJ."

"Hey J," she responds. "How's the farm?" I explain about the mix-up with the assistant and the driver. "Wait, Mr. Carville forgot to have his assistant arrange a ride for you? That's odd, considering how aggressively he pursued you."

"*Pursued me?*" I can't keep the outrage from my voice. Or the hurt.

"No, Jane, I didn't mean that—"

"He's seventy-nine years old and uses a cane!"

"That's not what I meant to say. Not even close." I try to let her words in, but I've been hearing this same "joke" in some form or another since I was fourteen, something Millie alone knows. The accusations still make me physically sick to my stomach. "I meant the *business* you. The CEO of Jane & Co. He was obviously, understandably impressed by how professional and competent you are. I've known your brilliance since that first day in Intro to Marketing, when you corrected that trust fund loser about what marketing entails. Do you remember? He was going off about advertising, and your hand shot up like Hermione Granger's." I smile, and the pang in the back of my throat lessens. "You went off about new product development, segmentation targeting, and a bunch of other stuff that I only understand now because you were such a good tutor. Jane, Mr. Carville hired you because you have a vision that other people don't have. You should be proud of yourself. I wish you would have told us after you hung up with him instead of the next day in a staff meeting, but still."

Her words soothe the sting, especially the teasing in her voice. Millie's big on words of affirmation, and it's working on me right now when I feel extra vulnerable and a little neglected by Mr. Carville. With the back of my hand, I wipe the moisture beading on my forehead. "Thanks, Millie. So does this mean that you'll come out and help rather than working remotely? Pretty please?"

"Not a chance, cowgirl."

Disappointment settles in my gut. "I understand. I never wanted to shut you guys out. I hoped the surprise would be as exciting to you all as it was to me."

"I know. And 'heavy is the head that wears the crown' right?"

I love Millie, but she has a tendency to play therapist and read too much into situations. I ignore it, like usual.

"Mr. Carville gave you a pretty hefty budget for travel expenses, right?" she asks. "If I can move around some stuff, maybe I could fly out in a couple of weeks to check things out. Sound good?"

"Sounds great," I say, not counting on it. I hear the beep of a horn and look up to see a barn red 1964 Chevy C-10 truck with the Sugar Maple Farms logo on it. The logo is everything that was wrong about design in the early 2000s. The classic barn and sugar maple are there, but so are three-dimensional block letters and drop shadows. It's almost blasphemous to have something so tacky on such a beautiful truck. "My ride is here, gotta run."

I grab my laptop bag and oversized suitcase. The lining in my light gray dress pants sticks to my butt and thighs, and as I snap back up, my butt cheeks seize.

No. Did I seriously forget to wear my granny undies, today of all days? I try to adjust without someone seeing, but it's no use.

I have a wedgie.

A wedgie in heat and humidity, which everyone knows is one of Dante's circles of hell.

Maybe that's why Southerners are so God-fearing, come to think of it.

I try to wiggle my underwear out as I turn, but I bump into a wall that I swear wasn't there two seconds ago. I fall back down to the metal bench, rubbing my nose, just to see a giant of a man standing where the wall was.

Oh. He was the wall.

"Sorry about that. Let me help you up." He puts out a muscular hand and pulls me up, and I'm struck by how the smell of strawberries clings to his t-shirt and how his t-shirt clings to his very broad chest and biceps. "I'm Tripp. It's a pleasure to meet you."

I look up to see stubble on a rugged jawline and green eyes so piercing, he could beat Clint Eastwood in a staring contest. His short, high, light brown hair reveals a slight widow's peak.

Holy Sergio Leone. He *looks* like a young Clint Eastwood. I nearly fall back to my seat, but with him still holding my hand, I only sway a little. "But I was told Rusty would pick me up." *Not that I'm complaining, but please don't secretly be a murderer.*

"He got caught up with the Farmer's Market, and my stall sold out early, so I offered to come pick up our newest guest." My Chicago sensibilities are on high alert, especially with how alluring his smile is, but the story adds up, especially with the company truck.

"In that case, thanks for coming. I'm Jane Harrington." His brow lifts just enough to show he heard my last name and immediately connected it to the famous socialites. Nothing new. "It's nice to meet you, too."

Tripp pulls my bag to the truck and hefts it into the back with a thud. I wince, thinking of how Millie and I hunted for luxury luggage at every thrift store in Chicago before finding this vintage-inspired SteamLine case. I got it for a (comparative) steal.

"That's a mighty big suitcase, Miss Harrington," he says, opening my door for me. "How long are you plannin' to stay?"

I slide onto the gray leather bench and quickly try to pull out my wedgie as he comes around to his side. I manage to shift the elastic around one cheek before he slides in beside me, closer than expected. The truck has plenty of room, but Tripp takes up a lot more space than most men. I'm not short, but he has to be nine inches taller than me and twice as broad. Jack Reacher's body with a young Clint Eastwood's face.

And he smells like strawberries and soil. When he closes the door, the scent fills the cab.

Never has a man smelt so good. Ever.

He's looking at me expectantly. What was the question? Oh right, how long am I staying. "I'm not sure yet." I expect him to start driving after we both buckle our lap belts, but instead, he leans against his door and fixes his gaze on me. He's so attentive, I feel like he's giving my very soul a once-over. "I guess I'll know better when I've had some time there."

"Smart thinkin'," he says. "The place isn't the height of fashion like it used to be, but it has more soul than about anywhere I've been."

"And where all have you been?" I want to kick myself for how flirtatious I sound.

"Oh, just about everywhere, ma'am." Even with Lou warning me that people would call me ma'am as a sign of respect, the word is off-putting. Do I look old? I hope the humidity didn't make my mascara run. Boy would that age me.

I casually rub a finger beneath one eye and find a streak of black underneath.

No.

No no no no no no.

Here is a man so hot I couldn't have dreamed him up if I'd tried, and I'm sitting next to him like some zombie reject from a bad horror movie. Of all the things Lou could have warned me about, why couldn't it have been waterproof mascara? Why?

"And what about you?" Tripp asks, still looking at me. I have half a wedgie and melted mascara dripping down my face. Can't the man do the polite thing and stop looking at me, already? "I'm sure you've done more than your share of traveling."

"Not as much as you'd think." I grab a tissue from my purse and dab it under both eyes. Yup. Black as Mom's toast. "You know, for someone raised with manners like yours, you could have told me that my Northern mascara lost the battle to your Southern heat and humidity."

Tripp chokes on a laugh. "My apologies, ma'am." I shake my head but can't keep back a smile. "If it's any consolation, you look even prettier without the mascara than you did with it under your eyes."

Laughter bursts from my lips. "Oh really? That's high praise."

"I think so."

I'm still laughing and wiping my face when a knock on the window startles me. A police officer gestures to roll down the window. Authority figures always make me nervous, even though I've never been sent to a principal's office or had so much as a parking ticket. I look at the door and, when I can't find a button, I glance at Tripp in alarm. He half-smiles and reaches a substantial arm across my body, grazing my own arm as he does. The touch sends a wave of tingles through me. Tripp grabs a handle that I somehow missed before and turns it. The window rolls down, and my cheeks are ablaze. After all the years tinkering on old cars with Grandpa, I somehow over-looked the window crank handle. Grandpa would have laughed himself to tears.

"What can I do for you, Officer?" Tripp asks, still leaning over me so he and the officer can see each other. His muscled neck is inches from my face. *Do not sniff his neck like a creep. Do not sniff his neck like a creep.*

"I hate to break up the reunion, but it's time to run along," he said.

"Oh, this is our first time meeting," Tripp says companionably. "But she's captivating. Rather than risk unsafe driving conditions, I thought it smarter to give her my full attention while we talk."

Yup. It's official. I am on fire.

The officer eyes me up and down slowly, a bucket of water dousing my flames. "Can't say I wouldn't do the same. But y'all can't stay here. Go canoodle somewhere else."

"Will do," Tripp says, but the warmth is gone from his voice, and the officer backs up as if Tripp is the one with the badge. Did the officer's leer bug him? Tripp cranks up the window and then returns his formidable presence to the driver's side of the bench. I miss the view of his neck.

As we pull onto the densely tree-lined freeway, Tripp asks me about the flight and about my background. I tell him about growing up in Chicago but skip over my family details. I've dated guys for a year before broaching that subject. He seems fascinated by my MBA from Northwestern and my experience with a big marketing firm before I convinced my friends to set out on our own.

Our conversation is both easy and compelling. He asks question after question and actively listens. I would feel guilty for talking so much, but even after an hour, I get the sense that he's still gearing up.

It feels good. Like, absurdly good.

"I'm sorry this is so boring and way more than you asked for," I say.

"Not at all. I wouldn't have asked if I didn't want to know. I wasn't lyin' to the officer about how captivating you are," he says, stealing a look. I smile when we make eye contact. Have I always been this smiley? My cheeks are starting to hurt. We've turned onto a smaller highway, and I can't figure out how he knew the turn was there for how thick the tree covering is.

"What about you?" I ask him, eager to learn as much about him as he has about me. "Are you from South Carolina?"

"I've lived in Sugar Maple since I was eight." I get the sense that if he were wearing a hat, he would tip it. But then his eyes widen, and I don't even have time to look forward before he slams on the brakes in the middle of the highway. He holds his arm out, catching my collarbone and saving me a millisecond before my face smashes into the dash.

CHAPTER THREE

TRIPP

*W*hen the truck screeches to a halt, Jane's eyes are wider than a barn door. I'm still holding an arm across her lean, toned shoulders, and her chest is heaving. "You okay?" I ask.

"I'm fine, but why on earth did you stop in the middle of a highway?" She speaks fast, like my Yankee friends from college, but none of them have her low, throaty voice. I feel the tenor of it up and down my spine.

I jut my chin out, indicating that she should follow me. We step outside and meet at the front of the truck, where a nine-banded armadillo and six babies are crossing the road several feet ahead of us.

"Aw," she gushes. The animals speed up when they see us.

"It rained this morning after a long dry spell, so they must be out looking for worms," I say. "They're nocturnal."

"They're actually cute with their little armor. Is it weird that I want to pet them?"

"Only if you don't mind getting leprosy."

I chuckle when she jumps back a yard. Her stormy blue eyes narrow, and I find I like the feel of her gaze on me. "You're messing with me."

"Exaggerating a little. It's rare, but not unheard of."

We watch the armadillo family scurry to the other side before continuing our last few miles to the farm. The sun is baking us, and I kick myself for not installing the AC kit in the truck when I had the chance last year. The shoulder belts, too. Jane rolls down her window and closes her eyes, sweat trickling down the side of her cheek. The wind whips some of her long, dark blonde hair free of her bun, and it's sexy as can be, especially with her contented little sigh.

Is she ... enjoying herself?

The only sign of any discomfort is the way she occasionally clenches her legs and shifts in her seat. She's otherwise so at ease, I can't stop myself from peeking at her when her eyes close and she breathes in deep.

My last girlfriend would have been panting and fanning herself, making a show of her long-suffering without ever coming out and saying it. And if I'd so much as acknowledged that her mascara had run, I'd have paid for it for days. The way Jane just teased me and wiped hers off? And the way she simply unbuttoned her blazer and propped her arm up on the truck door to cool off?

I've known some cool girls in my time. But not ones who make it impossible for me to focus on the road after over an hour in the car.

Of course, it would have been faster if I'd driven the speed limit. Or stayed on main roads. Or not taken a scenic detour.

Maybe I should install the AC kit if Jane is going to be around for a while.

I'm not making decisions based on a woman I just met or

anything. Although, she's the kind of woman *anyone* would want to make decisions for.

Shoot. I'm looking at her again, which is what nearly had me taking out the armadillo family back there. No woman should look that good with sweat beading on her forehead.

Eyes on the road, Tripp.

Jane asks me about my experience on the farm, and I tell her I've worked there in some capacity most of my life and that I'm sort of the jack-of-all-trades. I avoid any more details. Although the Harrington last name screams wealth, Jane feels different than the upper crust I've seen my whole life. I don't want to bring my family into this before I have to. She eats up every story of rural life. When I tell her about taking my prom date in a carriage senior year and my date and I slipping in horse poop, she laughs hard enough that I'm envious. She's not the least bit self-conscious. I can't remember the last time I wasn't worried about proving myself to someone.

We're turning off the main highway into the booming town of Sugar Maple, population 3,800, when I get a call from Anita. I answer with an apologetic look to Jane.

"What can I do for you?"

"Tripp, I finally got someone at Carville Industries to give me access to that terrible assistant's schedule. Looks like Tag had a meeting scheduled today at three p.m."

"It's a quarter past that right now," I say.

"Exactly my point. Fortunately, they're runnin' late, too. When you get home, dust off, throw on a shirt, and run into the office, will you?"

"Yes ma'am."

When I put my phone down, Jane is shooting off a text. She clutches her phone between her hands when she's done, seeming almost nervous. If we hadn't already blown through town in the minute I was on the phone, I'd have stopped to get her a Cheerwine and show her around

As it is, we're pulling into the farm now. Rows upon rows of freshly tilled dirt greet her, and she breathes in a little deeper. "It smells a bit like you." She clamps a hand over her mouth. "Wow. I cannot believe I said that out loud. I swear, I'm normally a lot more put together than this."

"I hope that's not the case," I say with a grin. "I like this version of you."

"Well, if I'm going to be here for a while, maybe you'll get to see more versions, and then you can make a more educated decision." She shifts a little.

"Sorry about the lack of air conditioning. I should've thought of that when I offered to pick you up."

"No problem," she says, as if wiping the sweat from her upper lip doesn't bother her in the slightest.

We pass more and more empty acres before reaching the fruit trees, which stretch out for another couple hundred acres, but I'll take her to the bed and breakfast before she can see the rest of the farm.

"I can't believe how good it all smells," she says, inhaling deeply.

"The peach trees are flowering," I explain. "It's too heady for me. But wait until the strawberries flower. That's the greatest smell on earth."

"If the strawberries haven't flowered yet, why do you smell like them?" Her face turns pink, and the flush is beyond appealing.

"We grow 'em in the greenhouse. Since the Farmer's Market started taking off last year, we're trying to keep some of the most popular fruits available year-round."

"That's smart," she says, turning her attention back to the view. She looks so enchanted by the rundown farm store we pass, I don't want the drive to end.

I've had a love/hate relationship with this place for the last twenty years. I loved it for the eight before that, though. It was magical then. A place of wonder where a young boy could get lost for hours without always fretting about someone else's expectations. I suppose it retained some of its wonder after it became my full-time home. I wasn't lying about how the place has soul.

Now it's the soul of an albatross around my neck.

"Would you mind taking me to the main house?" she asks with a look at her texts. "Mrs. Anita asked me to check in with her."

Huh. That's surprising, but Anita is the caretaker now and does run the B&B. Maybe she doesn't have time to get Jane checked in. "It's Mrs. Farnsworth or Miss Anita, never Mrs. Anita."

"You just made that up, didn't you? You all do not make this easy on a girl."

I love a girl who can bust my chops. She is doing something to me, all right. "About that. It's not 'you all.' It's 'y'all' or 'all y'all' if it's plural. Ma'am."

She side eyes me playfully. Would it be too forward for me to ask her out on the spot? No, judging by her suitcase, she's going to be around for a while. It's common for rich Yankees to come down to the South to find themselves. I've never heard of *Jane* Harrington, but the wealthy, socialite Harrington family is constantly in the news. She's probably a cousin, but with the classy way she carries herself, I can't imagine she's not connected.

At the main house, I introduce her to the housekeeper, who promises to get her to Anita. Then I make my excuses to go get ready for whatever meeting Tag put on the books without telling anyone. There are too many cars and workers around for me to guess who I might be meeting with. I take the stairs two at a time and rush around, washing my face and arms, fixing my hair, dusting off my jeans, and throwing on a button-down shirt so Anita doesn't pester me. Good enough.

Back downstairs, I don't see Jane anywhere. But Anita catches my arm when I turn the corner from the foyer to the hallway that leads to the office. "Where've you been?" she asks, leveling me with warm brown eyes a few shades darker than her skin. She's been a presence in my life since I first moved here. "Your three p.m. is now a 3:37 p.m. You and Rusty must have shown up right at the same time."

I didn't see Rusty, but that doesn't matter. "What's this even about, Anita?"

"You remember how you refused to be at the reading of the will last night, and you wanted me to catch you up on all the pertinent information? Well, there was a stipulation with your inheriting Sugar Maple Farms. Tag arranged for the farm and label to be rebranded by a marketing firm over the next year. As the new CEO, you have two choices: you can either sell it to Carville Industries now for pennies on the dollar or you can wait the full year for the rebrand to be complete and then do with it what you will."

"You aren't serious." I run a hand over my mouth and stubble. I'm mad, but I'm not surprised. Tag knew I wanted to work for Carville Industries. He knew I wanted nothing to do with the farm. In classic Tag form, he kept me from the company with the family name on it and saddled me with the crappy old farm. "So what's that got to do with the meeting he had set up?"

"The CEO from the marketing firm he hired is here."

"Well, I'll go in and explain that the situation has changed and we'll cancel the contract."

"No, you won't. Tag made sure the contract was signed, and he transferred the money to a separate account to pay out unless you sell the farm to Carville Industries now."

I mutter something I hope Anita can't hear, but I don't care what Tag said or did. This isn't happening. "Then I'll talk to Uncle Lawson. He'll make this right."

"Maybe," she says in a voice that screams *not happening*. "But in the meantime, you need to take this meeting. And Tripp, I don't know exactly where your head's at, but you do right by Tag, you hear?"

I refuse to lie, so I don't respond. Instead, I march toward the office, determination weighing down my movements. I cannot stay tied to this place for another year, let alone for the rest of my life. I wouldn't even be here now if I didn't have to be. This place holds too many memories, too much hurt.

A plan forms in my mind as I approach the French doors to the office. The curtain is drawn so I can't see who's sitting there, but I've known hotshot businessmen my whole life. I know how to make this problem go away.

I grab the heavy brass door handle, hesitating. Nothing good has ever awaited me behind these office doors.

Toughen up, buttercup.

I turn the handle.

Time to meet my fate.

CHAPTER FOUR

JANE

I am officially wedgie free.

Ahhhhhh.

Not having a wedgie is the best feeling since having Tripp hang on my every word in the truck.

If I'd had the time in the bathroom, I would have changed into my McLadyPants undies, but I didn't want to be any later for my meeting than I already am, and frankly, refreshing my mascara cut it close enough. I've only been waiting for maybe two minutes, and I've used the time to get my tablet up and my notes in order. Now that task is done, I really want to pry around the office, because Mr. Carville's walls are plastered with pictures. It feels like a grandpa's office, not the office of a multi-millionaire.

I'm about to reach around the desk to grab a picture frame when the door opens. I pop up and spin around, but instead of Tag Carville, I see Tripp. He's cleaned himself up and looks … I mean, he's stupid hot. He looks stupid, crazy hot, and part of me wants to just shove my face into his shirt to see if it, too, smells like strawberries and soil and maybe a hint of something else. Like kissing.

Not that kissing has a smell. Or that I should be thinking of kissing him after a single car ride.

Unless he's thinking of kissing me.

Head in the game, Harrington!

"Hey, what are you doing here?" I ask.

He looks as confused as I am. "I was about to ask you the same thing," he says, walking around the expansive mahogany desk. "I'm supposed to meet with someone in here."

"Funny, so am I," I say.

His face shifts suddenly. "You're the marketing hotshot. Of course." He closes his eyes for two heartbeats before whispering, "I'm an idiot."

My eyes dart around the room. "Am I missing something?" He shakes his head, gesturing for me to sit as he does. I don't sit, though, because I'm waiting for sweet old Mr. Carville to come in and explain what's going on. "Where's Mr. Carville?"

"Mr. Carville isn't coming."

My heart drops into my stomach. Why is Tripp acting so oddly? Is this all a scam? Does Mr. Carville want to cancel the contract? Or is he secretly some kind of gross old man who plays mind games with attractive, single women?

Oh my gosh, am I being Squid Gamed? I haven't watched it, but our intern gave us blow-by-blow details. Am I going to be competing against a bunch of other struggling CEOs for my life?

"I'm sorry to tell you this," Tripp continues, "but Mr. Carville passed away two weeks ago."

I drop into my chair. Relief and sorrow clash in me, but sorrow quickly wins. I think of how Mr. Carville told me he couldn't wait to see me breathe new life into Sugar Maple Farms, about how he made me promise to turn the farm into the place his grandson would want to grow old. All I can hope now is that I can do everything he wanted without the caretaker he was so worried about getting in the way.

"I'm so sorry," I say softly. "I talked to him two weeks ago. Two weeks and a day." Tripp's face is blank. I'm still not sure why he's the messenger rather than Anita. "Can I ask what happened?"

"He's had heart disease for years, but whiskey and cigars proved too much temptation for him."

He's so calloused that I flinch. "Wow. I'm sorry to hear that. And I'm sorry for your loss. Working here for so long, I'm sure you knew him much better than I did—" He snorts. He actually snorts. "Excuse me. Did I say something funny?"

"I knew Tag Carville as well as anyone alive." He sneers, and it's the first time I've seen him look anything other than spectacularly hot. "I'm his grandson. Tag Carville III, at your service."

I pause, blinking fast and making connections in my head. "Tripp, as in triple. Third." He nods. "You don't seem too happy about me being here, Mr. Carville."

"You can still call me Tripp." He says this as if he's offended that I would use formal addresses in a business meeting. Though, this is a pretty bizarre business meeting. "And it's not about you, it's about this job that Tag hired you to do."

"What do you mean?"

"I don't want you to do it."

"Sorry, what?"

He leans over the desk with a buzzing urgency. "I don't want this place rebranded. I want it to remain as it is."

I inch forward in my seat. "Last year was the farm's worst year since your massive crop failure of 1996, and the trend is only downward from here. Why wouldn't you want the farm rebranded?"

"I ... can't explain it."

"And I can't just *not* do the job."

"Why?"

"Because your grandpa already paid me a bonus to do it."

"But he's gone, Jane. If you agree to quit now, I'll let you keep whatever he paid you."

He can't be serious. "You have no idea how much that even is."

"It doesn't matter. It's worth it to me."

What is going on here? Why is he offering to let me keep money to let his farm stagnate? And why on earth am I fighting him? If we can keep 20 percent of a three-million-dollar account without having to do any of the work, that money can more than pay the bills. That kind of money would change my life. But the memory of Mr. Carville's bright smile after my presentation hits me. "I took the job and signed a contract. Not following through would be unethical."

"It's not unethical. I'm the new owner, and I'm letting you off the hook. You can go back to Chicago, buy yourself something nice, and move on to the next—"

"*Buy myself* ... are you serious?" I interrupt, my chest burning with the unjustness of what he said. Did he really tell me to *buy myself something nice*?

"Absolutely!" he says, missing my outrage. "Jane, take the money and run."

"I can't!" Can I? It's so much money! "I came here to do a job."

Tripp groans into his hands. "Nothing you can do will fix what's wrong with this place."

"You acknowledge that something is missing, but you don't even want to hear me out?"

Tripp drops his hands and clasps them on the desk across from me. He looks as irritated as I feel. "Fine," he says shortly. "Why don't you tell me what Tag wanted you to do?"

"Well, about that ..."

His eyes pop wide. "You don't have a plan? Did you even give him a proposal?" He shakes his head, muttering, "Classic Tag to give the job to the nicest pair of legs."

"Wow." I flip my hair like Elle Woods. "And we didn't even talk about how I did in the swimsuit portion."

He winces. "I didn't mean that."

"Then what did you mean?"

He shakes his head, looking away. "You wouldn't understand."

"Because I'm too pretty to be smart?"

His face scrunches. "No. Don't put words in my mouth."

"You know nothing about me, Mr. Carville. How dare you assume that I want an easy out so I can go back home and *buy myself something pretty*? You think I, what, seduce rich old men into giving me jobs so I can get paid faster when they die?"

"What? No!"

"But you've implied that I can't possibly have earned a single thing in my life."

I had him backpedaling a moment ago, but I must have backed him up against a wall, because he looks ready to fight now. "Well, you *are* a Harrington."

My laugh could melt a Chicago winter. "Oh, and you know all about what that means, do you?"

"Yes. Because I'm a Carville."

"So I'm not merely too pretty to be smart, I'm also too rich to know how to work. While you, on the other hand, are a surprisingly humble yet strapping jack-of-all-trades. Sound about right?"

"Stop putting words in my mouth."

"Then what is it?"

A low, guttural sound comes from his throat. "You wouldn't understand."

"Why, Mr. Carville?" I flip my hair again and bat my eyes.

"It's Tripp, and that's not what I'm trying to say!"

"Then why don't you want me to help you?"

I don't even know when it happened, but Tripp and I are both standing up, hands planted across the desk, and his chest is rising and falling as hard as mine is. The movies have it all wrong. There's nothing sexy about this feeling. I'm angry and hurt, and a part of me I've tried to bury for a long time is dangerously exposed.

We stare each other down, neither of us blinking for a long moment. Then finally, Tripp stands to his considerable height and folds his arms in front of him. "You're right, Ms. Harrington. I don't know you. But I do know Tag Carville. The man had more girlfriends at seventy than I had at seventeen. One of his girlfriends was about your age. Almost married her, in fact, until he pulled out a pre-nup. And sure, while he stopped dating altogether in the few years that I've been caretaker here, you'll have to forgive me for thinking that a leopard doesn't change his spots. You waltz in here looking like a cover model and tell me that he hired you without a proposal for what I'm sure is a multi-million-dollar account, and yes, I'm going to make some assumptions. I'm not ashamed of that."

"I had a proposal!" I argue. Defensiveness replaces outrage as my insides start to squirm. "Mr. Carville said it was too slick. He said he liked my vision but felt it was missing something that I would only be able to find by coming out here."

"Good for you. I assume he liked your portfolio, then, too? You must have rebranded at least one other orchard or farm, right? It must be what you're known for if he hired you?"

"No," I admit reluctantly. "Never."

Tripp's laugh is dark and a bit ugly. "Exactly."

I know my conduct was above reproach. I *know* it. My friends all worked on the finished presentation. Our evaluation and proposal were solid. Ash's initial logo mockup was enough to pique anyone's interest.

But my friends' teasing and comments and Tripp's accusations are in my head.

I got this job based on what, exactly?

And now when I think about what he said—how the moment he saw me, he knew he wanted me at Sugar Maple Farms—it feels … tainted.

Was he not the dear old man I thought?

"Listen, Jane, I don't want to waste your time. If he considered your firm at all, it's because you know your stuff. I'm not accusing you of anything, I swear. I'm accusing Tag. I don't know what he was playing at, but I won't ask for anything back. Take the 20 percent, no strings attached. Go back to Chicago and use the money to grow your startup. I'll take care of things around here."

I feel so small and stupid. Tripp is right. I should absolutely take the money and go. This is huge, life-changing money. My friends and I need this. And I didn't do anything wrong. I didn't flirt or lead him on or even give him one of my Mom's smiles. I worked my butt off, and my presentation was strong, even if it wasn't exactly what Mr. Carville wanted. It was strong.

Wasn't it?

My mom's voice creeps into my head, making me feel even worse. *Who cares how you got the job? Take what you can get while you can get it. Those looks won't last forever.*

How could I have thought that I landed an account on merit that the top firms in the country were falling over themselves to get? Did I really think my vision wowed Mr. Carville so much that he simply believed in me? I'll bet I wasn't his first choice. Maybe not even his second. If he knew he was dying any minute and he was really so worried about what his caretaker would do—

Wait. His caretaker?

Tripp's deep voice is placating. "Take the deal, Jane. I can drive you back right now, if you'd like."

"You mentioned that you were your grandfather's caretaker?"

"The farm's caretaker," he corrects.

"And did he have another caretaker or a nurse of some kind?"

"No. His death caught us all by surprise."

"You've been traveling a lot lately, right? You mentioned that you've been just about everywhere?"

He folds his arms again. "That's right. What are you getting at?"

"You want to know what I'm getting at? You are a snake." I stab a finger toward him for emphasis.

"What?"

"Your grandpa warned me about you! He said you would try to sabotage the rebrand. That's why he was in such a rush to get the contract signed." The realization is a lifeline when I was drowning. "I almost believed you. But you are a snake."

"No!" He looks almost as angry as I feel.

"I'm taking this job, *Mr. Carville*, and I'm not leaving until it's done. If you have a problem with that, take it up with my lawyer."

I spin on my heels and storm out the door. I stomp down the hallway, through the foyer, and down the stairs until I'm outside. I huff all the way to the parking lot before I realize that I didn't drive, I don't know where my bag is, and I don't know where I'm staying.

Oh, and my wedgie is back.

"Aaaarrrgggghhh!" I shout up at the sky.

A whimper and scuff of feet nearby pull my head down. Ten feet away stand a woman and a little boy of around four, clutching her leg. The woman is holding a bag from the store and looking at me warily.

"Momma, what's the crazy lady doin'?" the boy whimpers.

"We don't know she's crazy, bless her heart. Now run for the car." The two dart down a dirt path and into the trees.

When I whip around to go back inside, Tripp is waiting for me on the porch. He's leaned up against a pillar and may as well be eating an apple for how calm he is.

How dare he be calm after the crap he just pulled?

"Well, if you're stayin', allow me to take you to your cabin."

Tripp leads me back to his truck, and because I have no other option, I follow. While pointedly ignoring him. We drive in silence over one dirt path after another. A few families walk around the farm, but fewer than I'd expect for a Saturday. I want to ask Tripp about it, but I'm ignoring him, and he's a monumental jerk, so the question would be wasted on him.

Like his stupid hotness.

Why is it that jerky men are so hot, whereas kind women are so routinely beautiful? Evolution really should have fixed this problem.

I drag my attention from him and to my surroundings. The farm is enchanting, but it's not as accessible as the ones Parker and I have been to when we've visited her family in New England.

Thinking about Parker gives me a pit in my stomach, so I mentally shove the thought from my mind and instead focus on impressions. Right off the bat, I know I want to pave these trails. I'm sure it would cost a small fortune, but one of the plans Tag did like was the idea of making this place a wedding destination. Both of his children got married here, he told me.

I've always hated the idea of planning a wedding. Too many people's expectations to manage. Too much opportunity to offend or disappoint. It's the marriage that matters, not the ceremony. Any sane person would elope.

But this isn't my wedding I'm stuck thinking about, it's the idea in general. No bride wants to be covered in dust when she's walking down the aisle. Beyond that, though, no one likes dirt in their toes, and the few customers I've seen were wearing sandals. Sandals and the brightest, most patterned clothing I've ever seen. My gray suit and mint blouse are boring in comparison.

We take yet another, smaller path to a row of a dozen colorful little cottages. They look charming from far away, but the closer we get, the more disrepair I see some have fallen into.

"I'm not staying in the B&B?" I ask. We drove past it on the way to the main house, and it looked modern and adorable. Also empty.

"We don't know how long you're stayin', so it doesn't make sense to put you up there when you could have more space to stretch out. This is where people used to stay before the B&B was built."

"So these are currently …" *Condemned?*

"Vacant. And far enough from the rest of the farm that you'll have plenty of privacy and space to think. Is that a problem?"

Yes, because that one up ahead looks two broken windows shy of a horror film. "Not a problem in the slightest."

His brows crease for an instant, and I wonder what flashed through his head. But no way am I asking. The sweet, funny, magnetic man from the drive home never actually existed. He was always a lazy playboy who would rather jet set around the world than do any real work. His poor grandparents built Carville Industries from the ground up, starting with Sugar Maple Farms. But it seems Tripp doesn't care much about the work that created his new empire.

He stops at the most rundown cottage, like I knew he would. Before I've even collected my laptop bag and purse, he has my suitcase waiting at the door. A home sign above the knocker reads "Strawberry Fields." He unlocks the door and then hands me the key. "Welcome home."

"This is really how this is going to go? You're dropping me off at your most dilapidated cottage in the hopes that you can scare me away?" He doesn't answer, but he *does* squirm. "The fact that you're making this about you instead of the legacy your grandpa wanted to leave is pathetic." I don't wait for him to respond. I wheel my bag in and slam the door behind me.

And then I pull out my wedgie.

Ahhh—

My sigh stops short as I gag. Ugh, what is that smell? I look around in disgust and increasing horror. This isn't just rundown, it's practically a crime scene. I kick empty chip bags and beer bottles and pizza boxes and ...

Wait, is that a used—

I gasp.

Oh.

Oh no.

Oh my word.

I gag again and hold my blouse over my nose and mouth. I cannot believe he put me in this hole. He clearly isn't happy about my presence, but does he truly despise me this much? I tiptoe across the dank floor and something huge flies up at me. I swallow a scream. Is that a cockroach ...

With wings?

Every hair on my body stands straight up. Revulsion turns to terror. I shriek as the thing dive-bombs me again. I try to dodge it one way and another, but it's a MASSIVE FLYING COCK-ROACH. Its devilish senses lock on me, and I can't run from it because I keep tripping on the evidence of whatever crime happened here. With the kind of urgency only seen in horror movies, I throw open the door and slam it behind me, panting hard. The bright sun blinds me momentarily, stabbing my eyes. Tripp isn't here, but that's the only consolation. He would probably laugh to see a "Harrington" freaking out over a flying cock-roach in a dumpster. Catching my breath, I drop down to the porch swing, but cobwebs run up my arms and neck. I jump up with a squeal and wipe the silky, sticky threads off of me.

Nothing is safe. This place can't be real. I look up and down the row of cottages. Does a fresh hell wait in each one of them, or did he really reserve this one for me?

I want to call my friends and tell them I made a huge mistake. I want to change my mind, take the 20 percent, and go back home, exactly as Tripp said I should. My friends wouldn't begrudge me that. Not even Parker, who was still frosty when I left. Maybe if she knows I negotiated to keep the upfront money, it could fix whatever I broke. The money could fix everything for each of us. If I just tell Tripp yes.

Would that be so awful?

The voices of my mom and grandpa war in my head.

Take it! Worry about yourself, she would say. *Because no one else will.*

But my grandpa's voice edges hers out.

You made a promise. If you left, could you look in the mirror and like what you see?

I know the answer. As much as I would enjoy the easy way out of this, and all of that sweet, sweet cash, I wouldn't be able to look myself in the mirror if I took the money and ran. That's not who I am.

"Okay, Jane," I say to myself, because I'm an external processor. "Pull yourself together. What would Clint Eastwood do? Would he give up because it's hard? Would he run because he wasn't wanted? Would he crumple at the sight of a little—okay a huge—flying devil bug? No he would not. He would shoot the thing into smithereens. Or, you know, step on it probably."

I shudder. The idea of squishing that giant abomination underfoot makes my skin crawl. No. I will not step on one of those things ever. But my pep talk is working. This cottage may look like an episode of CSI, but our trailer wasn't always such a big step up. When I was too young to know how to clean, we had mice and roaches. Even if the roaches were tiny compared to these, Tripp has no idea who he's up against. Time to put on my McLadyPants, because this place is going to look like a palace when I'm done with it.

Over the next few hours, I learn that the AC is broken, the toilet and shower are clogged, and most of the light bulbs are missing. I find a package of (thankfully unused) rubber gloves in the kitchen and cleaning supplies in the bathroom (let's not talk about what else I find in the bathroom). I change into my running clothes, leave my suitcase and travel clothes outside on the porch swing (after clearing off the cobwebs), and I clean.

And clean.

And clean.

The place is small, maybe 350 square feet with only three rooms: the bathroom, the bedroom, and the sitting room/kitchen. The flying cockroach to room ratio is three to one. I ask each one of the little punks if they feel lucky right before I scream like a warrior and smack it with the broom.

None are left alive.

It's early evening by the time the cabin is clean. I am hot and red and so sweaty from working so long with no AC, I look like I've been in a sauna fully clothed. Bags of trash line the path ahead. I have no idea what I'm supposed to do with them. I fall to the porch swing, which is thankfully solid, and sit with a glass of tepid tap water.

Today has gone so differently than expected.

I wish my friends were here.

Millie would give me the world's best hug, sit with me, and let me feel all the feels. Lou would validate every ounce of sadness out of me and possibly draft a lawsuit against Tripp for sucking at life ... or breach of contract, at any rate. Ash would drive over to the main house, chew Tripp out, and steal the keys to his place. She would also put cling wrap on his toilet bowl or pull some other camp-style prank, and I would protest while secretly loving every minute of it. Parker, who's learned to thrive on being underestimated, would have renovations started on the place before Tripp was even awake the next morning. And she would start by demolishing his house.

A stab of longing for my best friend hits my gut. If I texted her, would she even answer? Before I can find out, a truck pulls up to the cabin, and a beautiful man steps out.

"Can I give you a hand?"

CHAPTER FIVE

TRIPP

"*U*ncle Lawson, this is Tripp. Again. I need you to call me back about Sugar Maple Farms, all right? I can't imagine this is working out how either one of us wants it to, so let's make a plan for how we can fix this. Call me."

I stuff my phone into my jeans pocket and walk inside.

I've spent the last two hours leaving increasingly desperate messages for my uncle and talking on the phone with our lawyers. Tag's will is iron clad. I can sell the farm now to Carville Industries at the discretion of the CEO—Uncle Lawson —or I can overhaul the place using Tag's marketing firm and then sell it off to the highest bidder in one year's time.

The farm is worth hundreds of millions of dollars, but I'll be lucky to get a fraction of that selling it to Carville Industries. And I couldn't care less. My parents weren't great with money, but my inheritance means I'll never have money concerns, especially if I go work for a competitor after selling the farm. I know my worth. I wouldn't start as Chief Sustainability Officer with

McNeal Family Farms or Pulse Agro, but I wouldn't be a grunt, either.

Anger at my grandfather burns through my veins.

I asked him for one thing. One thing! It wasn't a deathbed request, because I didn't know he was dying, but it was the only thing I'd ever asked. When I graduated with my master's in agribusiness, I asked him for a job with Carville Industries, and instead, he gave me the Chief Sustainability Officer's number and told me to work with him to set up whatever I wanted on Sugar Maple Farms.

I went to Bolivia with a non-profit called FEED, instead.

When I got back, I asked him if I could interview for the VP of Sustainability spot with Carville.

He made me caretaker of his farm, instead.

I went to work with FEED again.

Then he called me out of the blue two weeks ago.

Two weeks and one day.

"Tripp, my boy!" he said in a booming voice I hadn't heard from him in years. It sent a wave of nostalgia over me that almost made me forget how mad I'd been at him for so long. "How was your experience in Brazil?"

Experience. Huh. At least he didn't call it a vacation this time. "Good. The rainforest was incredible. The indigenous peoples could teach master's classes on sustainability."

"Tell me about it," he said, surprising me.

"Are you sure? Last time we talked, you seemed to think volunteering was a waste of time."

"I didn't see the vision in your work, but I did some research. You should be proud of yourself," he said a bit gruffly. "Helpin' people is never a waste of time."

You should be proud of yourself. The words shifted in my chest, as if trying to make room in the middle of all the years of disappointments and unmet expectations. I swallowed hard. "Thanks, Tag. You know, I could drive down to Atlanta tomorrow and tell you and Lawson about it. Maybe there's room to implement some things at Carville Industries." I was being heavy-handed. I'd wanted to work at Carville Industries for years. It wasn't just the family name, either. I'd studied about Carville in my under-grad and master's programs. Tag was the CEO, and he still spent most of his time at the Carville Industries headquarters.

"I'm not in Atlanta. I'm at the farm. What could you imple-ment here?" he asked, the words sounding choppy, like he was out of breath. Knowing him, he was probably tilling soil by hand. But then he coughed, and worry pricked my chest. He was fit as a fiddle, but heart disease was no joke.

I ignored his question. "You're at the farm? You know I'm in town, right? Stayin' at Duke's?" Duke was my best friend, and his house was more welcoming than the main house at the farm. That house was the loneliest place on earth. But the idea of Tag being there all by himself didn't sit well with me. "Why don't I swing by? I could give you a hand with—"

"No, no need to bother yourself," he said. He coughed again.

"Tag, I'm the caretaker. Or did you fire me without telling me?"

"I think the caretaker's supposed to take care of *this* farm, not farms all over South America," he said. I would normally snap back, but then he added, "But I know how you feel about being here."

In his prime, Tag was my height exactly, six-five, although he'd shrunk an inch or two with age. He was a presence, even now that I was taller than him. But he sounded small in a way I couldn't imagine.

"I can handle it."

There was a long pause, and then he said quietly, "I wish you could see what I see here."

"Yeah, and what do you see?" I asked through gritted teeth.

I braced myself for a lecture. I knew he and Uncle Lawson thought I was some slacker who couldn't finish a project, but they didn't get what it was like for me to be on the farm. Tag was so hard when I was growing up: so hard to please, so hard to understand, so hard to connect with. All I'd ever wanted was to make him proud, to feel like I was living up to his name.

The farm was a mausoleum where hopes of proving my own worth had died.

The lecture didn't come, though. "Do you remember when we picked strawberries?"

"I—sorry? Strawberries?" I was sure we'd done it before, but for the life of me, I couldn't remember a time we had. "No. What does this have to do with my failures?"

His sigh was bone-deep, and when he spoke again, I wanted my words back. "You're a good boy, Tripp. A good man. I wish you could see what I see."

"Tag, why don't I come over?"

"It's late," he said. It was barely nine p.m. "Come by tomorrow."

"Okay."

Except, there was no tomorrow. Not for Tag.

Did he know he was dying? That thought has haunted me for two weeks. The thought that he knew and didn't even want me there in his final moments.

But now, I wonder if he didn't want me there so he could call Jane and make sure that the wheels were in motion. Did he call his lawyer right after? Did he mastermind sticking me with the farm on his deathbed?

The idea of working for a competitor gives me a sort of spiteful glee that quickly fades into an oily guilt. But why should I feel guilty? Why should I put myself through the coming year of revamping this place? Is it just because not everything with Tag was bad? Is it the memory of the better times? Is it the love for my nana, for my parents, as complicated as that feels?

Or is it because of what Jane said, that Tag knew I would sabotage the deal?

Should I feel guilty?

I push that thought as far away as possible as I walk through the house. I'll talk to Uncle Lawson and we'll find a way to fix this mess.

"Where's Miss Harrington?" Anita asks when I reach the kitchen.

"I put her up over in the cabins."

"But the cabins haven't been renovated yet."

I shift. "She could be here for months, Anita. We have to keep the B&B open for potential guests, and the cabins aren't making us money."

She levels me with her gaze. "Nothing is making us money, Tripp. You know this as well as I do. But as long as she's not in Strawberry Fields, she should be fine."

"What do you mean?" I ask quickly. "What's wrong with Strawberry Fields?"

"Other than the AC going out? A few of the harvesters used it as a party cabin. We fired them last week but haven't had the chance to clean it up yet. As the kids would say, it's NSFW." And now the guilt takes a big bite. I drop my gaze from Anita's. "You did not."

"I didn't know!"

"You knew about the AC!"

"But I thought that's all it was. It's February!"

"In a heat wave."

"Barely. Come on, Anita. I'm not *that* bad a guy."

"Tell that to the elegant young woman you stuck in a hot, filthy cabin with heaven knows what layin' about!" She shakes her head and pulls out her phone.

"Who are you calling?"

"Rusty. I'm gonna have him move her to another cabin."

I stiffen. "Why Rusty?"

"Because he drove her here and is sweet as sugar, so at least she'll have someone familiar to help her out."

Rusty is one of my best friends and the type of guy Tag always wanted me to be more like. Studious, thoughtful, hard working. I could be those things, too, mind you. But when Rusty's dad broke his leg and needed help running the fruit stands, he left his dream job in Atlanta and came home to help.

When Tag got sick, on the other hand, I ran. It's not like I could have helped. It's not like anyone wanted me around. My parents made it clear where I fell in their priority list: somewhere after flight lessons and jet skiing but before church. I was never enough. I was the weight that tethered them to the earth when they wanted to fly.

For a while, I thought it was different with Tag. He wasn't warm, but I didn't cramp his lifestyle. At least, I didn't think so. When I got to high school, he started taking the occasional trip. When I went to college, he practically vanished. He must have been so relieved to be rid of me. He all but moved to Atlanta to spend more time at Carville Industries headquarters … and with Uncle Lawson and his family. Then a couple of years ago, he moved back into the farmhouse and paid me too much to become the caretaker. But I knew what he was really doing. He was trying to keep me under his thumb and control me, like my dad always said Tag did to him. He was trying to turn me into a mini Tag so that I wouldn't embarrass him or ruin his legacy.

If I had only been more like Rusty. Solid as an oak and twice as humble. Jane will love him.

"Don't bother Rusty. He was caught up with the vendor, so I offered to pick up our guest. Jane doesn't know him from Adam."

Anita looks like the living embodiment of long-suffering. "You're tellin' me that you drove that young woman here and never got around to asking *why* she was here?"

"I thought she was another Yankee comin' down for a week of self-discovery."

"You make this right, Tripp." Anita doesn't know what I said to Jane, but she knows me too well *not* to know that something is up.

I swallow the shame creeping up my throat. "Yes, ma'am."

The sun is getting low as I drive the few minutes to the cabins. To show that I'm not a complete scumbag, I grab some food for her. I should have probably told her where the seasonal workers have dinner, but she has Anita's number. I'm surprised she hasn't checked in with her since I dropped her off, come to think of it.

Turning onto the cabin row, panic spikes in me. A black truck is parked outside Strawberry Fields. Jane is totally isolated out here, and even though we typically have good seasonal workers, we don't background check everyone. Anita firing a group of them is proof of that.

If something happened to Jane, I'll never forgive myself.

I slam on the brakes and spring out the second it's in park. I rush to the cabin door and try to open it, but it's locked. I pound a fist and hear Jane say, "Coming!"

The door flies open, and Jane's eyebrows shoot up. "Can I help you?"

I look past her to see who's with her, but the bedroom door is closed. Is someone back there? Who? "Just wanting to see how you're getting settled in." I try to move past her, but she puts hands on both sides of the doorframe.

"I'm doing *great*. I *really* appreciate you putting me up in such a *clean* and *safe* cabin, Mr. Carville. Your *thoughtfulness* astounds me."

Why is she speaking so oddly? Emphasizing certain words like this? I watched a movie once with my ex where the woman kept speaking in some sort of code, and it turned out that she was being held hostage in her own home. I fell asleep before it finished, but Jane is putting out that same vibe right now. And the way her eyes are digging into me?

She's not safe.

I put a finger to my lips and push past her, in spite of her protests. Although it *is* weird that she's vocally protesting as I creep across the floor toward the bedroom. Shouldn't she be quiet so I can get the jump on the guy?

"What are you—?"

I shush her as I grab the door handle.

"Don't!" she cries as I shove the door open.

I meet immediate resistance. Something smashes painfully onto my head, and I drop to my knees. Lights swirl in my vision, but a man's work boots approach me across the hard-wood floor. I jump up and tackle him onto the bed. He lands with a loud "oof" and the bed cracks beneath us. His hat falls over his face, and I dig a knee into his stomach. I wind my arm back and am about to punch his face in when he pulls the hat off.

"Tripp, what the—"

"What is wrong with you?" Jane yells from behind me at the same time. I scramble to get off the bed—which has broken under the weight of me and one of my best friends.

"Rusty?" I pull him up, and he rubs his gut. Rusty's a few inches shorter than I am, but he can hold his own. At least when he doesn't have 240 pounds of muscled madman on top of him.

The bedroom is tiny, but that doesn't stop Jane from shoving past me and checking Rusty for any sign of injury. "Are you okay? Do you know this jerk?"

Rusty doesn't seem to mind Jane's attention in the least, gingerly putting his arm around her shoulders, as if he didn't take harder hits than that in football on the regular. "I do. He's one of my best friends."

"I'm glad you weren't attacked by an enemy, then," she says sharply.

I look around the cramped room. The ceiling is barely a foot and a half above my head, and the crawl space flap is open. A stepladder, toolbox, and industrial lantern flashlight lay on the floor. But I notice something else, too.

"The AC is working."

"That's what Rusty and I were working on," Jane says. She doesn't add "you idiot," but I can see it in her eyes.

When I hurled the door open, I must have pushed Rusty off of the stepladder, causing the flashlight to crack down on my head.

"You were working on the air handler?" I ask him.

He nods and looks between us. "I'm sorry about the mess, Jane. Let me tidy this up."

"No, I'll take care of it," I tell him. I apologize, but he brushes it off, as he always does. "I'm sorry, Rusty. Honestly. Let me handle it."

He nods, reading something in my eyes that I'm not saying. "Okay. I should probably get goin', then. The fruit stands won't open themselves tomorrow," he says. "Nice to meet you, Jane."

"You too, Rusty," she says. I step out of the way so Rusty can grab his tools and get past me. With a quick glare, Jane follows him. "Thanks again. How about I play the white knight next time, okay?"

Rusty laughs and the door closes behind him.

I brace myself for impact in 3 ... 2 ...

"How dare you come in here like you own the place?"

"Technically, I do." I want to bite my tongue the moment the words are out. What is wrong with me?

"Wow. Real mature." She folds her arms. Her hair is up in its high bun still, but she's wearing black running shorts and a white tank top, and I absolutely will not admire how good she looks, because I may be a jerk, but I'm not a creep. "Listen, I get it. You don't respect me, you don't like me, and you don't want me here."

"You don't understand."

"So I hear. Again. You *shushed* me, Tripp. I tried to stop you from marching into a room where your friend was helping me out, and instead of listening, you *shushed* me."

"That's not what ... I thought someone was ... I thought you were—"

Jane's gasp stops me. "First off, that is so not my style. But if it were—"

"Would you stop interrupting me?" I bellow, in spite of the irony of my interrupting *her*. "I thought you were *in danger*. You don't know anyone here except Anita and me, and I thought you may feel isolated over here. I came to check on you."

Jane bites her lip, and the last thing I need right now is to be thinking about her lips. It is the worst sort of cosmic cruelty that the first woman I've been interested in for years is also the last person I want around. And the feeling appears to be mutual. "I don't understand you. You dump me in the equivalent of a condemned No Tell Motel, yet you clearly feel guilty about it. You've been very upfront that you don't want me here, and yet you came to check on me. What do you want?"

I rub my forehead, feeling cramped in this tiny space. I give up. If anything, I've just made the situation with her worse. "Nothing. You have Rusty and Anita's numbers, right? I'll clean up and then get out of your hair. I shouldn't have bothered you when you were obviously doing fine on your own." I rush outside, stopping halfway to my truck. I mutter, "I'm sorry," and keep walking.

"Tripp, wait," she says as I'm rounding my truck. I pause and risk a peek at her. She stands on the outside of her bare feet as if she's trying to touch as little of the ground as possible. It makes her look vulnerable. Is there a chance she can forgive what a tool I've been? "Who should I contact about getting a new bed?"

CHAPTER SIX

JANE

*I*t's nearly midnight when I've finally showered, unpacked, and eaten the sandwich and salad Tripp begrudgingly gave me (it was delicious, and I assume Anita was responsible). I lie in bed and video chat with my friends, who are an hour behind me in Chicago.

After I reminded him about the bed he broke, Tripp instantly opened the cottage next to mine. The place was dated and a tad worse for the wear, but it was clean and tidy and did not look like it was haunted by the ghost of Spring Break Past. I wanted to make a snide comment, but Tripp's conscience appeared to be doing its job, based on his inability to look me in the eye. I helped him remove my broken bed and replace it with the one from next door, although I'm not sure he needed me. He carted everything away without comment. Watching him casually toss the broken frame into the back of his truck was as annoying as it was impressive.

Just remembering it makes me hot under the collar. The man is a specimen.

A work of art.

And I hate him for it.

"You don't hate him," Ash tells me.

"He shushed me, Ashley Jane. *Shushed.*"

"I'm not saying it wasn't annoying. I'm saying you don't hate him. You haven't stopped talking about him for like twenty straight minutes. When you hate people, you eviscerate them and move on. You're not moving on, you're fixating. Am I right?" She looks at Millie, who holds up her hands in a "no comment" kind of way that makes her my current favorite best friend. "I'm right," Ash says. "Which means you liked him before he went all Dr. Jekyll and Mr. Hyde on you."

"I already told you how nice he was on the drive."

"Here, talk to Parker," Ash says. My stomach plummets as the video jostles. Quiet mumbles and hisses sound from my phone's speaker, and I know exactly what's happening. Ashley is telling Parker to take the call. Parker doesn't want to. She's been avoiding me, and if there were ever a time for an *I told you so*, now is it. "Will you grow up and take the call already?"

After a scuffle, Parker's face appears.

"So, good first day, huh?" The angle is awkward, and I'm pretty sure that Ash is holding the phone up to Parker's washed face. Parker wears makeup like armor, so she always seems more open right before bed. Her features are naturally dark, but her lashes don't look like hundreds of tiny stiletto heels when the mascara is wiped away.

"It's not even my first day," I say, my mouth dry. "It's the day before the day before the first day."

Parker stifles a yawn, covering her mouth with her hand. This isn't our most comfortable conversation ever, but at least we're talking. "You're not afraid of hard work, even if it's interpersonal. Do you need this guy to like you to do your job?"

"I don't know," I admit. "Mr. Carville must have made a pretty ironclad provision in his will about the farm, or I think his grandson already would have sent me packing."

"So the turd grandson can't fire you, which means you can do the work with or without him. So do it. The faster the job is done, the sooner we get paid."

She's right, of course, even if she doesn't have all the facts. I haven't told any of them about Tripp's offer to let us keep the upfront bonus if we drop the job altogether. I'm not sure why, either. I'm doing this as much for them as I am for me. We all need the money. The business needs the money.

The business! If it were only about the money, I'd be on the first flight home tomorrow. "This job is so much more than a payday, though. Think about how good the Sugar Maple Farms account will look in our portfolio. The accounts we'll get based on the name alone are going to change everything for the firm. You see that, don't you?"

"You're not wrong. You're never wrong. It's what I love and hate most about you."

I half-smile, some of the tension between us easing. "Okay, I gotta hit the hay, as they probably say here, because I'm on an actual farm."

"Look around the place tomorrow," Parker says. "Go into town. Talk to customers and farm workers. Ask them what they'd like to see."

"Bless you and your beautiful brain."

If I want to find whatever Mr. Carville thinks my proposal was missing, I need my boots on the ground.

CHAPTER SEVEN

TRIPP

*a*fter a week, I'm still too annoyed and ashamed to go anywhere near the cottages, and Uncle Lawson still hasn't called me back. He's visiting all of the company's global holdings, so I understand, even if the rejection stings. Every morning, I see Jane out running at 6:30 a.m. while I take care of whatever stupid thing Anita has asked me to take care of. This morning, though, Rusty is running with Jane.

I spot them up ahead and curse.

The memory of my first encounter with Jane clashes with the memory of our second. I've never had a conversation with someone that clicked like that first one did. I've never felt as charged talking to a woman as I did in that hour.

Why, of all the firms in the world, did Tag have to hire hers?

All I want is to walk away and let this place fall apart. All she wants is to do the opposite.

If we'd met under any different circumstance, I'd have asked her out by now. Twice. As it is, I never want to see her again through no fault of her own.

Rusty hears me driving behind them. He turns and waves as I pull to the opposite side of the dirt road. Jane looks over and her face falls the moment she lays eyes on me. It fills me with the petty urge to speed up and spit dirt their way. I consider it an accomplishment that I simply drive past with a wave.

I park in the lot near the main house, call my uncle again, and get his voicemail. Again. I hang up and drop my head. Why won't he call me back? We've always been close. Is he angry I skipped the reading of the will? Or that I declined to say any last words at Tag's funeral?

I get out of my truck and walk up to the house right at the same time as Rusty and Jane. At Anita's beckon, Jane bounds up the stairs in one of those running jackets with thumbholes and a pair of extremely distracting black leggings.

Rusty waits for me. "You two sure look chummy," I say.

His face is already red as an apple from his run, but his flush deepens from Honeycrisp to Braeburn. "I'm not interested, if that's what you're gettin' at. I'm just trying to help her out. That okay, Boss?"

"Stop with the 'boss' nonsense."

"You got it, Chief." I fake a slap toward his possibly bruised ribs, and he dodges. "I guess it's not okay, then."

"It's not that. I don't trust her."

Rusty folds his arms, wearing an uncharacteristically skeptical look on his face.

"She's here from Chicago looking to 'rebrand the farm,' whatever that means."

"You know exactly what it means," he says. Rusty studied graphic design at Clemson, and he was working for an ad agency in Atlanta up until last year, when his parents asked him to "stop sowing his wild oats and come home, already." As if

Rusty has a wild side. When he first got back and was still humming with big city energy, he suggested modernizing the logo, signs, typography, all of it. I'd bet that's what gave Tag the idea to rebrand the farm altogether.

Sugar Maple Farms started out as the flagship orchard of Carville Industries decades before I was born. But after Nana died and the mother ship had amassed farms and orchards globally, Tag separated his family farm from the rest of the business. I've never known why. Uncle Lawson was chosen as Tag's successor of Carville Industries and me as successor of Sugar Maple Farms. He'd planned to retire from both next year—at eighty—so he could finally "enjoy his old age."

I always told him that my first act as CEO would be to sell it back to Carville Industries so I could leverage the sale to become the Chief Sustainability Officer. Tag always waved it off and muttered something about my not knowing a good life when I saw it. Sometimes those conversations felt almost playful. Other times, not so much.

Knowing he didn't take my objections or wishes seriously hurts. I may not love the farm, but I respect the work. I got my Master's in Agribusiness so I could improve our precision agriculture among the dozens of commercial farms in our holdings. He was happy to use my ideas, just not happy to let me be the one to implement them.

I'd hoped Uncle Lawson would care more than Tag, but now I'm not so sure. He became CEO upon Tag's passing and put his oldest daughter, Kayla, over Sustainability last week. His three sons have been sprinkled throughout the company for the last few years, too. I would happily work under any of them, even though I have more education than Hunter and Wes.

It's hard not to think about what might have been. Had I been born to Tag's younger son.

I need Uncle Lawson to call me back so I can sell the farm to him ASAP. Come to think of it, maybe Rusty has an axe to grind in all of this, too.

"I'm sorry Tag cut you out of the rebrand," I tell Rusty. "If he hadn't written up an ironclad contract, I'd get rid of her and give you the account."

"I do graphic design, Tripp. I'm good at it, but I don't know how to do a rebrand," he says. "Tag did right by me and my family with the fruit stands in his will. But I don't think you need to worry about Jane. She's good people."

We'll see about that.

We find Anita chatting with Jane in the big, open kitchen, where huge platters of eggs, bacon, biscuits and gravy, and grits are spread out. Anita looks as enchanted with Jane as Rusty is, talking faster than normal with an excitement I rarely see from her. How did Jane manage to get Anita prattling away in only two minutes? Jane accused me of thinking she was too pretty to be smart, but the woman she's talking to is proof that beauty and brains are never mutually exclusive.

Anita waves us in when she spots us. "Y'all sure dilly dallied long enough out there. Come on. Let's eat."

We join Anita and Jane at the big farmhouse table in the dining room and tuck in the moment Anita finishes saying grace. I'm still not sure how we all came to be here at the same time, considering Anita didn't coordinate anything with me, but over the years, I've learned not to argue with Anita.

Anita and her husband, Booker, have run the B&B for the past eighteen years. Since I promoted her to caretaker upon inheriting the business, the main house really should be theirs and I should move to Tag's estate in town on the other side of the river. Problem is that the main house isn't wheelchair accessible like their house off the B&B is. Booker was an expert horse rider, but even the best of riders can be thrown, and in Booker's case, it was a miracle his spinal cord injury wasn't fatal. He lost muscle function in the lower half of his body and has been a wheelchair user ever since. I know it's far harder than they let on, but Booker seems unchanged, mobility aside. His personality is as constant as rain in August. He's as gruff as they come, and that exterior hides an even bigger jokester.

Tag modified the B&B and built a house adjacent to it for them after Booker's accident. He bent over backwards to make sure that Booker and Anita were taken care of. I'll do the same for as long as I'm here.

As we eat, Anita explains all that she and Jane have been talking about in the last several days. Jane tells us about her team in Chicago and the consumer research they're already working on. She talks about her goal to make our brand match our world-class quality, and even though this is off-the-cuff, she shows us some of her team's research on her phone. "Your current branding screams pre-packaged processed foods rather than fresh, healthy, or organic." She swipes, showing our existing 'Nature's Fast Food' slogan alongside one that looks clean and modern. "And while your slogan could still work, the style has dramatically dipped in popularity."

"It was ugly then," Anita says, making Jane grin. "But that mock-up is gorgeous!"

"You can see it on a fruit stand, can't you? On a package of dehydrated apple slices that no one could confuse for Doritos?"

Rusty chuckles.

I glance at him in surprise. He's hanging on Jane's every word. Anita is, too. This isn't even a real meeting, but the woman holds the room spellbound as she sits in front of a plate of bacon and grits, holding a phone with as much confidence as if she were wearing a power suit in a boardroom.

And it's sexy.

"And let's talk about restoring some of the spirit of this place. Rusty, you told me about your third grade class coming to the farm on a school field trip."

Rusty nods. "It was the whole class's favorite trip."

Jane shares research about how school outcomes improve across the board for students who go on field trips and separate research about how kids who spend more time in nature have healthier eating habits. She talks about the power of associating those patterns with Sugar Maple Farms. The data alone could persuade school boards across South Carolina to invest in the effort with us.

And if the data is delivered by Jane?

Fish in a barrel.

If I let myself, I could get caught up in the magic she casts. She's sharp and well spoken, and she has a way of making eye contact when she talks that makes you feel like you're in this with her. Even me, and she's barely looking at me. When she brings up an interesting point, she makes us feel smarter for understanding and agreeing with her. I can only imagine how much more of an ego boost we'd all get if she had a formal presentation. She could make us think we invented fire.

She could almost make me want to stay. See this rebrand through.

I sit up straight, alarmed by the traitorous thought. *Don't let her suck you in,* I warn myself. *Yes, she's swimming in talent, but you do not care. You* cannot *care.*

Anita and Rusty are clapping, and I realize Jane has finished her impromptu presentation. They tell her how much they love her vision for the updated brand, how perceptive her research was, how they love the idea of recapturing the community spirit. Jane asks Rusty for his thoughts on their logo ideas, and he, surprisingly, has plenty to say. What is it about her that empowers him to use his voice so freely?

When Anita asks me what I think, I can't be honest. I can't tell her that I agree with Jane's assessment, because I don't want any changes to happen here. I don't want to admit that her ideas make me rethink this place, because I don't want to be *in* this place.

"You have a lot of interesting thoughts, but Tag was right. There's something missing," I say. Then, before Anita can tell me off or I can let the hurt in Jane's face sink in, I put my napkin on my plate and excuse myself. "Thank you for breakfast, Anita."

And I walk out, feeling like the biggest jerk in the world.

CHAPTER EIGHT

JANE

*T*ripp Carville is the biggest jerk in the world.

That's all I can think of for the whole next week. Every free moment, my thoughts turn to Tripp and his big, stupid jerk-face.

Rusty and Anita took turns showing me around the farm my first week, but since then, I've wandered the farm on my own, talking to workers, to Rusty's parents, who run the shop and the fruit stands. I talk to Anita and Booker, to the housekeeper, everyone. Wherever I go, I hear comments about fruit season being the toughest time of year, and they're not even harvesting anything yet.

It all sounds hard, and that makes me feel useless.

I hate feeling useless.

Anita lets me shadow her while I strategize, which means some time on the farm and a surprising amount of time in her office. She and Booker have a wheelchair accessible house that is almost like an annex to the B&B. A covered ramp connects the two buildings, but where the B&B is all accessible, homespun charm, their home is state of the art. The professional kitchen is built lower to the ground, with cutouts and gaps beneath counters for a wheelchair. Booker insists on making me breakfast and lunch while I'm there, and he maneuvers with the same ease that he jokes with.

He pushes shrimp and grits or applewood smoked pulled pork sandwiches or some other delicious creation on me every time he sees me. I try to protest, but he eyes me.

"I don't trust a woman with elbows as sharp as yours." His eyes twinkle against his deep brown skin. I can easily imagine how handsome he was when he was younger. He's a silver fox as it is. He's bald, but his black beard has streaks of gray.

"Your wife's elbows are this sharp," I remind him.

"Exactly my point," he says with a wink.

In her spacious office, Anita has explained planting schedules, market condition, disease and soil management, farm workers, and more. She wears jeans, boots, and a t-shirt to work, yet she exudes more confidence and competence in that than I do in my wide-legged linen slacks, wedges, and sleeveless blouse. I feel like an overdressed fool, but it's better than the dress suits I brought.

Somehow, my imposter syndrome convinced me that it would be better to be overdressed than underdressed. On a farm. My only other real option is my running gear, but I can't feel professional in spandex. I just can't.

Anita tells me that she wishes she could keep her top seasonal harvesters from year to year but work needs don't justify it. "Having to recruit and train new harvesters is a constant thorn in my side," she says, "even with a management company doin' most of the work."

"Have you considered incorporating agrotourism into the business model? With the reservoir, the forest, and the river running through, I think you could organize farm hikes along with glamping or camping grounds. Maybe things like a ropes course for people to book family reunions."

She rubs her chin. "Could work. I imagine those activities would be most popular in summer or during school breaks. We'd need to find trained help for those areas, which would be its own hassle," she says, and I want to kick myself for not having anticipated that. My face warms like I'm sitting in front of the space heater Grandpa gave us when I was nine. "But I'm interested. What else have you got?"

I hate offering the wrong solution to a problem. For the hundredth time, I wish my friends were here. I need to talk things out, to bounce thoughts off of others. I thrive on brain-storming and then reinterpreting ideas when they come back to me. No matter how crazy the notion, my friends always see my process through, because they know the end result is worth it. Anita isn't Parker, who I miss more than ever, but she's intelli-gent and conversational. I'll take that over Tripp's intelligent-but-stubborn any day.

I pull up some figures on my tablet. "Sugar Maple Farms used to hold pumpkin patches every year up until about ten years ago, right? So if you started holding a pumpkin patch and a couple of other festivals like, say Christmas lights or Bunny-land, would those generate enough revenue to justify keeping on some of the top workers?"

Her eyes skip across the screen, and I sense excitement. "It's a very good idea. The setup and takedown alone would require a lot of extra help. Maybe more than I'd want to keep on. I'll need to do some research."

"You could consider recruiting help from the local high school to run booths, take tickets, that kind of thing. I under-stand community involvement used to be pretty strong, so it could help revive that same spirit."

She nods. "That's good. I'll make some phone calls to see if it's even possible before we get too much further, but you're on to something."

What? No. Stupid external processing. I didn't mean to give her more responsibility. I should have looked into the logistics before presenting it to her. She has enough on her plate. "No, please, allow me. This is my proposal."

"But it's my job, hon. I don't mind putting in the work when I'm getting the paycheck."

She's smiling, but my palms go sweaty at the idea of inconveniencing her.

"I insist," I say. "We're a full-service boutique, and I should have made sure the plans were viable before presenting them."

She eyes me like I'm on display in a museum. "You don't like accepting help much, do you?"

Wow. She does not pull punches. Our proximity feels too close now, like she can see too deeply into me.

Because she's exactly right: I *hate* accepting help.

Anytime someone—anyone—did something nice for me, my mom made it feel dirty, like I'd descended into her ranks to get ahead. It didn't matter who it was or what it was, if my mom found out about it, the help became something greasy and suspicious. So when Tripp said that I hadn't earned this account ...

I swallow hard. "I like feeling self-sufficient."

"That's your pride talking." She turns back to her laptop. "When you're humble, you know that there's no such thing as self-sufficiency. We're all here by the grace of someone or something. A grandparent, a friend, a teacher. God. The stranger who slammed on his brakes when he saw us jaywalking. More often than not, greatness comes from having the graciousness to accept help when it's sincerely offered."

This mark is begging to help you! Take it! Mom's voice screams.

"That's a good reminder," I say, even as my skin crawls with the need to make this conversation stop. I don't think help makes you weak or prideful, but it makes people talk, and in my experience, that talk always comes down to the same implication: you only got this because you're pretty.

That professor who mentored me throughout grad school? Everyone said it was because I was pretty. The internship I got that most of our class went for? I only got it, they said, because I was pretty.

This job I'm in no way qualified for?

Tag only hired me because I'm pretty.

It's not your brains they like, Mom would say. *Use those looks to your advantage,* Mom would say. But I can't let Anita, of all people, think that way—a former Miss South Carolina who is so quick and beautiful and competent. I *need* her to feel the same way about me. I need to prove that I'm not a leech like my mom, that I'll contribute above and beyond what's required.

I've spent my life trying to carry more than my fair share, to show that I'm not some opportunist who's just in it for myself. That was my mom. Drop dead gorgeous and couldn't care less about another living soul.

That. Isn't. Me.

"I've been in your way long enough. I'm going to start looking into the events and festivals and put together a firm proposal. Thanks, Miss Anita."

I'm out of the house before she can protest or agree. I'm not sure which I'd prefer.

The mid-morning sun feels too warm, even though it's a milder day than when I first arrived. I walk into the sugar maple forest that surrounds this part of the farm, my wedges sinking a bit too far into the soft dirt. I feel like I'm choking, like I need to loosen my blouse, even though my top two buttons are already undone. A plane flies low overhead, the dull roar of the engine taking the edge off the worst of my self-doubt. I walk deeper and deeper into the woods until, finally, I feel like I can breathe.

No one needs me out here. My success or failure is irrelevant to these trees. I can't disappoint them like I can the people I work with. And for.

Mr. Carville made me promise to find a way to make his grandson want to stay. I made that promise before knowing how stubborn and miserable his grandson is, but I made it, all the same. I can't let him down, not even if he's beyond the grave.

The worst part is that I can't stop thinking about Tripp, can't stop thinking about how he considers my plans for the farm lacking. I hate that he said it in front of Anita and Rusty. I hate even more that he's right and that, if he were any other CEO in any other setting, his words wouldn't have bothered me at all.

And I hate that I can't stop thinking about the Tripp who drove me here as if he were a different person.

Speak of the devil …

I've walked far enough along a little path that I'm well past the homestead and forest and am back in farm country. Empty fields sprawl all around me, and there's something so peaceful about being alone. At least until his truck pulls up alongside me, spitting dust all over my linen pants and blouse. "What are you wearing?" He shakes his head and barks over the sound of the plane. "Better question: *what in the world are you doing out here?*"

My nostrils flare with the effort to stay calm. "I'm brain-storming."

"Well you need to do it somewhere else. Now."

"Do you have to be so cantankerous?"

"Do you have to be so contrary?" he snaps back. "You can't be out here, Jane."

"I get it, Tripp! You don't want me here! You've made that abundantly clear."

"No, that's not—" He puffs his cheeks in obvious frustration. Then he steps out of the truck, rounds to my side, and opens the door. "Get in!"

I dig my heels in. "Don't you—eek!" I scream as his Hulk arms pick me up by my waist and heave me over his massive shoulder. I beat my fists against the thick muscles of his back for only an instant before he tosses me into his truck, darts around to his side, and starts driving.

"Wh-what are you doing?" I stammer. *He picked me up!* "Are you looking to drop off the dumb Yankee outside of town to see if I can't find my way back?"

"No, I'm lookin' to protect the dumb Yankee who was about to get doused with pesticides. Did you not see the crop-duster above you?"

"Huh?" I whip around to look out the window, and sure enough, the little plane I heard is dumping chemicals all over the field I was just wandering past. "I thought you guys were certified organic! You're lying to everyone?"

His spine stiffens, and he looks upward like he's praying for patience. "Pesticides don't make a farm organic or not, it's the sourcing of the pesticides. Unfortunately, 'organic' is one of those buzz words that everyone gets behind because they think it's healthier or better for the environment, when that's not necessarily the case. Some of the pesticides used by organic farms are even worse for the environment than the ones in non-organic farms."

Whoa. Is Tripp venting about something? I stay quiet, hoping it will keep him talking.

It does.

"Did you know that if all farms were to shift to organic farming that the number of people suffering globally from malnutrition and hunger would jump by *500 million*? I love a lot of what small, non-industrial organic farms do, but if you're looking to feed the world, organic farming has a lot of catching up to do."

"But Sugar Maple Farms is organic, right?" I say softly, trying not to draw attention to myself. Tripp holds the steering wheel with both hands, navigating quickly but carefully along the dirt roads.

"For the last ten years, yes. We've been pioneers in biodiversity and moving away from monocultures, but if we don't embrace the best of technology, we'll be nothing more than a producer of luxury goods. Organic sounds fancy, but it's not always better."

"So why not start a more affordable, non-organic line? Start small at first, but implement some of these technologies to see the impact it has?"

"Huh." He taps a finger on the steering wheel. "That's not a bad idea."

I ask more questions, and Tripp's stiff shoulders slowly relax. He's in his element as he talks about his dreams of combining the best of organic and technology. He's passionate, too. A continuation of the Tripp I met two weeks ago. It's like he's forgotten that we're sworn enemies and is excited to have someone to brainstorm with. Something I understand completely.

His enthusiasm is magnetic and draws me back in with every word. Even if it's … well, boring.

"And that's to say nothing of the benefits of full coverage irrigation coupled with cover crops. We don't even need fertilizer anymore thanks to that one change."

"You don't care about farming at all, do you?"

Tripp chuckles. "Not at all."

"No, seriously, tell me how you really feel."

"Ha ha." He gives me a wry half-smile. "Don't pretend you weren't hanging on every word."

"Oh, I was. That part about micro irrigation systems?" I fake my mind blowing. "That was … whew! Riveting stuff. Really."

"Bustin' my chops," he mutters with a shake of his head. "I bet I could start you on some marketing topic and you'd be like a wind-up toy going on and on."

"Obviously. Market segmentation is the sexiest topic known to mankind."

"Sexy? Whoa there. This here is a family operation. You keep that dirty talk to yourself."

I feign a zipper across my lips.

"There's no way you started a business you didn't need to start if you didn't love it."

"No one *needs* to start a business."

"You know what I mean."

I know what he *thinks* he means. He thinks I'm richer than dark chocolate, a notion I would gladly disabuse him of if he didn't run so hot and cold. "It felt like a driving need at the time. I love helping people and businesses grow. Generating ideas with an open-minded client is satisfying, but nothing feels better than seeing those ideas come to fruition."

"Tell me."

I don't even know where we're driving anymore. I get the feeling that Tripp is taking the long, scenic route in order to prolong our conversation, so I comply. I tell him about the McLadyPants account, one of my favorite accounts in ages. The ad dropped only a few days ago, and it's already reached twenty million views on social media. McLadyPants's sales have gone through the roof. The Blanche Knows Best line is completely sold out, and people are signing up for backorders.

Best of all? Jane & Co. has received four new client inquiries already because of the success of the ad, calls I'm struggling to fit into my schedule as is. None of them are huge companies, but they don't have to be huge to keep the lights on.

Which makes me wonder if we needed this account as badly as I thought we did. Did I need to take such a drastic step? Did I need to sign a contract late at night and fly out two weeks later to save my company?

My friends and I bought a pressure cooker last year and it sat in the cupboard for months because we were all too afraid to use it. After years of being the sole provider at home, I'm relatively comfortable in the kitchen, so I finally worked up the nerve to try it.

I closed the pressure valve like the tutorial told me, and then I let the pressure cooker do its thing. At the end of the cook time, though, I was supposed to manually release the pressure to keep the food at the right temperature. I was terrified. I put on oven mitts, reached out holding tongs, and flicked the pressure release valve, sure the whole thing would explode.

It didn't.

Is there a chance that if I let some of the pressure release inside of me, things wouldn't blow up?

I finish telling Tripp about the account, and he promises to look up the video later, something that makes my stomach flip.

"You seem to love your job," he says. We pulled up to my cottage at some point, and now we're just talking across the cab to each other. It feels like it did on that first day.

"I do. And we've already established that you love farming." He nods. "Then why won't you let me help? Why can't we combine our two loves and make something spectacular?"

What I said sounded so innuendo filled that I blush, but instead of teasing me, Tripp closes up faster than a golf course in a lightning storm. "I'll let you off here."

Stupid Jane. You had to push it, didn't you?

Actually, I did.

"Mr. Carville, enough. You need to help me do my job."

"Please stop calling me that." He closes his eyes and grips the steering wheel. "I don't want you doing your job. So looks like we're at an impasse."

"You do realize that the longer you refuse to help me, the longer we're both stuck here, right? Unless you're *trying* to keep me around, you should make my job as easy as possible."

"Yet you've been here two weeks and we've hardly seen each other."

"UGH! Fine, then I'll ask Rusty."

He shifts to look at me, a Jack Reacher kind of energy that has me way too aware of how close we are to each other and how brutally hot he is. I'm almost sweating under the heat of his gaze. "Rusty's too busy."

"And yet he offered. Twice."

"An offer you've refused. Twice."

"Until Anita told me that you'd be no help because your 'knickers are in a knot over Tag's will.' I'll see if I can get a pair of McLadyPants in your size right after I text Rusty."

I pull out my phone, but Tripp covers it with his hand. His fingers brush against mine in the process, and ...

I don't hate it.

"Stop, Jane." He huffs. "You are not makin' this easy on a guy."

The words are playful yet pained, and the combination softens my frustration. He lost his grandfather only a couple of weeks ago, and their relationship didn't seem particularly solid. No matter what else is going on, I should show some compassion.

"Does that mean you'll help me?"

"It means I'll give you access. It's as much as I can do for now."

"Thank you."

He side eyes me. "That's it? No argument? No lecture? Just a 'Thank you'?"

"The lecture will come later. We've finally reached the hands-on portion of today's outing."

When I say "hands-on," Tripp's gaze flickers to my bare shoulders for a split second, and a flash of heat burns through me. His eyes jump back to mine, and we both pause, the air in the cab growing charged. Is he thinking what I'm thinking? Am *I* thinking what I think I'm thinking? That getting hands-on with Tripp wouldn't be the worst thing in the world?

Not by a long shot?

Tripp reaches his massive arm out. Is he going to grab me? Kiss me? No way I want that. Right?

Before I can so much as exhale, his arm passes me, opens the door, and practically shoves me out into the sticky humidity.

"Put your board room clothes in the back of the closet for the rest of the stay, will you? You work on a farm now. Change into something you can move in, and I'll be back in twenty," he says before taking off.

I watch him go, wondering what in the world just happened.

And when did his truck get air conditioning?

* * *

I rush into the cottage. Hope bubbles up in me, spilling over until I pull out my phone and call one of my friends. I put it on speaker and drop the phone to the bed as I rush to get changed. The phone dials—

Shoot!

Did I call *Parker?* End call! End call!

I try to stab the red button, but she answers before I can.

"What's up?" she asks, sounding distracted.

I scramble to pick up the phone. "Hey, sorry, I must have butt dialed you," I lie lamely.

"Okay, talk later—"

"Wait! While I have you, how are things going?" I ask, trying not to sound as desperate as I feel.

Her silence stretches over several heartbeats. "I'm really busy, so unless you need something, I should probably go."

"Parker—"

"Yes?" The word cuts like a knife.

"I know I should have told you about the account before I took it, but he didn't give me a choice. Can't you understand?"

A huffing sound is all the answer I get. "I need to prep for another call. We can talk about this later."

"When?"

"Later. Bye, Jane."

I'm hurt and angry as I stare at the blank phone screen.

"Don't do this," I tell myself. "Focus on turning the farm around. You fix this place, and you'll fix whatever's going on with you and Parker."

Several minutes later, Tripp pulls up in some kind of off-roading vehicle that looks like a utility golf cart with windows. As much as I hate it, I've changed out of my work clothes and into sneakers, yoga pants, and an oversized, half-tucked t-shirt (I won't admit how long I debated between a full-tuck and that half-tuck).

It's not hot outside, but it is humid. How does he not get sweaty wearing jeans all of the time? Thinking of his jeans makes me notice how they hug his exceptionally muscled thighs.

Why does he have to be so hot? Why does he have to be so hot? "Why does he have to be so hot?"

"Beg your pardon?"

Fun fact: I talk to myself. It's part of my whole external processing thing. When something is on my mind, sometimes it escapes, especially when it's distracting me from other things.

Tripp's hotness is distracting me from everything.

"Why does it have to be so hot?" I ask, as if I'm repeating myself.

"It sounded like you said 'he.'" The corner of his mouth tugs upward.

"Oh, did it? How funny." *Drop this, please!*

"'He' who?"

I look out the window to hide my burning cheeks. "Hmm?"

"You definitely said 'he.' 'Why does *he* have to be so hot?' I'm wondering who 'he' is?"

Um, hello. Is he flirting with me? "Rusty," I say, wiping the smirk right off his face, even though I'm not interested in Rusty,

73

and he doesn't seem the least bit interested, either. "That man is too pretty for words. Have you seen the bursts of green in those hazel eyes? Whew! Is he seeing someone, do you know?"

"Don't know."

He's surly now, which means he was absolutely, definitely flirting. The brat! He doesn't get to flirt after one civil interaction, no matter what's going on beneath the far too impressive surface.

Ugh. Why does he have to be so hot?

"Well, your all-terrain golf cart has great air conditioning," I say.

Tripp snorts. "You must have spent a lot of time at the country club if you call a side-by-side an 'all terrain golf cart.'"

Just like that, his hotness disappears.

"You sure have me figured out," I say sarcastically. In point of fact, I did spend a lot of time at the country club. Just not remotely in the way he thinks. With a last name like Harrington, everyone assumes they know me without knowing a thing about me. Tripp seems to think he dunked on me with the way he acts as tour guide now. His deep, rumbling voice sounds smug as he points different places out. The farm is empty of the nostalgic touches it was once known for. Other than the small store selling preserves and fruit butters and the iconic red barn and sugar maple tree from their labels, it looks more like the ghost of a farm than one of the most recognizable brands in fruit spreads. Everywhere I look, I see possibilities, beyond the obvious farm-to-table restaurant.

I went to a half dozen farms and orchards to prepare my proposal to Mr. Carville. The customer experience was either hip and modern or nostalgic and folksy, but never both. Is it even possible to do both with Sugar Maple Farms?

Tripp is right. I've never worked on so much as a flier for a fruit stand. My team can research with the best of them, but there's no substitute for experience. The memory of Mr.

Carville saying that something was missing rattles through my brain. And that makes the memory of my mom's taunts echo along with them.

If someone's paying you attention, girls like us know exactly what it's for. Take what you can get while you can get it.

Never, I would tell her with my hands balled into fists.

She would just laugh.

Something is missing. But don't worry, Mr. Carville told me. *You'll know it when you see it.*

Watching Tripp point out sight after sight, I hope Mr. Carville knew what he was talking about.

CHAPTER NINE

TRIPP

I have whiplash. Every conversation with Jane tosses me around worse than a roller coaster at a county fair. I am constantly on my toes with this woman.

I hate it.

I love it, too.

Why did I have to meet her like this? Of all the times and seasons in my life, why did it have to be now? We are so compatible, yet everything we want is at odds. It feels like Tag's final *Carville test*.

That's not my interpretation of how he acted, either. That's legitimately what he called the difficulties I faced in life: "A Carville test." When I got wrongly accused of vandalizing my prep school's auditorium, I asked him for help. He put his hand on my shoulder, stared down his nose at me, and sternly said, "This is a Carville test, Tripp. I trust you'll know how to handle it."

When I injured my shoulder senior year and my chances at a

football scholarship went down the drain, I came home angry and heartbroken. He looked me in the eye and said, "You gonna let this make you bitter or better? This is a Carville test, Tripp. I trust you'll know what to do next."

It was always the same with him. The good things that happened were never Carville tests. Not winning a big game. Not earning an academic scholarship. Not getting accepted into the program of my dreams. Only the bad stuff. Everything that hurt, everything that didn't work out. It's like he only noticed my faults and mistakes. Like I wasn't allowed to mess up if I wanted to be worthy of the Carville name.

But it wasn't only me. My dad used to complain about Tag constantly. He would grumble about what a killjoy he was, about how controlling he was. In fact, the first time I ever heard mention of a Carville test was from my dad. He had just bought his prop plane and had called my grandparents to see if he could keep it at the farm so they could watch me while he flew.

Tag must have launched into a lecture because my dad snapped. "Duty? Come on, Dad, learning to fly a plane doesn't take away from my duty. I'm never going to live up to your expectations, so spare me the *Carville test*."

The men in my family could never measure up.

It didn't matter that I was named after him or that Carville was on my birth certificate. If I'd been adopted like two of my cousins were, it would have been the same. A Carville test wasn't about DNA. It was about some nebulous idea of *character* that only Tag could identify or approve of.

Rusty? Carville-approved. Self-sacrifice and a work ethic like his have a tendency to turn people into fans of his right away. Tag was no exception.

Jane? Obviously Carville-approved. Determined, whip-smart, and creative enough to work around my objections? How could I have thought that Tag only hired her for her looks?

I'm ashamed even thinking about our interaction from that first day.

What is it about Jane that makes me say the exact wrong thing? Rather, what is it about *me* that makes me say the wrong thing when Jane was around? I'm not used to feeling flustered by a woman. Tag was the only person who ever made me second-guess myself, but even that was nothing like this. With Tag, I was always waiting for the trap. With Jane, I keep stepping in landmines while forgetting where I dropped them.

She makes me stupid.

No, I'm stupid for her. Over her. Around her? Something with a preposition.

Like the comment I made two minutes ago about the golf cart. I thought it was funny, but her frosty answer has me wondering what I said wrong. She's a *Harrington!* If she can't joke about her upbringing, she's not the woman I thought she was.

Oh right, because you joke about your upbringing all the time?

Shut it.

"What am I missing?" Jane whispers to herself. "What is the essence of this place?"

I smile at her self-talk. Her question makes me wonder the same thing that she's asking herself, though. What *is* the essence of Sugar Maple Farms? If I weren't actively rooting for her to fail, what would I say?

What did this place represent to me when I was a broken eight-year-old boy?

My phone rings, the sound shaking me violently from my thoughts.

It's Uncle Lawson.

"I have to take this." I pull over, throw the side-by-side into park, and jump out. I'm grateful I brought the UTV with the full-cab enclosure. Jane won't be able to hear how desperate I am. "Uncle Lawson, thanks for calling me back."

"Tripp, my boy," he bellows, sounding so much like my dad, my throat aches. "What are we going to do about that farm of yours?"

I saw Uncle Lawson at the funeral, but that was before the reading of the will. If I'd known then what I know now, we wouldn't be in this mess. I tell him about the will, including that Jane's company has been hired to rebrand the farm and product line. He knows it all.

"You're now the proud owner of one of the most esteemed farms in the country. Your papa hired a firm to revamp it, so the financial trends should flip around. I fail to see the problem here."

"The problem is that I don't want the farm. You saw my proposal about agricultural drones. Let me implement this wide scale. I want Carville Industries to be the global leader in efficient, sustainable agriculture."

"We want the same things, Tripp, but I'm sorry to break this to you: you haven't earned it."

"What do you mean? I have the degrees, I have the proposals—"

"But you don't have the experience. You've been the caretaker at Sugar Maple Farms for how long, and you haven't done a thing? Tag gave you years to show that you could implement your proposals on a small scale, and you chose to backpack across Europe instead."

I squeeze my free hand into a fist and kick at a rock. Dirt flies up around my jeans. "It was *Venezuela*, and I was teaching villages how to expand community garden programs with fewer resources."

"And then it was on to Bolivia and Brazil."

"Again, to help them. It's not like I was sitting on a private beach, sipping margaritas."

"I miss alcohol," he says. He gave up cigars and alcohol shortly after Tag's diagnosis. While Tag said he was too old to care, Lawson said he was too young not to. "But that's not the point. I'm not saying you were wasting your time or doing anything wrong. I'm saying that you've never seen a single project through. We gave you chances. We offered to put you on projects, and you prioritized your volunteer work over your job, work that someone else dictated. You're asking for a seat at a table when you've never even finished a meal."

"Uncle Lawson, please," I beg, not caring how desperate I sound. Sweat drips down the side of my face. "I didn't choose volunteering over the company. Tag only offered me jobs I didn't want."

"And what happens if *I* give you a job you don't want or ask you to do a project you don't like? That's what work is, Tripp: doing stuff you sometimes don't want to do for the good of a company. But now you can have it all. Every idea you wanted to implement across our global holdings you can implement at your own farm. You're free to innovate, to do whatever you want without a board of directors or a boss putting you on something else. Why wouldn't you jump at the chance to do so?"

He's right on paper. Everything he's saying makes logical sense. Emotionally, though, nothing adds up. "You know what this place represents for me. I have to get out of here."

He breathes softly into the phone. "I know, Tripp. I only wish I understood why. After your parents' accident, the only place in the world you wanted to be was Sugar Maple. I'm not sure when it changed for you, but I think you need to be exactly where you are."

A hard lump forms in my throat. "I don't, Uncle Lawson. I want to sell. I'd rather it be to you than to McNeal or Pulse, but I don't care how much I get for the farm if I don't have to wait."

"You'd give up hundreds of millions for spite?"

"Not for spite," I correct him.

"Then for what?"

"I don't belong here."

"You own the place. You can change that," he says. I don't answer, because we may as well be speaking Greek to each other at this point. Lawson drums his fingers on the table, judging by the sound coming through the phone. "If I were to buy the farm tomorrow for peanuts, what would you do?"

"Leave," I say, because it's the only thing I know for sure. I'd rather work for Carville, but I know people at some competitors. I have connections and could be working soon enough. The importance of my next job matters a lot less than dumping this one.

After a long pause and another puff of breath, he says, "You're desperate to sell. I hear you. But I'm not desperate to take on a farm and label that are losing money. You hear me?"

"Yessir." The lump in my throat doubles in size. Uncle Lawson has a point, one that makes me feel like an idiot to one of the few people in the world I care to impress. If I hadn't felt like a failure before, I definitely do now. I want to end the call, but he clears his throat.

"So how about this," he says. "I'll come back to the farm at the end of August."

"August?" Hope swells in my chest.

"Six months is better than a year, isn't it?" he asks, not realizing his words are rain after a drought. "Work on the rebrand, Tripp. Throw yourself into it, and we'll see how far you've come. If the rebrand looks promising, we'll have another conversation then. If it's good enough, I may even approach market value. Sound good?"

I pump my fist. "Yes, sir. Thank you, Uncle Lawson."

"I'm not making any promises, Tripp," he cautions, but I feel lighter than air. "You have to give it the old Carville try."

"I will," I say, the expression not quite as distasteful to me as usual. We hang up, and I practically float back to the side-by-side. I'm grinning when I squeeze into the driver's seat.

"Good conversation?"

I startle. "Geez Louise, I forgot you were here."

Jane looks like a kid on Christmas morning. "*Geez Louise?*" She throws her head back in laughter. "Okay, Grandma."

"Don't you make fun of phrases like that around Anita," I tell her, buckling up and pulling out. "She'll roast you on a spit."

"Wouldn't dream of it. But you'd better believe I will around her husband."

"You've met Booker?" I give her a quick glance and see confusion on her face.

"What do you think I've been doing for the last two weeks, Tripp? Apart from cleaning out a filthy cabin, fixing a toilet, and unclogging a shower drain?"

Heat pricks my neck. "Right. Sorry again about that."

She shakes her head and looks out the window. "You really didn't know?"

"I knew about the AC," I admit, the warmth spreading up to my face.

She snorts. "That's better than I thought, at least."

I want to go back in time a week and punch myself in the face for dropping Jane off at Strawberry Fields. I just got the kick in the pants I needed to let the rebrand march forward, and now I'm paying for being a spiteful idiot.

"I was angry at Tag," I say, "and I took it out on you. I'm sorry."

She side eyes me. "Thank you," she says. Graciously. What I did was pretty messed up, yet she has the manners or breeding or good nature to accept my apology. "But you're not forgiven quite yet." She shudders, so I ask her what, exactly, was in the cabin.

When she tells me, I feel even worse. "You must have thought I was the lowest person alive," I say with a groan. "I swear on my Momma's grave, I never would have stuck you there if I'd known."

Jane's sarcastic smile falls from her face. "I'm sorry about your parents."

Did I mention my parents earlier? "It was a long time ago," I say, shrugging it off. I don't want to get into my sob story.

Out of the corner of my eye, I can see her looking at me. She opens her mouth, and I say a silent prayer that she'll drop it. Mercifully, she does.

We pull up to the farm's processing factory—a large, red brick warehouse a couple of miles outside of town. We employ hundreds of people in town here, not including the ones on the farm. The lot is full, but that doesn't stop Jane from whispering, "I knew it. I knew you'd find a remote place to chop me up and dump my body."

"You just walked past someone passing out balloon animals to children. Does this place really scream murder factory to you?"

"I wouldn't put it past you."

"Only because you don't know how hard it is to sanitize a jelly production line," I deadpan.

"That's very reassuring."

"You're safe, Jane." I hold the door open for her. "For now."

She slaps my abs as she passes me to walk into the factory.

Progress.

CHAPTER TEN

JANE

*I*t's not like I'm thinking of Tripp's abs three hours and a factory tour later, or anything. I definitely paid attention during the tour. I pointedly was *not* thinking of how his stomach felt like a washboard while he was talking about products and units sold and other things I absolutely need to know to do my job.

Okay, I'll just read up on everything I missed later.

The factory has a customer-facing store with a line of a half dozen people. Sugar Maple products are found in most grocery stores, but for a local, it's as easy to get it here as the Piggly Wiggly in town. Tripp talks to a production line manager while I wait for a slice of bread with their famous pumpkin butter. My mouth waters. I'm not a big foodie, so for the last week, I've mostly survived on protein shakes and meals that Booker has insisted on feeding me. Anita also dropped off a few bags of produce ... along with a farm truck for my personal use. I've used the truck to run into town a few times, but the smells in here tell me I should have prioritized the grocery store over the hardware store.

Also, I forgot to eat this morning. It's typical for me. Breakfast was always a turbulent time at home, what with the constant fear of seeing some new guy slipping out to get to work. I got used to skipping it as often as possible. The habit has never left me, and nowadays, I can call it "intermittent fasting" and people nod their heads like they admire the sacrifices I make for my health. But it's not about health. I'm just stuck in an old routine that I don't know how to shake.

My phone buzzes with a text from my sister asking for money. Yet another old routine I don't know how to shake.

The clerk hands me my bread, and it smells so good, I can almost forget my sister and financial problems. I take a bite of the bread and pumpkin butter on the spot. I moan, and Tripp flashes me a knowing smile before gesturing to get him one. I grab two more (one for him, another for me) and make my way to his side. The bell above the lobby door rings, and habit from my server years turns my head.

A very blond, very handsome, very desperate looking Hemsworth of a man strides through the door a few yards from us. He's holding a toddler in his arms. Her messy brown pigtails bounce with every stride he makes toward Tripp.

The way he walks is both frantic and controlled, screaming urgency and a need to hide the urgency from the girl at the same time. When Tripp sees the man, he sends the production manager away.

"Duke, what's going on?" Tripp asks. Duke? As in ... oh my gosh, it's Duke Ogden. The NFL quarterback. "This is Jane. Jane, Duke."

He nods to me. It's clear he doesn't have time for small talk, yet he keeps his voice as calm as a summer's morning. "Can you take Lottie for a few hours? Grammy and Pop are in Hilton

Head, and I need to run a quick errand." He gives us a smile that looks false with how wide his eyes are.

"My pleasure." Tripp takes Lottie from her dad's arms. "Everything good?"

"Oh sure, everything's fine. Just need to go check in with Walters." Then he slowly, deliberately mouths, *"Lump."*

This conversation is way outside my pay grade.

Tripp's brows shoot up, and he gestures to his friend to go. Duke kisses Lottie's head and exits the factory. The moment he's out the lobby door, he runs for his car. "Well, Lottie-Bot, you and I are going to have a grand time today, aren't we?"

But Lottie has shut down. She clings on to Tripp and instantly starts crying for her dad. The more Tripp tries to shush her, the more upset she gets.

Something Lottie and I have in common, come to think of it.

The customers in the shop are watching Tripp try to comfort Lottie, so I grab his thick arm (how is this thing real?) and pull him outside. Duke had the good sense to leave the car seat right next to Tripp's military golf cart thingy. Side-by-side? What a weird name.

The humidity makes my skin prick with moisture, but Lottie is crying so hard, her face is red and sweaty. After trying everything we can think of to calm her down, Tripp pulls up a TV show about a family of dogs in Australia and hands her his phone. That buys us enough time to get her in the car seat and to keep her in a haze until we're back to the farm.

When we pull up to the main house, I turn around to see that Lottie is asleep, Tripp's phone in her hands, her head to the side in a way that would have me needing a chiropractor. Tripp starts talking, and I clap my hand over his mouth.

"Shh!"

He tugs my hand down gently. "It's okay. When she's out, she's out."

"You watch her often?" This surprises me. Tripp nods and

looks at her in the rearview mirror. I unbuckle and turn to face him, tucking my knees beneath me on the black leather seat. "Is your friend going to be okay?"

"I'm not sure. Can you be discreet?"

"Of course, but you don't have to tell me anything."

He taps his thumb on the steering wheel. "Chances are you'll hear something around town, and if you're going to be here as long as you say you will, I'd rather you know the truth over the rumors out there."

"Okay."

"But this cannot go *anywhere*. Do you understand? You can't tell your friends or your family. No one." He seems both reluctant and earnest, so I reassure him, and he continues. "You know who he is, I'm sure? And you know he missed the season before last?"

"Yeah. Rehab for his shoulder, right?"

"That's the official story. The unofficial but true story is that Duke was diagnosed with Hodgkin's lymphoma. They found it early and treated it aggressively with chemo and radiation, and he's been cancer-free for about a year now. But he just said he found a lump. Walters is his oncologist in Columbia, so he must be going in for an emergency scan. Normally his parents or sister would watch Lottie, but they're all over in Hilton Head for the week. If Duke has to check in to the hospital, I'm sure they'll be back tonight."

"And what about Lottie's mom? Do I remember right that he's divorced?" I'm a pop culture fan, but I follow sports more than the athletes themselves, so I rarely know anything but the biggest headlines when it comes to athlete's personal lives.

"Don't get me started on Carlie." He peeks back at Lottie, and his face is so close to mine I can smell his aftershave. It's woodsy, but I miss the strawberry scent. Not that I care what he smells like. "While Duke was doing chemo, Carlie up and left in the middle of the night. She said his illness was too upsetting for her, but it turned out that she flew to Europe and hooked up with some pro soccer player."

Shock and outrage make my mouth fall open. "She left her baby while her husband was getting cancer treatments ... for an international hookup?"

"That isn't the half of it, but it's the part that got Duke full custody. He's a good dad, and Lottie is the best kid in the world. And I'm not just saying that because I'm her godfather."

I lay my cheek against the headrest. "I'm surprised you've had time for her with all your globetrotting." I mean it in a teasing way, but once it's out, it sounds cold and accusatory.

And maybe it is. Tripp has managed to be a part of his three-year-old goddaughter's life, but he couldn't help his own grandfather take care of the multi-million-dollar farm he was to inherit?

"That's not fair."

"Yeah, you've mentioned that. Yet you haven't given me a reason to think otherwise."

Tripp looks out the window, and it's like he's a million miles away. "I loved this place as a kid. It was better than Disneyworld. When my parents would drop me off, Nana would always take me here."

"Didn't your grandparents live here?"

"No, they were already beyond rich when I came around. They had a big house in town. But Nana made sure that I knew the farm as well as my dad did, and she made me work alongside her, too." He lets out a soft chuckle. "We stayed in the main house rather than in town because we'd get up so early. Chores were a great equalizer, in her eyes. She said, 'status doesn't much matter when you're up to your armpits in fertilizer.'"

Tripp's accent gets thicker when he's talking about his grandma. I haven't heard this tender note in his voice before. "She sounds really special."

"She was."

"When did you lose her?"

"About twenty years ago. In the same accident that took my parents."

"Oh, Tripp." I grab his hand and squeeze. He lets me, which is more than I expected considering our constant push and pull. He's so solid, but this conversation is revealing softness, too. That much heartache in such a short time surely left a deep mark. "No eight-year-old should have to live with that much pain. I'm sorry."

Tripp's eyes move to our hands, and mine follow. "Thanks," he says. I'm not sure if it's me or him, but the next thing that happens changes everything.

Our hands shift and spread until our fingers are interlaced, and there's a feeling of something clicking into place. The right- ness of simply holding Tripp's hand somehow reaches across the universe, through the cosmos, into our galaxy, and then zips all the way into the vehicle, where we're sitting side by side. The feeling seems to hit us both at the same time, as our eyes meet in unison.

"Jane." It's only a word—my name. One single syllable. But it's laden with paragraphs of subtext, all of which I long to read.

His eyes flit down to my lips, making my breath hitch. He's like the Pied Piper, because that simple gesture makes me lean forward, even as he does. I don't know where he's looking anymore because all I can see is his mouth. And now all I can taste is his breath. And as I close my eyes, all I can—

"DADDY!"

Lottie's voice shatters the air, and Tripp and I fly apart.

CHAPTER ELEVEN

TRIPP

ottie will not stop crying.

My goddaughter is inconsolable, my best friend is going to find out if his cancer is back, and I almost kissed Jane Harrington in a side-by-side. My mind is a mess of emotion, but not even the memory of Jane's lips parting in anticipation can numb me to the feeling of Lottie weeping in my arms.

I've tried every sort of bribery the house has to offer: TV, food, candy, my phone, bubbles, even the playground behind the house. Nothing is working.

Worse, Jane disappeared on me five minutes ago, and if anything, that's only made Lottie cry harder.

Her little body is curled into my shoulder, but she keeps her hands in front of her mouth to cover her sobbing, which makes me hate Carlie even more than I already do. I sway and make shushing noises like Duke taught me to when Lottie was an infant, all the while rubbing small circles on her tiny back.

"No girl likes being shushed, in case you need the refresher." Jane's expression is arch when she returns to the kitchen. She gestures to me to join her at the kitchen table.

Lottie twists in my arms when we sit so that she's looking at Jane. Her first two years of life were marked with disappearances, and she seems to remember it to her soul. Her mom leaving and just not coming home. Duke being gone for hours and days getting cancer treatments. As soon as she likes someone, she clings to them in so desperate a way, it turns the cracks in my heart into fissures. For Lottie's sake, I hope she doesn't like Jane that much.

And yet, now that we're at the table, I look to Jane like she's going to save us all. Once she knows that Lottie's looking at her, Jane pulls a surprise out from behind her back. It's a baby chick. She holds the tiny ball of yellow fluff in her hand so Lottie can see it. When Lottie's cries lessen slightly, Jane puts the chick on the table a few feet from us.

"Do you want to know something awesome?" Jane says in her naturally low voice. She's not even trying to speak over Lottie, and Lottie's cries quiet even more. "Baby chicks are born with a tooth on top of their beak. A tooth! Can you believe that? They use it to peck their way out of the egg. It falls off a few days after the chick hatches."

Lottie takes a break from crying and gulps air in a hiccup that makes her tiny frame shake. She's a mess of tears and snot and sweat, and I hug her closer. But as Jane points out the tiny white tooth covering the chick's beak, Lottie's tears cease and she takes another gulp of air. Jane lets Lottie touch the chick with one finger, and the little girl is entranced by the magic of new life.

"Can you imagine if we had to peck our way out of an egg?" Jane crosses her eyes and pretends to peck with her nose. It's arresting to see someone so stunning willingly look so silly.

"How big do you think Uncle Tripp's egg would have to be?" Jane asks, making her arms go as wide as they can.

"As big as a din-a-saw egg!" Lottie laughs. I catch Jane's eye in a brief flash of excitement before Jane laughs with Lottie. They spend the next few minutes teasing me about being part dinosaur or part bear, etc., and I do my best impression of whatever animal they call me.

I'll admit it: my buffalo needs work.

But Lottie is coming out of her shell, laughing and squealing, and I'll be a goofy half-buffalo man for as long as it takes to keep her happy. When Jane's phone vibrates, she leads us out the backdoor into the yard where, somehow, a petting zoo has been erected, complete with a portable fence.

"How did you do this?"

"I know a guy." She shrugs.

"*You* know a guy?"

"What do you think I've been doing for the last two weeks, Tripp?" Jane winks. True to her word, her "guy"—Rusty—is standing inside the fence, ready to show Lottie the animals.

"Hey there, Lottie," Rusty says to Lottie's squeals. Everyone knows that Lottie has a crush on "Uncle" Rusty. I try not to be annoyed that Jane called him in her time of need. I pass Lottie to him over the fence, and the moment he puts her down, she's off and petting some of the kid-friendliest of baby farm animals: goats, llamas, and alpacas.

Jane thanks Rusty, but he's too occupied with Lottie and the animals to stay and chat.

I step beside Jane, close enough that Lottie can't overhear us. I drop my head toward her. "How did you know to do all of this?"

"My friend Millie. She's the consumer behavior specialist with Jane & Co., but she's a licensed clinician and takes on private practice clients here and there. She's incredible. The most empathetic, nurturing person. But, boy does she cheat at cards."

I laugh. "A therapist who cheats at cards? There has to be more to that story."

"She is the most sneakily competitive person you'll ever meet. You'd think it would be Parker, because she's so obviously brilliant and hates being wrong, you know? But no, Parker plays games like there's an ethics review board watching."

Jane's smile fades, but I ask her more questions. She tells me about her friends in aching detail. It's obvious how much she misses them.

"Tag's will mentioned that your team would do the rebrand," I say. "Why didn't they come with you?" At the mention of the will, Jane stands straighter. "I'm not threatening to fire you over it; I'm just curious," I stress.

She looks like she's biting her cheek. "They have other accounts to finish up."

"So they're coming later, then? When they finish those jobs?" I ask. Jane squirms. "Are they coming at all?"

She folds her arms. "No. They consider 'all-hands-on-deck' to be equally as effective when remote."

It figures. The minute Uncle Lawson convinces me to embrace the rebrand is the minute I find out that infighting at Jane's company is going to slow this whole thing down. "But Tag specifically said 'You'll know it when you see it.' How are they going to *know* anything when they aren't even here?" I ask.

Jane cocks her brows way up. "And why do you suddenly care, when you don't want any of us here in the first place?"

Before I can respond, Lottie is jumping up and down at the fence in front of us, insisting that we come in and play with her. But not even the cuteness of watching my goddaughter ride an alpaca can distract me from my frustration with Jane and her team. She doesn't seem any happier about it than I feel, but she's the CEO. She should do something about this!

My frustrations linger until Duke finally returns around supper. Lottie, Jane, Rusty, and I are eating picnic-style by the backyard playground when Duke comes out the backdoor. Lottie sees her dad before he can open his mouth, and she runs to him faster than Duke does when he's running a quarterback draw.

"Daddy!" She squeezes him tightly and tells him all about her day, pointing to the remains of the petting zoo and telling him about the ride Rusty and Jane took her on in the side-by-side while Uncle Tripp cleaned off the alpaca poop he slipped in. No mention of the brownies I made or the piggyback rides I gave or about how I only slipped in the alpaca poop because I had to break her fall from the very same alpaca.

Cute little ingrate.

Duke listens with a grin on his face and they join us on the blanket. But as soon as they're down, Lottie is bouncing up again and asking Jane to push her on the swing. Jane complies like we all do with any of Lottie's commands.

"The scan came back clear. Doc said I have a sinus infection, so my overactive lymph nodes got a touch too excited," Duke says, and Rusty and I both whoop and give Duke an awkward seated hug. We don't need to talk about how worried any of us were. The relief is enough. "She didn't cry when she saw me," Duke says, watching Lottie swing with Jane. "How did you do that?"

"Jane's therapist friend gave us some tips," I tell him. At the alarmed look on his face, I reassure him. "Jane didn't give her any details. She just asked about how to help a three-year-old with separation anxiety."

Duke exhales loudly. "Thank her for me. And Rusty, I'm guessing you helped with the petting zoo, considering we all know what happens when Tripp gets around baby farm animals."

"Pigs are omnivores, Ogden, they bite," I protest.

"And yet none of the rest of us got bit," Rusty says.

"Because none of the rest of you were the ones opening the pen," I say.

"Uh huh. Sure. Whatever you have to tell yourself, Pig Bait," Duke says.

"Shut up, or I'll sit on you." I say, but they only laugh. At six-five, I have nearly an inch and a half on Duke and four on Rusty. When your friends have more dirt on you than a farm, you take every advantage you can get.

"And I'll bench you," Duke says, throwing a strawberry at me. I catch it in my mouth. "So that's the woman Tag hired to rebrand the farm. She seems terrible. No personality at all. And uglier than a mud fence. I get why you're so angry with Tag now."

Rusty snorts.

"Shut up," I repeat. We watch Jane chase Lottie up the stairs and down the slide, growling and giggling in turn.

"Do you remember when Tag built this thing?" Duke asks. "We were what, nine?"

"He put it in right after the accident," I say. "Probably looking for a way to get rid of me."

A V forms between Duke's brows. "I don't know about that. He spent hours pushing us on those swings, even though we were all big enough to swing by ourselves."

"I remember the day he finally finished putting it together. You were up in your room," Rusty says, gesturing to the window on the second floor that overlooks the backyard, "and he hollered at you to come down and see the surprise he built you."

I rack my brain, but nothing comes. "I don't remember any of this."

Rusty picks a blade of grass. "That makes sense. It was a hard time for you. It was fruit season, or I probably wouldn't remember it so well." Rusty tries to shrug off his constant presence, but he practically lived at the farm from early spring to late summer. Whenever Tag was in his shed, Rusty found his way over. Tag would hand him a tool and expect him to figure it out. "Tag let me carve my initials in one of the beams," Rusty says, pointing to the tower.

Envy creeps up from my gut to my throat, extending down my arms to my fingertips. Rusty spent a lot of time building things with Tag when we were in middle school and high school, but why am I surprised that Tag let Rusty help him, even then?

Because while he let me in his office, he shooed me away from his shed if I got within ten feet of the place. When he told me it was "too dangerous for a twelve-year-old," he actually meant he didn't want me around. I don't remember Tag building the playground, let alone pushing us on the swings. The shock of the accident was too much for me to bear for a long time, and even now, my memories of the months following it are foggy at best.

When I came out of the fog, it was to find that my grandfather had permanently moved us from his estate in town to the farm, and my life was gone. I was lucky to meet Rusty and Duke as quickly as I did. Life with Tag was too bleak, too quiet, too strict.

A rustle pulls my attention. Jane and Lottie's playing has moved closer to the blanket, and Lottie is hopped-up on the juice boxes and brownies I made for the picnic. She buzzes around us with such an energy that I have to wonder if, somewhere deep down, she knows that her dad is okay. That's all that matters. Not my childhood trauma.

As the evening winds down and my friends clear out, Jane stays on the porch with me and helps me clean the remains of the picnic. We work wordlessly. I'm not sure what I even want to say except that I couldn't have managed this afternoon without her. The feeling between us isn't the usual jolt of electricity that could either revive or electrocute me. The tension is more emotional than physical.

When the last of the dishes is loaded and the final napkin is thrown away, the moon is already coming up. The sky is spectacular on the farm, and the view from the kitchen window is straight out of a Norman Rockwell painting. Jane brushes her hands off on her leggings. They're a lot dustier than they were this morning. "I should get going."

"I'll drive you," I say. "We gotta make sure all that fresh bread and pumpkin butter from the factory get home safely, after all."

The drive only takes a couple of minutes, and we're at the cottage before I've been able to process what I want to say. But I don't want her to leave without things being different between us.

We take the food into her cottage, and I stop. "Were the walls always this color?"

"No," she says. It's been years since I've been in Strawberry Fields, or any of the cottages, but given the state Jane and Anita said the place was in before, I'm surprised to see how nice it looks.

Jane walks me to the front door, and I hesitate before opening it. The place is so small I feel like I'm taking up too much of her space, and yet I don't want to leave. "Thanks for everything today, Jane. You made a difficult day for Lottie into one she'll always remember."

"It was my pleasure. She's a sweetheart. You're really good with her."

"So are you." I pause. "I'm going to get out of your way."

"Okay. Have a good night." She's reaching for the door, and I realize she didn't understand me.

"No, I mean, yes, I'll leave you to the rest of your night, but I meant that I'll get out of your way *here*. With your rebrand. I know you'll do a good job, and I don't want to keep you from it anymore."

"Cool."

Why does she sound so sarcastic? "Cool?"

"Yeah, Tripp. Super cool. Thanks a ton. I uprooted my entire life, created a rift with my best friends, and crossed the Mason-Dixon line to take a job where you, as CEO, are telling me you'll no longer actively try to prevent my doing it."

"Isn't that a good thing?"

"I've never taken a job where *not stopping me* was the best that the leadership team could offer."

"Jane—"

"I need more. I need your perspective. You know this place better than anyone alive—"

"Not better than Rusty."

"*Yes,* better than Rusty. He went home at the end of the night, Tripp. The cicadas didn't sing him to sleep like they did you. The rooster didn't wake him up. Like it or not, this place has formed you and you it." She looks away. "Do you know what your uncle told me when I called him?"

"You called Uncle Lawson?"

"I repeat: what do you think I've been doing for the last two weeks?" She raps my head lightly with her knuckles. I pull her hand down and hold it for a split second longer than I should. "Your uncle said that after your parents died, he and his family had planned for you to live with them, but you *insisted* that you would only live on the farm. He didn't say it outright, but the sense I got was that this was the only place that could help you heal."

So that's how she knew about my dad. My uncle had time to take her call but not mine. But is what he said true? I have no memory even resembling that. "Heal, huh? I'm not so sure."

"Well, Lawson said that Sugar Maple Farms has a soul unlike any other place, and that he was counting on us to uncover it."

"Us? As in you and me?"

"Yes. He seems to think I'm the Tripp whisperer."

"Shouter, you mean. Yeller. Holler-er," I say.

She rolls her eyes, but it's almost affectionate. Almost. "Tripp, I'm good at my job. My team is top notch. We could put together something that will stop your slow bleed and get you back on the map, no problem. But that's not all this job is about. I need *you*, Tripp." Her face looks warm, but she stares straight in my eyes. "You have to give me more here."

Her words aren't easy to take, especially what she said about Uncle Lawson. I don't remember any of what he told her. I can believe that I asked to live here, but I can't imagine choosing Tag over Uncle Lawson and Aunt Jolene and their family. He wouldn't lie about it, though. I know that for certain.

Jane's eyes are searching, pleading, and my answer to her is the most natural thing in the world. "Okay. I'm all yours."

CHAPTER TWELVE

JANE

For the next week, Tripp and I drag each other everywhere. He talks to customers with me; I inspect crops with him. We look at the mock-up labels Ash sends us. We even run a fruit stand together when one of Rusty's guys gets sick. The seasonal workers are used to seeing him get his hands dirty—I'll say that much. But he doesn't know a single name.

"Thanks for the pumpkin butter, uh"—his eyes flicker down to the name tag of the woman who runs the farm store—"Paige."

I snicker as we take the bag out of the store and into the sunlight.

"Paige has run the farm store for two years. How do you not know her name?"

"Gee, yet another person for you to harass me about not knowing. What will come next?" he asks in mock surprise. "I get it. I was negligent in my duties as caretaker, okay? Can we move on from the public shaming already?"

"I'm not ready to commit to that."

He shakes his head. "What am I going to do with you?"

I stick out my tongue and turn him around to face the store. We both agree we need to expand the store, but I'm also trying to convince him that we need a farm-to-table restaurant.

"So we can charge sixteen dollars for an omelet and offer a list of desserts normal people can't pronounce? No. That's not who we are. No hipster nonsense."

"Hipster? Farm-to-table is *not* hipster."

Okay, maybe it's a bit hipster, but I razz him because I like hearing him say "we." The more he defends his ideas, the more he identifies with the farm. The more protective he is of it.

The closer I get to fulfilling my promise to his grandpa.

* * *

After a week of being joined at the hip, I'm finally ready to put in more work on the cottage. I've been catching up so much on Jane & Co. business at night that I haven't had time to do anything else. Parker offered to run point on meetings with our new clients, but I can't ask her to do that. She's busy and overburdened enough. And still ending our calls the second any business talk is through.

Oh, she's cordial enough. She pretends to be interested in our group text thread when I send pictures or updates, but it's not the same. *She's* not the same.

I miss her. I miss all of them. Getting lost in work is the only thing that helps, especially when I can talk to my friends *while* I work. Win-win!

I haven't told Tripp about my project yet, but he was right that the walls aren't the same color anymore. Nor are the cabinets. Working on the cottage at night refreshes me. *A change is as good as a rest,* Grandpa used to say. When I'm done, I make myself cinnamon tea, pop some popcorn, and watch a movie on the wall-mounted TV.

Or I watch Jack Reacher.

The gorgeous, genius giant makes me think of Tripp far more than I should. But when I watch nothing at all, I think of him far more than I should, anyway.

It's not right how vexing the man is.

"He's vexing *and* sexy, though. Vexy," Ash tells me. She and Millie are out on the town, based on the crazy sounds of people and cars in the background. I have my earbuds in, a scarf around my hair, and a scraping tool in my hand so I can remove the nasty popcorn ceiling. I've finished the bedroom and bathroom in the last hour and have the kitchen/sitting room left. I mist the ceiling with a sprayer I got from the hardware store in town and then scrape away one area at a time. I should have scraped before painting, but I've never renovated a cottage before. I'm handy, thanks to Grandpa's years of tutelage, but a house is different than a car. This isn't replacing bushings or brake pads for the neighbors in the trailer park. This is fixing up a cabin where a bride will one day stay the night before her wedding, if my plans work out. It has to be perfect.

I may not enjoy thinking about weddings, but the challenge to make a space meaningful exhilarates me, even as the pressure of getting it exactly right stresses me way the heck out. I think the soft coral walls and the sage green cabinets look beautiful together—like an echo of a strawberry patch—but I should have asked someone with a design eye before doing all of this. I tell myself repeatedly that I can't make a mistake too big to be fixed, but I don't know how well I believe it.

"Vexy?"

"Vexy. Yes."

"Stop trying to make *vexy* happen, Ash."

She cackles. "Nice try. It's happening. He's vexy! He's literally fireman calendar hot. *Literally* literally." Millie yells her agreement into the phone. The background noise is getting insane. Is someone yelling on a megaphone? "And not even you can deny it, Miss 'I dated an actual male model.'" I hate when they bring that up. That guy was as pretty as he was shallow. We went out twice until I dropped him and his fake tan. "Check your phone. I found pictures from Tripp's frat days."

"What??"

I drop the scraper and pull up my texts, where Ash has sent me a picture of Tripp in a dunk tank.

He has an eight pack. A soaking wet eight pack.

I zoom in and flush hot from head to toe. Is my AC broken again? "I bet he raised a lot of money for charity."

"He probably saved a small country," Ash agrees. I lose myself in zooming and staring until Ash clears her throat. "Jane? You still with me?"

I let go of the screen, and Tripp's picture pops back into place. "Sorry, what?"

"I asked how you liked the latest logo? It's testing well, but I think it still needs tweaking."

"About that: one of the guys here worked in graphic design for a few years. Because he knows the farm and the business, do you mind if I have him send over some feedback?"

"The more the merrier." One of the best things about Ash is that her confidence makes her humble. She knows she's great at what she does, and the greatness of others doesn't threaten her.

A knock at the door pulls my attention. "Hey, I've gotta run. Company."

"Company? Ooh, tell me it's Hotty McGrumpypants."

I get down from the stepladder and walk to the door. "It's not Hotty McGrumpypants. Love you, Ash."

We hang up just as I grab the door.

It's Hotty McGrumpypants. He's changed out of his usual jeans and t-shirt into black running shorts and a white t-shirt that clings to his every muscle. How many abs can one man have? Eight, that's how many.

I tug my eyes up to his. "Tripp? What are you doing?"

He takes in my hair kerchief, the scraper in my hand, and the state of the cabin. But he waits on the stoop like a vampire, needing to be invited in. Looks like someone learned from his mistakes. "Sorry, did you have company? I thought I heard a voice."

"I was talking to Ashley. Why don't you come in before you let those freaky flying cockroaches in?" I wrap my long hand a quarter of the way around his bicep and pull him inside before slamming the door.

"Palmetto bugs are nasty," he says.

"Is that what they're called?" I shudder. "Have a seat. Do you want something to drink?"

The place is covered in dust and drop cloths. He leans against a covered armchair. It looks like a child's toy beneath him. "Water's fine. Are you renovating Strawberry Fields? I thought Anita was hiring contractors for the cottages."

"She is for the others," I say, handing him the water and leaning against the counter. "I asked if I could do this one, and she didn't have a problem with it."

"No, why would she?" He looks around and takes in the walls and cabinets. The cabinet doors were woefully outdated, with a cathedral arch and that shade of builder's oak that can never actually be in style. Rather than get new doors, I took them off, stripped and painted them a subdued sage to match the cabin's theme, and hung them upside down. Now they look unique, cool, and cozy. "I like it."

"Don't sound so surprised."

"I don't mean it like that."

"Sure you do. A *Carville* can install an after-market air conditioning unit into a 1964 Chevy C-10, but you're surprised that a *Harrington* can renovate a cottage. Am I close?"

He cocks his head playfully. "Someone's been doing her homework on classic trucks." I shrug, letting him think what he wants. I won't tell him I changed the oil and filters in the farm truck Anita's letting me use. He would never believe I find oil changes relaxing. "I mean it, Jane. The cabinets and walls—I like what you've done."

"Well, wait till you see my plans for the bedroom—"

Tripp's eyebrows pull up. I clap my hands over my mouth.

"I can't wait." The look he gives me makes my cheeks flame. I throw a rag at him, and he catches it with a chuckle. "Don't make promises you don't intend to deliver on, Miss Harrington."

I take a long drink of water, hoping my face will cool down in the meantime. "So what brings you here at eight at night? Unless you finally realized that your apology for sticking me in Caligula's cottage was woefully insufficient?"

He wrinkles his nose. "I really am sorry."

"Go on."

"As soon as Anita told me, I came to move you into Orange Crush next door. I brought the food as a peace offering."

I smile behind my glass. "And then you saw your best friend being nice to your new enemy before you could apologize? You are such a brat."

"Guilty," he says, bowing his head. "And sorry."

"Apology accepted," I say. "Now did you say what you came for already?"

"I didn't, no." He takes a long drink of his water.

"Um, were you planning to?"

"I was, yes. You distracted me with your bedroom talk."

A laugh bursts out of me, and he grins in response. He looks so appealing that I need a distraction. Now. I put my drink down on the counter, go mist the remaining popcorn ceiling, and climb back up the stepladder.

"Looking good."

It's right now o'clock when I realize that I must look like an exhibitionist, reaching up as I am in my tank top and baggy shorts that are almost falling off my hips. "Shut up and use your giant height for something good, will you? There's another scraper on the counter."

A moment later, Tripp is scraping right next to me. His scraper has a ten-inch handle, but it's still absurd how easily he can reach an eight-foot ceiling. He is so tall.

I love it.

I mean, I don't actually care. Good for him for being tall. Nothing to see here. La-dee-dah.

After ten minutes, we've finished the rest of the room. He helps me with the clean up and then I drop to the floor to stretch. He gestures to the loveseat, but I shake my head, my hands hovering over one foot before moving on to the other.

"You're a floor-sitter, huh?" He smiles when I nod. "My mom was, too. On the rare occasion we would watch a movie, I would always lie down on the couch. I'd put my feet on my dad's lap and my mom would rest her head on the couch right beside mine. She liked to sneak a kiss on my cheek while we watched Bambi or Lion King or whatever movie about parents dying." He sniffs wryly. "It's a wonder I didn't see it coming."

"If your future is based on the movies we watched as kids, I think we're all in a lot of trouble. Roald Dahl?" I grimace.

"Better that than Dr. Seuss."

"What do you mean? Dr. Seuss is classic! The Grinch? The Lorax? Those movies killed me!"

"Have you even read the books?"

I bat my eyes and puff out my lips like a Tik Tok influencer after getting filler. "Books? What are books?"

He pushes me with his foot so that I tip over. I laugh and pop back up. "Of course I've read the books. They're classics."

"*Horton Hears a Who*, sure. But *Green Eggs and Ham* is like a how-to guide for assault."

"What?" My laugh is almost a cackle. "Assault?"

"Sam-I-Am is the worst! I would punch that dude's throat so hard if he kept shoving those green eggs and ham in my face. 'Would you try them here or there?' NO! I would smash the plate in your face, you creep!"

I'm clutching my stomach from laughing so hard. "You're serious! You hate Sam-I-Am that much?"

"I hate him. He's a pusher! He doesn't respect personal boundaries and he has zero concept of consent. He's a walking lawsuit!"

"You're reading into it too much! It's about food!" Tripp gives me a pfft that only makes me laugh harder. "Imagine that he's an old rancher talking to a hipster vegan, then."

Tripp snorts. "In that case ... "

"He's just a guy sharing his love of protein with the world."

Tripp pushes me with his foot again. "So is that what you were watching in your princess suite? *The Lorax*? *The Cat in the Hat*?"

I sigh. I know I should correct him, but pride is a funny thing. Tripp and I have made some headway, but he hasn't earned the right to my life story. Not yet. "No, my sister and I were usually tucked in our blankets early Saturday morning watching *Beauty and the Beast* or *Snow White* or some such movie where a man rescues the princess while my mom laughed 'Yeah right,' into her fl-frappuccino," I say, barely covering. I was about to say flask.

"It's a wonder you didn't see your man-eating ways coming," Tripp says.

"Now you get it." I lean back onto my hands. "You know, you never did say why you came by tonight."

"I was passing by on my run and saw your light on," he admits.

"And you were hoping to stay for my nightly movie?"

"You watch a movie every night?"

"Usually, yeah. I watch while I go through my notes, proposals, plans, what have you. It's the only way I can feel both productive and like I'm relaxing at the same time."

"I don't think you're supposed to feel both of those at the same time."

"No, you don't think *you're* supposed to. *I'm* definitely supposed to."

One corner of his mouth quirks up. "Are you always this obstinate?"

I shake my head. "Yes. You?"

He nods. "No."

He holds my eye, or maybe I hold his. Either way, our gazes are locked, and the temperature in the cabin just spiked about ten degrees. How is it that a look can drill into my core like that? And why can't I glance away?

Tripp blinks first. "Um, so what movie were you going to watch tonight?"

Released, I get to my feet and pad into the kitchen to make popcorn. "*In the Line of Fire*. Clint Eastwood."

"Never seen it."

"It's not *Unforgiven*, but it's a classic for a reason."

"I've never seen that one, either."

"What? But you've seen Clint Eastwood ask someone if they feel lucky, punk. Right?"

"Is that what that's from?"

"What? No!" I close my eyes and slow-breathe. "I can't even look at you right now. Do you not know who Sergio Leone is? Pioneer of the Spaghetti Western?"

"I know what a Spaghetti Western is, but I've never seen one. And now probably *isn't* the time for me to admit I always fall asleep during movies, is it?"

"Oh, come on."

"Always," he repeats.

"Tripp Carville, if you fall asleep during this movie, I will give you a wet willie so disgusting, you'll wear earmuffs for the rest of your life."

"I repeat: don't make promises you don't intend to deliver on."

"Not a promise, a warning, boyo."

"Boy-o? Is that Chicagoan?"

"Welsh. My grandpa taught me well."

Tripp's forehead wrinkles, and I bet he's wondering how on earth one of the Harringtons of global fame could have lived in Wales under the radar. He lets it go, and I find myself disappointed he didn't ask. I guess our truce is a bit tremulous to him, too.

"I haven't done movie night in a long time, you know, on account of the sleeping. Should I run to the house and grab some snacks?"

"No need. In fact, while I have you here, why don't you look over PJ's latest projections while I pop some popcorn."

"PJ?"

"Parker. Parker Jane. PJ for short."

He reaches for the figures on the coffee table. "That's a funny coincidence that she's Parker Jane and you're ..."

"Just Jane. My mom wanted me to keep my maiden name as my middle name whenever I got married," I say, angry at my traitorous cheeks for once again flushing. *It's not like you're asking him to get married by mentioning this fact, weirdo. Calm down!* "No, but what *is* a coincidence is that they *all* have the same middle name."

"No."

"Yes. Millie Jane, Parker Jane, Ashley Jane, and Lucy Jane."

"Lucy? Who is Lucy?"

"My lawyer." I don't mention her YouTube fame.

"Your lawyer is a round, bald guy named Lou who wears pinstripe business suits."

"That's how you imagined Lou?" I laugh and pull out my

phone to show him my screensaver. It's each of my friends and me on our first day in the Jane & Co. offices. We're standing in front of the building, arms around each other under our sign.

I watch his expression as he identifies each of them, putting faces to names. Millie with her stunning red hair and light sprinkling of freckles that make her look as trustworthy as she is lovely. Her perfect hourglass figure is hidden in a sweater dress, but her snakeskin ankle boots are classic Millie. Parker's an Ariana Grande look alike, if less of an ingenue. She has deep chocolaty eyes and the kind of eyebrows and lips women pay good money for. Her long black hair is always in a high ponytail that makes her look about two inches taller than she is. Combined with the four-inch heels that have become her constant companion, she's as fierce as she is secretly kind-hearted. Ash is the only one that seems to fit Tripp's perception: her mass of Felicity-Season-One curls match with her electric blue lipstick and glasses. She calls herself "cute" or "adorkable," but it's a defense mechanism. Her quirky look is armor every bit as much as Parker's makeup is. Lastly, he sees Lou, looking like a shorter, more ethereal Taylor Swift, with her natural ice blonde hair and light blue eyes.

"So this is Jane & Co.," he says. I have yet to date a guy who could keep himself from commenting on how attractive we all are. Tripp hands me back my phone while the smell of popcorn starts filling the room. When I take the phone from him, our pointer fingers touch, and a current of electricity flows through my body. "You all look really happy."

He's still holding the phone, and I'm still letting my finger rest on his, and the energy in the room is still heating as much as the popcorn is. If I don't stop this soon, it's going to be my heart POP! POP! popping. "They're the best friends I could ask for." I'm standing while he sits leaning forward, so we're close. Close enough that I would barely need to lean down to smell him.

Strawberries and dirt and sweat.

My stomach literally growls at the thought, and the sound makes him smile. He lets go of the phone, leaving my hand cold. "Popcorn smell makin' you hungry?"

"Something like that."

CHAPTER THIRTEEN

TRIPP

*J*ane is sitting on the floor in front of me, and it's everything I can do not to touch the nape of her neck. She has a scarf in her hair that makes her look like the hottest Rosie the Riveter to ever walk this earth. I never realized before that I have a type, but I do.

It's Jane.

Jane in her sexy power business suit.

Jane in her workout clothes.

Jane in her paint-splotched basketball shorts that I suspect she stole from an ex-boyfriend. Or current boyfriend. She couldn't have a boyfriend, right? The possibility makes me irrationally jealous.

As irrational as her closeness makes me feel. If she was trying to find a way to ensure that I'll never fall asleep during a movie, this was it. She sat on the ground at the far edge of the couch first, but I complained about having to reach for the popcorn. I could easily have suggested she get another bowl, but the truth is, I don't want my own bowl. I don't care about the popcorn. I care that my hand and Jane's are in the popcorn bowl at the same moment.

Because I'm a fourteen-year-old boy with his first crush.

I stifle a groan. This is pathetic. I should ask her out already, like I'd planned to in the truck on that very first day.

"Okay, you have to watch this," she says, elbowing my knee across the loveseat. She keeps it there so that her elbow is touching my leg, and all of my plans rush out the window, because I don't want to do anything that could jinx this. "He's about to put his foot in his mouth. You know, like you."

The two characters—played by Clint Eastwood and Rene Russo, according to Jane—are sitting at the Lincoln Memorial, and he's telling her that female secret service agents are just for show. Ouch. "Do you always spoil scenes seconds before they happen? Because I can take a quick nap—"

She whips around and pinches my knee. "Don't you dare!"

I jump like a farm cat, and she gasps. Her face is every bit as delighted as Lottie riding an alpaca. "You're ticklish!"

"Am not. I have a bad knee."

"Really?" Her flat tone tells me she ain't buying it. "From what?"

"Foot-ing. I mean farm-ball," I stammer. "I mean farming. And football."

"Obviously. But if you really have a bad knee, why don't I massage it for you?" She pinches it again, and I squeal like a baby. And again. "Stop!" I grab her hands before she can torture me. "There's no injury. You caught me. I'm ticklish, okay? Legs, arms. All of it."

She bites her lip as if she's debating her next move. I almost regret telling her to stop, because now she's going to respect me, even if I would gladly brave the indignity of being a grown man who giggles whenever she touches my knee.

"So I definitely shouldn't pinch you here again?" She twists, but before she can get me, her eyes scrunch as if in pain. She leans forward and rotates her arm.

"You okay?" I ask.

"Yeah, totally fine. I just slept weird last night and wrenched my upper back."

"And then you decided to scrape a ceiling with a sore back? Smart."

"Exactly. I'm very smart, Tripp. I don't know how you haven't caught on to this yet." She loops an arm around her neck to rub her upper back.

"Come here," I say, scooting forward in the love seat.

She eyes me like I'm a copperhead snake. "Why, are you going to dump your ice down the back of my shirt?"

"Tempting, but no, I'm going to massage the knot out."

"Ha, no. I don't need a massage."

"Are you in pain?"

She lifts her shoulders in a shrug, but the way she tenses tells me the movement hurts. "No."

"Liar. Why don't you want help?"

"I don't need help."

"I didn't ask why you don't *need* help. I asked why you don't *want* help."

Her eyes move from mine. "I guess I'm used to taking care of things myself."

Her answer feels a lot weightier than some sore muscles. The way she didn't look at me when she said that makes me wonder if she told me more than she meant to. "Maybe it's all the injuries I got growing up—"

"Foot-ing and farm-balling?"

"Precisely. But I'm a firm believer in rehabbing the problem before it becomes worse. And for a back, that means stretching and a massage."

"I'll stretch—"

"No." I snap my fingers and point in front of me like Anita

would when I was avoiding a haircut as a kid. "Come. What's your pride worth?"

She glares but slides across the hardwood floor. "Fine, but I've got my eyes on you."

I put my hands on her shoulders, noting how soft and silky her skin is. She's wearing a tank top, and I'm trying not to let it be too big of a deal that my skin is touching so much of hers. This is therapeutic, after all. Or at least it's supposed to be. But as I press my thumbs on either side of her spine, her muscles tighten rather than relax. What is she fighting? Giving up control, maybe? Letting herself be vulnerable in front of me? I'm not sure what she's pushing back on, but this massage isn't working.

"You have to relax, Jane," I say softly. On the TV, Rene Russo is standing up. "If you can't loosen up, it won't do anything."

She exhales loudly, still wound tighter than a two-dollar watch. But on the screen, the actress is walking down the stairs of the memorial, and Jane whispers, "This is my favorite part." Clint Eastwood watches her walking away and mutters to himself that if she looks back, that means she likes him.

She looks back. As soon as she does, Jane's tightness relaxes enough that I dig my thumbs into the golf ball-sized knots in her upper back.

A sound issues from her throat, something between a groan and a sigh. "Too hard?" I ask.

"No, it's perfect."

CHAPTER FOURTEEN

JANE

$\mathcal{I}$ have never had a massage before. Not from a masseuse, not from a boyfriend, not even from a roommate.

I am such a fool.

Parker is a massage junky, and I finally understand why. It's amazing. It's like a good stretch after a workout—the right kind of pain—but so much better, because Tripp's hands know how to target every sore spot. I wonder if he plays an instrument for how delicately and precisely he works. With every push and prod, my stresses float away more and more until I couldn't name them all if I tried. The longer he massages, the deeper his touch reaches. It's not merely the physical depth and relief, though; this feels mental, too. Emotional.

Since Grandpa died, I've never had someone take care of me. Not like this. Not like *anything*. My friends are amazing, but as the person who convinced them to start a business, the burden of success or failure has rested squarely on my very tight shoulders. I don't know if I realized until right now how heavy things have felt and for how long. It's like Tripp is unknowingly digging into the pain of growing up as I did.

I don't know how much of it I want to let go.

My thoughts fly back to watching a movie with my sister, Meghan—a horror movie we had no business watching. But I was eleven and thought it was cool, and Mom had just laughed at the Redbox when we asked for it. Almost immediately, the movie proved too mature and disturbing for us, but Mom was too busy giggling and texting her boyfriend of the week to notice that Meghan was quietly crying. I asked if we could watch *Sleeping Beauty*, instead, and she told us to shut up and watch the movie. So I whispered to Meghan that we were going to pretend we were in Harry Potter and cast a Riddikulus spell on every creepy monster. We had to imagine the silliest, most absurd thing we could do to the monster to make it so embarrassed that it would disappear. We made it through the rest of the movie, and Mom said, "See? Told you that you could handle it," as if she'd done us a favor.

It's one of a hundred stories I could have referenced when telling Tripp about my movie viewing habits as a kid.

After that, we went back to princess movies. Mom loved those princess movies before going out and hated them when she woke up. She was always looking to attract a "new daddy for you girls" at night and was raging about how women have gotta look out for themselves in the morning, after whatever guy she'd brought home had sneaked out. Her hope and cynicism were a dizzying emotional roller coaster that paired appallingly with her negligence. She'd refuse to cook or clean for months and then rally for a few days or even weeks. Each time, I would wonder if this was the time that she would finally start acting like a real mom. Someone who cared about her kids; someone who was willing to put forth basic effort to even open up a can of chili and heat it in the microwave for us.

But no. It never lasted. By seventh grade, I knew better than to hope. And I had a sister to take care of. Besides, I had Grandpa, too. He cared. He lived off of a small pension from working for one of the big American car companies for so many years, and he always managed to slip us groceries or utility money, in spite of things being tight for him, too. He became the trailer park's de facto mechanic and handy man, and I suspect he did so to better watch over us. Without him, I don't know how we would have survived. Mom was too spiteful to even get us on food stamps. She thought "being on welfare" would hurt her chances of finding a man, seeing as she was already saddled with two kids.

I was fourteen—barely old enough to work—when Grandpa died. His life insurance covered the funeral and paid our rent for a few more months, tiding us over until I started paying the bills.

Scholarships, grants, and student loans covered my college and MBA. My job covered rent on the trailer until my sister moved out.

I stopped paying rent the next month. The guilt of it still eats me up sometimes, but of all the burdens I willingly take on, Mom is no longer one of them.

Tripp's thumbs find the muscles around my shoulder blades, and each new push is an old memory. Grandpa's funeral. My first job out of my MBA working eighty hours a week. Watching the balance in my checkbook increase for the first time in my life just to have Meghan ask me to pay for her esthetician program. Finding out Mom had Meghan lie about how much the program cost so she could pocket the difference. Cutting Mom off. Not having the strength to cut off Meghan. Applying for my first credit card. Then my second …

Every memory reminds me how emotionally exhausted I am. And I've been exhausted for a long time.

"Are you okay?" Tripp asks softly, pulling me back into the

present. It's jarring, coming back to reality from how deep I was in my head.

"Fine. Thanks." I clear my voice of the emotion clogging it.

"Do you want me to keep going?" he asks. I do and I don't. My back feels so much better but facing all of this emotion feels like a burden of its own. My hesitation seems to say something to Tripp. "Do you want to talk?"

I put my hand on one of his. I mean it as a "that's enough" gesture, but he takes it in one of his and squeezes softly. We stay like that for a moment. And another. What do I say? I would love to talk to someone. Millie is the only person I've ever opened up to about anything, and that's only because of her super magic clinician powers that help her ask questions when I haven't had the strength to lie.

Tripp is doing that same thing right now. Asking the right question at the wrong time. Right time? I don't even know. All I know is that, even with Millie, I've never *wanted* to talk before. But with Tripp, I almost do.

No. I *really* do.

I twist around to face him. "Actually—"

A knock at the door interrupts me. Tripp curses, and I silently agree.

He follows me to the door more closely than he would have a couple of hours ago. And I don't push back the way I would have earlier. I'm too raw to be relieved by the interruption. I'm only annoyed by it. Disappointed.

That is, until I open the door.

"Surprise!" Ash and Millie exclaim in unison. I'm awash in shock, but they pull me into a hug, and I feel like I could cry over the squeezes and squeals.

"What in the world? How are you here?" I turn back to look at Tripp, but he looks as clueless as I am.

I'm teary-eyed as I usher them into the cottage and make introductions. Ash isn't subtle at all about how taken with Tripp she is, while he and Millie seem to size each other up while they shake hands. My friends explain how they arranged the trip with Anita, how they're only here for the weekend, how they're staying in "Apple Turnover." Tripp offers to take my friends' bags to the cottage next door as the rest of us sit at the table

The moment he steps outside, Ash's mouth falls open. "Is he *real*? How are you alive right now? How has your body not burst into flames from his hotness?"

"Oh, come on. We've all seen hot guys before." I look at Millie for support, but she's pretending to fan herself.

"Not like that, we haven't," she says.

I shake my head, but my friends catch the smile I can't quite hide. "You two would make the most beautiful babies. Please tell me you're going to make beautiful babies together. I know you pretend to hate him, but he is even better looking in real life than his picture. I am shipping you two *so hard*." Ash wrings her hands dramatically, making her wealth of spirals bounce from the top of her head to her shoulders.

"Down girl." Millie smiles. "So, was the surprise a good one?"

My heart is full to bursting, both from the massage and from my friends sacrificing their time to help me. "The best. I can't believe you guys came all the way here."

"You know the others would have come if they could," Millie says. Lou always has some secret project she's working on, but we both know Parker could have made it if she wanted to.

Which means she didn't want to. My full heart empties a little.

"We love you," Millie continues as Tripp comes back in, "and we wanted to come get a feel for the farm. Our research is missing some demographics. Is it possible to draw out the people in Charleston and Asheville while still appealing to the people in Winnsboro and Gaffney?"

"Gaffney? Wow, you've done your homework," Tripp drawls from behind me. I look up at him and am, once again, in awe of his presence. He's both a force of nature and something more down to earth at the same time. "I don't know if we can do both."

"And I don't know if that's even the dichotomy we're looking at: urban hipster versus rural folk." Millie taps her lip while Tripp tells my friends how nice it was to meet them and says he should get going. I walk him to the door.

"Thanks for your help with the ceiling. And for the massage." My whole body warms when I mention it.

"Thanks for the movie," he says quietly. "Maybe we could finish it sometime?" His grass green eyes dig deeper than his thumbs do.

"Think you can stay awake?"

"I'm willing to give it a try." He grabs the handle. "Good night, Jane."

"Night, Tripp," I say, and he's gone.

When I'm back at the table, Ash and Millie look like detectives in a movie, all crossed legs and intense stares. "You were watching *In the Line of Fire* with him, huh? That's like fifth date territory for you," Ash says.

"He came over to ask something and I roped him into helping me scrape the ceiling, so I let him stay."

"He can scrape my ceiling anytime," Ash says. "And no, I have no idea what that means figuratively or literally."

* * *

The next day is Saturday, and Tripp texts me in the morning.

TRIPP: Have fun with your friends

JANE: Too afraid to show your face?

．　．　．

TRIPP: Yes. I think Ash bit my direction when I left last night.

JANE: You weren't meant to see that.

TRIPP: So it did happen. I knew it.

JANE: Don't be too flattered. She has a long-standing crush on the Jolly Green Giant.

TRIPP: Now you're buttering my biscuit. You know the Jolly Green Giant wears the heck out of a leafy tunic.

I laugh and send him a GIF of a green giant doing a ridiculous dance. He sends back a GIF of a laughing baby.

Ash sees all of this and teases me for the rest of the day.

I've been here long enough to know the lay of the land, so I show my friends around the orchards, the store, and the B&B. We go to the barn where we stop at the pens of goats, pigs, alpacas, and a pregnant llama. Millie is a puddle of goo looking at them.

"You didn't tell me there were animals!" She leans down to pet a baby alpaca. It's much taller than the goats and piglets are, but its face is so goofy and cute that I can see why she's gushing. I like animals, but I'm more of a traditional pet person. Millie, however, did an internship at an animal therapy practice, and her heart has never really left it. "I have a few clients who would love you," she coos to the alpaca. "You're so soft and peaceful, aren't you, boy?"

"How does she know it's a boy?" Ash mutters to me.

"Therapist magic," I say.

"It has a penis," Millie says, still petting the fuzz ball.

"Huh." I tilt my head. "So it has."

After Millie gets her fill of animals, we drive into town to get lunch at Sugar Maple Diner. Not the most original name, but it gets the point across. And they've managed to sell me on cheesy grits.

As we wait for our food, Ash goes "woman on the street" and starts interviewing every patron in the diner. What comes to mind when they think of Sugar Maple Farms? What do they like about it? What would they change? A couple of girls mention Tripp by name when asked what they like. I roll my eyes, something Millie notices.

Ash is the perfect person to ask these questions. She's sunny and approachable, and the naturally warm Southerners open up to her like she's one of their own. I listen to her conversations raptly, taking mental note of everything people say. When our food arrives, Ash asks the server the same questions.

"All you Yankees think of when you hear Sugar Maple Farms is the label. Jams, butters, preserves," the server, Tia, says. I've talked to her a few times, and last time, she told me how her grandparents moved from the Philippines when her dad was a teenager. He met and married a White Southerner, and her cousins in Manila love to tease her for speaking Tagalog with a Southern accent. Her accent is thicker than butter.

"Can I admit something to you?" Ash whispers. "Jams and jellies and all that? I don't know the difference between any of them."

Tia smiles. She's maybe five or ten years older than me at most, but she talks with the air of someone much older, much more connected to her surroundings than I've ever felt. I'm envious listening to her.

"Well, get you to the factory and they'll give you the tour, already. But when folks 'round here think of Sugar Maple Farms, we think of our community. We think of how Tag and Helen Carville brought this town back to life when they started that farm. My grandparents started working there right away as seasonal workers until the town grew enough that my lolo started his plumbing business."

"Lolo?" Ash asks.

"Grandpa in Tagalog," she explains. "Before the farm, there were three grade levels *per class*. K through third, fourth though sixth, et cetera. Now there are four classes per *grade*."

"And when they started their food line?" an older man who introduced himself as Mr. Beaty says from a table nearby. "The factory gave us stable jobs."

"And benefits," Mrs. Beaty, adds. "Sugar Maple Farms paid for me to go back to college and get my teaching license. I've been teaching fourth grade for twenty-two years thanks to Mr. Carville."

"Tag wasn't a perfect man," Mr. Beaty says. "He was a tough boss, and he didn't tolerate any unsafe behavior on the production line. He had a two-strike policy. Strike one sent you back to training. Strike two gave you a week's severance. Made him unpopular with a lot of people, but we all understood. He was no nonsense about safety. Lost too much."

"He lost too much," his wife echoes with a sad shake of her head.

"So if you had one word to describe what Sugar Maple Farms means to you," Ash asks, "what would it be?"

Tia taps her fingers on her notepad. "Community."

Mrs. Beaty says, "Opportunity."

Her husband says, "Hope."

Healing, I think, imagining Tripp as a lost little boy who refused to go anywhere else. "One farm can't change the world," I say, "but it can change yours."

Tia shows us her arm. "Y'all, that gave me chills!"

Me too, I think, but I don't say it out loud. Ash would never let me live it down.

After a meal that makes my friends consider relocating, we walk around the cute downtown. It's quaint and charming and offers so much more than Tripp described when we first drove through. I still don't know what his beef is with this town or with the farm, but he doesn't see either accurately. The town is near enough to a main freeway, but the factory attracts more tourists than the town itself does. A bit of marketing could change that. Jorge's pecan fudge is a slice of heaven, and Natalie's antique shop is as good as some I've seen in Chicago. Nico's thrift store even has a vintage section worth tweeting about, if you're into that kind of thing (tweeting, not vintage. Everyone should be into vintage). With a facelift, the gazebo would be worthy of Stars Hollow itself. Part of me wants to put together a plan to promote the whole town, to make Sugar Maple a destination to rival Beaufort.

Focus, Jane. You weren't hired to rebrand the town, just the farm.

We tour the factory in the afternoon and rent bikes to ride along the river that cuts through town, something I discovered on my first trip into town to buy supplies for Strawberry Fields. We get back to the farm in the early evening, and on the door to our cottages, we find a note from Anita and Booker asking us to meet them at the B&B for dinner. We clean up and head over.

As Tripp requested, I've put my boardroom clothes at the back of my tiny closet and ordered some pieces that I hope are more appropriate. I'm not sure what the dinner party attire is, though, so I put on jeans, a white t-shirt, and a navy blazer, but I pair it with Western booties I found at Nico's thrift store instead of my normal heels.

The dining room in the B&B is hopping, busier than I've seen it. Rusty and his parents are there, along with Tripp and ...

"Lottie?" I say. The girl is hiding under the table, elbow deep in cheese she's stealing from the charcuterie board on the table above her, and I get the sense that her dad doesn't know. But as I look around the room, I don't see Duke anywhere. Lottie gives me a defiant look, as if daring me to pry the cheese from her fist or tell someone. I give her a wink, but she whips around so her back is to me and shoves the cheese in her mouth.

"I like her style," Ash says, walking past me to mingle.

"Who's that sweetheart?" Millie asks, looking at Lottie.

"Lottie, Tripp's goddaughter. He watches her sometimes for-for her dad," I say. I'm not sure why I don't mention Duke or why I don't tell Millie that Lottie is the little girl I called her about. Millie is the most trustworthy person I know, but it feels like a betrayal of Tripp to tell her anything without his say-so.

"She's darling," Millie says, watching Lottie pull the entire board under the table. I hear the tug in Millie's voice. She wants to be a mom more than anything, but she'll have a hard time ever getting pregnant or being approved for adoption with her medical history. The look on her face shows how much she aches for a baby, even if she rarely talks about it.

"She's a doll," I agree.

Tripp holds up a hand in greeting when he sees me. He's talking to Booker and Anita, and he squeezes Booker's shoulder before walking toward us.

When he's near, he asks, "Y'all haven't seen a three-year-old girl anywhere, have you?" To Millie and Ash, he says, "I'm watching her for a friend, and my charge isn't in the best mood."

We all point to where Lottie is hiding six feet away. He drops down to talk to her, but she just pulls the tablecloth over her head and grabs more cheese.

"I hope she's not lactose intolerant," Ash tells Millie, who smiles rather than laughs. Anita waves us over, so we join her, but Millie keeps stealing glances at Lottie and a visibly frustrated Tripp. When it's time to eat, Lottie still hasn't emerged, so Millie offers to take a turn watching over her while the rest of us go outside to the patio, where Anita and Booker have dinner waiting.

I glance back at Millie and see that she's fully under the table with Lottie. The last thing I see before following Tripp out the door is Lottie offering Millie a piece of cheese.

CHAPTER FIFTEEN

TRIPP

*O*ver dinner, Jane and her friend Ash hold court as they talk about Sugar Maple Farms. I get the sense watching them that Ash is an extrovert at heart whereas Jane feels more like an outgoing introvert. Ash tells everyone about her conversations with people in town, and then she asks our opinion about Jane's tagline:

"One farm can't change the world, but it can change yours."

The words are a punch to the gut. Anita covers her heart with her hand, while some of the others around the table nod or "aw." All I can think of is how my grandfather brought me here at my apparent request, and how it went from my happy place to the place I resent most in the world.

Jane looks at me. "When people think of this farm, they think of opportunity and community, of hope and healing, all concepts that fit well with the farm's vision and purposes."

Anita and Jane think it's important to update things like the company's vision. Even knowing I should be on my best behavior to try to help the rebrand be a success, I struggle not to comment. Cheesy business jargon isn't my style.

"It works perfectly with our mission," Anita says. Rusty seems alight with possibilities, and while his parents talk to Anita and Booker, he leans over to Ash.

I take the opportunity to snag Jane's attention. She's directly across from me at the table. "Healing, huh? I seem to have heard that somewhere before."

"I think it's fitting. And you promised you'd help me bring this vision to life, remember?"

"I remember. Why don't we talk with your friends tomorrow, firm up some plans and get the ball rolling."

Jane sits taller, the only indication she's excited. "Great. Their flight leaves mid-afternoon, so why don't you come over to Strawberry Fields tomorrow morning?"

"I have a better idea. Why don't I take you and your friends to my favorite spot on the farm for brunch? I'll pick y'all up in the ... all-terrain golf cart?"

"It's a side-by-side," she corrects, leaning across the table.

My pose mirrors hers. "Of course. I feel so silly."

"No one should feel silly not knowing something. They should feel silly being a butthead to someone who doesn't know something."

"I'm gonna stitch that on a pillow," I say. Her smile draws me closer still.

"I'm surprised it's not stitched into your soul, Mr. Southern Gentleman."

"I'll fix that right away, ma'am."

"Good boy."

Her eyes are so warm and inviting that it takes the table digging into my stomach to stop my forward motion. Everything around me is an annoyance. The table, the other guests. They're all getting in the way of what I want: more Jane. More,

more, more. Can she tell that's how I feel? Can she see me being pulled into her orbit?

I frown at a tap on my shoulder, but I wipe my face clean when I see Millie holding Lottie on her hip. The young girl is playing peek-a-boo with Millie through her hair, and it's so sweet and maternal that I'm glad Duke isn't here. Seeing what both he and Lottie are missing would hurt too much.

Millie mouths to me, without making a sound. "Diaper?"

"Lottie-Bot." I stand and reach for her, but she leans into Millie. "Can I change your diaper, sweetie?"

"No, Miwwie," she insists. Lottie sometimes says her r's, but her l's are nowhere on the horizon, something anyone with a heart finds endearing as all get out. She nuzzles her face into Millie's shoulder, and Millie's eyes widen. I can't read her reaction, but she's responding, all right.

"Are you comfortable changing a diaper?" I ask.

"Yes, but do you mind being there? I'd hate to make her parents upset that a stranger is changing their daughter."

"Don't mind at all," I say, impressed by her thoughtfulness. I join her in the house with Lottie's diaper bag. I'm only watching Lottie till tomorrow because Duke has an in-and-out meeting in Orlando, and his parents and sister are out of town again. She hasn't slept over since Duke's last round of chemo, so I think being here is triggering some fears that she doesn't even know about, let alone know how to process.

Millie is a pro at changing a diaper. We don't talk much, as she's busy distracting Lottie. Lottie was potty-trained before she was two, but after Carlie left and Duke's cancer treatments started, she regressed. No one talks about it or pressures her into using the toilet. We're all too protective.

Lottie jumps into Millie's arms the moment her bloomers are pulled up, and Millie tickles Lottie's back, causing the little girl to squeal and giggle in a way that always makes me excited to be a dad. And this time, it makes me look outside at Jane, who is talking excitedly to Rusty and Ash.

"She's a special girl," Millie says. I'm not sure if she's talking about Lottie or Jane, but I agree.

* * *

The next morning, I take Lottie and Jane and her friends to the reservoir the river runs into. I haven't been here in years, but last night, I had a memory of the first time I found this place: right after Tag brought me to the farm after my parents and Nana died. He had to go talk to someone—an attorney, probably—and I ran off rather than watching the movie he had set up for me in the main house. I took my bike out and quickly got lost riding. I was thirsty and scared, and when I found the river, I followed it until it got to the reservoir. Tag found me three hours later, asleep underneath one of the sugar maples, tears staining my cheeks.

Even as the pain of that memory stings my chest, however, more memories come to mind. Happy ones. Nana teaching me how to swim. The first time Tag took me fishing. Uncle Lawson and my dad shooting off fireworks from the pier on the Fourth of July. Kayaking with Rusty and Duke. Hours and days playing on the rope swing.

I breathe in the fresh, earthy smell and hold the air in my lungs for a few seconds. I listen to the chirr of a robin and the rustle of the leaves in the breeze. When I exhale, peace washes over me. Healing, as Jane would say.

Jane's team has a full presentation, which is even more impressive considering how they manage to do it in between bites of grits, ham and collard green quiche, and biscuits with fresh preserves. I know a lot of what's coming, but Jane has some surprises, too, and it's those surprises that make me almost want to keep the farm. The hipster restaurant is gone, replaced with rotating food trucks from local vendors. Glamping and camping space. Community gardening classes. School tours and summer camps. Dorm-style housing on the property for seasonal workers, and longer-term modular rentals for annual employees or those with families. Ash brings up an idea that's straight out of the Bible: allowing people in the community to come pick the last of the crops after harvesting ... for free.

"Or maybe we have boxes of fruit available once a month at a 'pay what you can' stand?" I suggest, excited by the idea. They love it.

They talk about trying to book a big wedding before the end of the fall, when the sugar maples will be at their deepest red, but considering most brides plan their weddings a year or two in advance, they acknowledge it may be necessary to start with smaller ones.

Each concept is better than the last, but Millie's final proposal grips me. "Everyone loves their goat yoga these days, and while I think that could be a fun option for you here, I see something much bigger." She shares her vision of the farm part-nering up with a mental health facility to offer animal therapy. Her passion when she talks about the healing role of nature and animals is enough to sell me on the spot. She even offers to help me find a clinician to set it up.

My mind whirls with possibilities, and for the first time in a long time, I can see past the years of hurt and loneliness, the deep pain of never being enough for my own family. And I see potential. Looking at Jane, I could even imagine a future. She glows from the joy of a job well done. I can't believe I was ever so stupid as to think she got the job because of her (stunning) looks. I've never been as good at anything as Jane is as CEO of her company. I've never been as excited about anything as she is to present these plans, for Pete's sake.

Watching her smile on a picnic blanket as she gestures

STRAWBERRY FIELDS FOR NEVER

animatedly, a half-eaten plate of food by her knees, the warm sun streaming down on her, illuminating her dark blonde hair and stormy blue eyes as the water ripples around the reservoir … it fills my heart with both heat and contentment. A swirl of butterflies and a calm breeze.

I don't want her to disappear when the rebrand is done.

But what does that even mean? She'll head back to Chicago when she's done. Would I follow her? McNeal—our biggest competitor—has offices in Dearborn, Michigan. A mere four hours away. Or maybe Lawson will be so impressed by the rebrand that he'd offer Jane a permanent position. She could be a marketing exec, and I could be a senior manager in sustainability.

You're getting ahead of yourself again.

"This will more than turn things around for the farm," I hear myself saying. "This will revolutionize our brand. Launch it past the twenty-first century without sacrificing the core of who we've always been. It's brilliant. You've done it, Jane. Janes," I add.

I mean every word.

Get a handle, man. Overeager isn't a good look on you.

Jane blushes, and the color on her cheeks is so honest and pure, I want to kiss her. "Let's not jump ahead of ourselves. There's a lot of work to be done still."

Good point. Listen to the smart, beautiful woman.

"You already emailed me the presentation, right?" I ask Jane. "Can y'all sit tight while I make a call?" I look at Lottie, but she ignores me. She hasn't moved from Millie's lap since we got here, and she doesn't notice when I step away to forward the presentation to Uncle Lawson. I call him a moment later, and, to my surprise, he answers on the second ring.

"Tripp, my boy. What can I do for you?"

I give him the run down of everything Jane and her team

presented. I try to keep my enthusiasm in check so as not to overplay my hand. He's impressed but cautious.

"Do you want my opinion from an acquisitions perspective or an uncle's perspective?"

Why does his question fill me with dread? "Acquisitions?"

"Never mind," he says immediately. "I can't separate the two with you. I think you should see this through the way *you* want to complete it. That's the goal, remember? Letting you see a project through?"

"It is, but I don't want to do anything that will make you change your mind."

"Do a good job, and you won't. But I'll tell you this: only implement the things you could handle managing if our deal doesn't work out. If I'm not interested, you'll have another six months of seeing this all through. Don't go bigger than will make you happy. Animal therapy? Whew. That's some out-of-the-box liability right there."

He mentioned cutting the one thing that's non-negotiable to me. I don't care if there's an animal therapy practice two miles from here, I want it at the farm. It would have made a world of difference when I was a kid, and after seeing how it soothed Lottie only a couple of weeks ago, I know we need it. *I* need it.

I feel like I have two brains fighting against each other: my rational brain and my Jane brain. My rational brain thinks in seeds and sales, in produce and profits. It will take years for the housing to pay off with how low the rent will be, and much of that cost would fall on Carville Industries, if Uncle Lawson agrees to purchase it after all.

My Jane brain reminds me that every project she works on keeps her here longer, and every day she's here increases the chance that *we* have a chance.

A real chance.

Wherever that may be.

Slow down, Tripp. You have to update the farm, anyway. Follow Uncle Lawson's lead.

"I think I want to do all of them," I say. I slap my palm against my forehead.

"All of them? You want to implement every single proposal?"

No, Lawson's right. This is so much bigger than we need to go, my rational brain says.

"Yes, all of them," that voice of mine says.

"Son, this is a lot of risk. Sugar Maple Farms is failing, but it hasn't failed yet. The changes to the label will probably fix the financial problems right there. You sure you want to take such sweeping action?"

Am I sure? If Jane weren't Jane and I weren't so bitter, what would I do? Tag earmarked a lot of money for the rebrand, but what I'm considering will cost even more. Am I willing to jeopardize the sale to Carville Industries completely?

Lawson said not to go bigger than would make me happy. The fact is, these ideas energize me. Imagining walking around the farm in Jane's vision reminds me how much I love this business and how magical this place can be. Besides, if Lawson doesn't want the farm at the end of this, these changes could make it more desirable to potential buyers.

Or not.

But they'll also give me more time with Jane.

"I'm positive."

"Why, Tripp?"

I look over at Jane, who smiles when she sees me. Any reluctance even my rational brain could hold vanishes. "I think it's what it needs. Sugar Maple Farms should be a place of opportunity, community, hope, and healing. Those are the pillars that hold us up. Anything less than a full commitment threatens to put us on shaky ground."

"Your farm, your pillars," he says. Is that a smile I hear in his voice? "Keep me posted."

When I tell Jane that I want to move forward with all of the plans, her smile beams so bright, it could give me a sunburn.

*　*　*

A half hour later, Lottie insists on taking a walk around the reservoir. She wanders off, leaving Ash and Jane to catch up with her. "I'll follow in a sec," Millie calls behind them. Half of Lottie's brunch ended up down the front of Millie's floral dress, so she dabs at it with a wet napkin. When she's done, she offers to help me clean up, and we talk while we work.

"So, this is where you grew up, huh? I bet you have a lot of complicated memories walking around here."

"Why do you say that?"

"It's a farm. Even if your family is perfect, growing up on a farm means backbreaking responsibilities and sky-high expectations at a young age. And if your family is anything like mine, it *wasn't* perfect."

"Ha," I say. "Understatement of the century. Before they died, my parents used this place as a daycare for me. And we lived in North Carolina, so they had to drive all the way down to drop me off before they could take whatever trip they had planned."

"Ouch." It's a small word, but the way she says it hits me. No judgment, just empathy. It's like she *felt* that pain just from what I said. And that opens me up to tell her more.

"And then when it was just Tag and me, even when he was here, it was lonely in that big house and he was ... aloof. Hard to read and harder to please. I was so starved for his attention that I probably acted out in stupid ways that made him too angry to even look at me. So he stopped looking at me."

"In what way?" Her voice sounds like it aches with concern.

"He was still the CEO of Carville Industries, so after years of doing most of his work remotely, he started traveling to Atlanta a lot more and leaving me behind."

"You've been left behind a lot in your life. That must have hurt," she says.

A familiar, painful lump forms in my throat. I focus on folding the picnic blanket. "It was one of his 'Carville tests.' An opportunity for me to figure out how I would spend my time, who I would be when there was no one watching. He may have seen it as a test, but to me, it was one more example of how I was never enough."

"Never enough for what?"

I place the blanket in the back of my truck with the remains of the picnic and slam the tailgate. My lungs feel painfully tight. "For someone to stay, I guess."

"Oh, Tripp. What a crappy way to feel all these years. I'm sorry."

"Thanks," I say.

"You've had a lot to carry for a long time," Millie says as we start for the path. "You should be proud of yourself for how much you've accomplished, regardless of your last name."

"Ah, the burden of privilege," I say self-deprecatingly, because I know there are few things tackier than a rich guy complaining. And because I can't believe how much I've spilled. "You've probably heard all about that from Jane, though."

Millie's head snaps to look up at me. "What do you mean?"

"She's a Harrington. She knows better than anyone what this is like."

"Ah," Millie says, nodding her head only slightly. "You think Jane is one of *those* Harringtons."

"Is there another kind?"

"Tripp," she says delicately, and it's the first time I've sensed an ounce of judgment from her. "Harrington is probably as common a last name as Carville. And you know better than anyone that your tenth cousins aren't multi-millionaires. Yet you thought that because Jane is beautiful and accomplished, she must come from privilege instead of poverty. I don't air my friend's secrets lightly, but the only thing your upbringing has in common with Jane's is suffering."

Hot shame creeps up my neck. "I've teased her about it a half dozen times, at least. Why didn't she say something?"

"Why didn't you ask?"

"But all her jokes about golf courses—"

"Were a defense mechanism to someone making assumptions about her. She knows her way around a golf course because she worked as a server in a country club to pay her family's bills."

I have never wanted to punch someone in the face as much as I want to punch myself right now. How could I be so stupid? "I had no idea."

"Jane has to work twice as hard as any man around her to prove that she deserves a seat at the table. When someone like you graduates second in his class at Northwestern, everyone assumes it's because he's smart. When someone like Jane does, everyone assumes she slept her way there. An attractive, successful woman has to prove her intelligence while simultaneously disproving other's assumptions. You've let me know a bit about what it's like to grow up a Carville. It sounds both easy and exhausting. Take away the ease and double the exhaustion, and you'll have a small idea of what it's like to be Jane."

I am humbled. Humbled, embarrassed, and even emotional to think of how I fed right into the very assumptions that Jane has been disproving her whole life. What Millie has said is enough, and yet she's not done.

"Jane's mom is as beautiful as you would imagine, but that beauty was the only thing that mattered to her. Whatever her past, her experience with being so beautiful made her heartless. Totally narcissistic. She didn't care about anyone or anything, including her daughters."

"I didn't know."

"You didn't ask," she corrects me. "The only lessons Jane's

mother gave her were in how to take advantage of people, how to get whatever she wanted whenever she wanted it. Human cost was meaningless. She teased Jane for acting like the mother to her younger sister, told her that all that mothering would *age* her. As if total neglect of a child would be preferable to a few premature wrinkles. Can you imagine? You don't feel like you'll ever live up to being a Carville. Jane is terrified that all she'll ever be is a trailer park Harrington with a pretty face. The success of her company and this job couldn't matter more to her professionally or personally." Millie's eyes bore into mine. "Do you understand?"

"I do." My voice cracks. "I do."

"Good." Millie steps over a fallen log. "Jane doesn't talk about this, so maybe I shouldn't, either. But unfortunately for all of us, I'm a bit of a meddler." Her smile is sharp but not unkind. "You're going to be working with her for months. She deserves to be seen for who she is."

We're close enough to see Jane, Ash, and Lottie now. A light breeze stirs, blowing Millie's red hair into her face. She ties it with a rubber band from her wrist.

"Thanks for the free therapy and the free perspective," I tell her. "I appreciate you setting me straight. But man, I wish I'd have asked her."

"You still can. But it's my pleasure. Any friend of Jane's is a friend of mine."

"I don't know that Jane would call us friends. Frenemies, maybe."

She smiles. "Nah, you're good people, Tripp."

"You too, Millie."

She stops me a few yards from where Lottie is throwing rocks into the water.

"Now it's my turn to ask you something ... "

* * *

139

Lottie has a tantrum when Millie and Ash get in their rental. She screams and begs and cries for Millie not to go. I see the pain on Millie's face as she waves at Lottie, but they don't have a choice but to leave. Lottie is inconsolable. Jane asks if I want help, and although I do want her to stay with me, I feel bad putting babysitting duty on her, on top of everything else. Truthfully, I also feel sick about all of my assumptions. So I let her off the hook. I can't tell if she's relieved or bummed when I do.

Unfortunately, I don't have time to think about Jane's reaction. Lottie grabs on to me and won't let go. She cries so hard and for so long that my shirt is soaked. She screams that something is going to happen to Millie, to her dad, to Grammy and Pop or Auntie Reese. She falls asleep in the middle of crying on me and wakes up crying again. Neither Rusty nor Anita nor the animals can help her this time. It isn't until Duke gets to the house at ten p.m. that she finally lets go of me. She collapses into an exhausted heap on his shoulder, screams for Millie, and falls asleep right away.

Duke looks alarmed. "What happened? What's a 'Miwwie'? I thought she'd been doing well with you."

"Not Miwwie, Millie. She's Jane's friend. Lottie was fine until she left earlier. You'd have thought it was Carlie leaving all over again," I tell him. And then I mention what Millie told me by the reservoir, right before we reached Lottie. "Have you considered she may have separation anxiety disorder?"

Duke's features harden. "Of course she has separation anxiety. All three-year-olds have it."

"I mean something beyond typical toddler behavior. She's experienced a lot in three years, Duke. It may be of some worth for you two to talk to someone."

Duke tightens his hold on his daughter. "Tripp, you're like a brother to me, but you're not her father. I know what Lottie needs, okay? She's just tired. She'll be fine after a good night's sleep."

I back off, nodding and telling him he's probably right. Since Millie brought it up several hours ago, though, I know this isn't the last time someone will have this conversation with Duke. Lottie is hurt and scared, and she needs help. I hope Duke will be more receptive to the idea in the future, but I also know he can't hear this from me.

"How did things go?" I ask. "Did they try to negotiate?"

"Not as hard as I did." He gives me a wolfish smile. "Five years, $200 million, fifty guaranteed."

I pat his shoulder, congratulating him on the monster contract. Duke is one of the top quarterbacks in the NFL, and the Carolina Waves have a good chance of making the Super Bowl next year with him leading. When Duke heads out, I'm left in the house where I grew up, alone with my thoughts, wishing Jane was here.

On a whim, I text her to ask what she's doing. She responds saying that the kitchen sink is clogged and she's working on it. Then, after a pause with three dots, she says that my auger and I are welcome to join her.

I'm running before I've even put my phone away.

CHAPTER SIXTEEN

JANE

*W*eeks have stretched into months since my friends left, and already, the farm has come a long way. Tripp has teams of contractors renovating, updating, going to work. A second barn is being built for the animals so that the famous white barn by the maples can be converted to the wedding venue. The new barn will have an annexed space for a licensed therapist to work, too.

The cottages are well on their way to being renovated. All except mine, which is slowly coming along as I have time … and a helper in Tripp.

We've reached out to local colleges about having education majors intern with us for future education programs. We have a huge interest list. Schools and daycares are coordinating summer day camps at the farm, which will start in under a month.

Tripp has an office in the plant, but we've set up shop in the office in the main house so we can focus. The mahogany desk is so large that we can share it facing each other and still have room to breathe.

Well, not breathe, exactly, but work, at least. Because sometimes, I'll glance up and catch Tripp looking at me, and I think his hotness is sucking the air out of the room. That's what heat and fire do, right? Feed on oxygen? Tripp's fire feeds on the oxygen in my lungs.

The metaphor is getting out of hand, but the point is that getting to know Tripp so well has allowed me to freely pitch my tent back in Tripp-is-too-appealing-for-words territory. Him being funny, smart, and hot is distracting in the best and worst possible ways. Especially since he's gotten to know the real me.

"Jane, can I ask you something?" he asked a few days after my friends left. "You're not related to the famous Harringtons, are you?"

"Sure I am," I said. "We're sixth cousins twice removed."

He shook his head. "I'm sorry. I projected my own issues on you."

"It's understandable. You're not the first person to do it. It happened all through college and grad school. Honestly, it was easier to let people think I got where I was because of my family than because of … "

"Your pretty face?"

"I wouldn't put it that way."

"I would. I *did*. And I'm sorry," he said. "You deserved better, *especially* from me."

It was that *especially from me* part that struck the deepest. Hearing him distinguish himself from other people in relation to me felt significant, like he was trying to tell me something.

I was listening.

Since then, we've spent every day together for almost two months. We go on morning runs to brainstorm and we work through dinner. During the day, we bicker and brainstorm nonstop. At night when we have time, he helps me with whatever project I'm working on. Our bickering becomes more like banter, and that banter has progressed from playful to flirtatious to downright electric.

Tonight we're retiling the shower, and the bathroom is cramped enough that we keep bumping into each other. He's wearing his running shorts and a t-shirt that looks like one of those Batman's abs shirts, for the way it defines his each and every muscle. I wonder if he has to special order clothes that fit him. Jack Reacher always manages to step into a second-hand store and the closest outfit he can find is just a bit too tight, for all of our benefit. Tripp has the same luck.

And by Tripp, I mean me. It's my luck.

He pops out a two-by-two-inch square tile, and the small movement uses muscles in his neck that I didn't even know existed. Without meaning to, I put my hand on his shoulder and lean closer. He turns his head back to look at me in confusion, but my face is too close because I was ogling his weirdly sexy neck, so now I have to try to think of some way to save face.

"Good work," I say stupidly. "That was good work."

His eyes drop down to my lips and then back up to my eyes. We're only a few inches apart, so I get an extreme close up of how sexy his smirk is.

"Thanks. I appreciate your *close* supervision."

He pops out the last few tiles and then puts down the chisel and ball peen hammer. I finally remove my hand from his shoulder—yes, I kept it on; yes, it bordered on caressing; no, I didn't hear him complaining.

He wipes his sweaty forehead and leans back and we both come to a stand. Then he turns to face me where I'm backed up against the sink. We're so close, but with his height, his lips are out of reach. And so tempting.

"That was … um." What am I saying? Am I talking? "That was good work."

"You said that."

"I meant it."

"I couldn't have done it without your helping hand."

"Always happy to help."

"Always?"

"Always."

My eyes wander his face territorially when he leans in.

He puts one hand on my waist, lighting a spark that only grows at his touch. His eyes watch my lips as he bends down. I inhale sharply, eagerly. Just as my eyes start to flutter closed, his face moves three inches to the right and his free hand snakes past me. His cheek brushes against mine, sending a thousand pinpricks of desire through me.

"Just grabbing my water," he drawls in a low, strong voice.

And I dissolve into a puddle.

Okay, not a literal puddle, but my bones are at least puddle-adjacent.

Rein it in, Harrington.

But I don't rein it in. I gape as Tripp guzzles water. A drip of condensation from his bottle rolls down his chin, streaming past his neck and under his shirt. I imagine that it continues between his absurdly rock-hard pecs and somehow zigzags around each of his impossibly chiseled abs. I can make out all eight—EIGHT!—of them through his sweat-damp gray shirt. I don't even pretend not to stare, but he's looking away from me while he drains the bottle.

I need a shower. Ice. Cold.

"What?" he asks, putting the bottle down on the counter behind me.

I look up. "Huh?"

"Did you say you need an ice-cold shower?"

My face flames up like a marshmallow left in the fire too long. "Yeah, because I'm sweating buckets, obviously."

I should be embarrassed to admit how sweaty and gross I am, but Tripp's face isn't the least disturbed by my admission.

His eyes drop down to my neck and shoulders, which are, in fact, sweaty from the work.

"And here I thought I was the only one who needed cooling off," he says, his lips twitching into the sexiest hint of a smile.

"Oh really?"

"You know, the reservoir is pretty nice this time of year."

We're still standing in the tiny bathroom, only inches of space between our bodies, more between our faces because of his height. But with the poor ventilation, his breath mingles intoxicatingly with mine. He's inviting me to go night swimming with him in a secluded place, and never has anything been more tempting. The heat between us sizzles. We've become familiar and a little handsy over the last several weeks, and our banter has gone from subtle hints to bold innuendo.

But we haven't even gone on a date. I'm not about to jump to a watery make out with the man—

Jump! My body begs. *Think of the muscles! The muscles!*

My hand reaches out, and I'm almost shocked to see my fingers touch his abs. Suddenly, the ventilation in this room has gone from poor to nonexistent, and the temperature has ratcheted up to planet destroying. I'm on Alderon and Tripp's body is the Death Star incinerating me.

What a way to go.

My hand has taken up residence on his torso. If it has its way, it will build a home here on his abs and never leave. Tripp places his hand over mine, and then his fingers trace all the way up from my fingers to my shoulder. I explode in goosebumps, in spite of the heat. He looks at me expectantly, enticingly.

Oh, I still haven't responded. Suddenly, the magnitude of his invitation hits me like a wrecking ball. He invited me to go swimming with him. At night.

"I think that would be getting ahead of ourselves." I drop my hand from his abs, but he takes it again. His hands are so strong. I let my fingers explore the calluses on his palms and fingertips.

My grandpa always had calluses. *Calluses are the sign of an honest day's work,* he used to say.

"Jane, I'm not asking for anything more than swimming. Cooling off, remember?"

"*Just* cooling off?" I look at our clasped hands, at how well they fit. My fingers are like my legs—too long for my body—but they look exactly the right size next to his.

"Unless you'd rather stay hot ... "

My face flies up to his. I hold my smile back. "It is hot in here, isn't it?"

"You should talk to the owner about getting a new air conditioner."

"I'll bring that up with him when we go swimming." I'm getting a kink in my neck from looking up at him so much. I hop backwards onto the counter and cock an eyebrow at Tripp, who looks like he's more than ready to take that dip with me. The look on his face tells me he's done with banter and, as my chest starts to heave, I realize I am too.

It's about to get a lot hotter in here.

I lean back, biting my lip as he takes a step closer to me. But the bathroom counter is tiny, and in the process, I slip into the basin and wrench down too hard on the old faucet. The faucet and my upper half both fall into the sink.

And water explodes from the pipes like a geyser.

Tripp screams like a child, and I would laugh if I weren't slipping ... and flipping over. The water hits me right in my face, squirting up my nose as I scramble to extricate myself from the sink. But the countertop is too slippery to even get my bearings. Every time I put my palm down to try to move, I slip back in. "Help!" I scream. Or try to scream. The water shoots in my mouth, gagging me.

In the scramble, part of me knows that everything is going to be okay, that this is probably as funny as it sounds, based on Tripp's chuckles, but I have a fire hose to my face, and the rest of me thinks I'm absolutely drowning. "Tripp!" I try to cry.

Tripp's strong arms are around me in an instant, pulling me out of the sink and away from the gushing water. He cradles me to him and takes a quick step, but unfortunately, the wet tile is trickier to navigate than dry tile, especially when holding another human being. His foot slides out from underneath him. I curl into a ball in his arms, tucking in my limbs as we go down. His butt lands right before the back of his head cracks against the tub.

I jerk my face up in time to see him wince and his eyelids go heavy. "Tripp! Tripp, stay with me," I beg, slipping against his wet, silky running shorts as I spin around on top of him, trying to get into a position where I can inspect his head, help him in any way. But the water is still exploding from the broken faucet and I can't get to him until the deluge has ceased.

Instead of trying to climb up him, I slide down, toward the faucet. I throw open the cupboard door and twist the shut off valve. The water stops immediately, and I'm able to stand up and plant my feet around Tripp's hips in order to examine him. He's blinking in confusion when I put my face in his, looking at his pupils.

"I'm lost at sea," he whispers.

"I'm right here," I say, not sure what he's talking about. I feel the back of his head and find a massive knot, but no blood. I cover his eyes for ten seconds before moving them away. He's too dazed to even ask what I'm doing, and he just stares at me when I study his pupils.

"Your eyes are dilating," I say. He groans and starts to push himself up. I stop him, putting my hand on his wet shirt, pushing his chest firmly enough to make sure he gets the message. "Don't try to stand. You could slip again."

He nods and the movement makes him whimper. His eyes

go wide before fluttering. I panic and lunge to hold his head. "Tripp, don't go to sleep. Stay with me."

"Okay." He sounds groggy. "But can I keep my eyes closed? The light hurts."

Uh-oh. Sensitivity to light is a bad sign. "Can you sit up at all? If I can help pull you up?"

His laugh is rumbling. "You can't pull me up."

"Moms can lift cars off of their kids. I can handle this."

"I don't think I like you thinking of me like that." His eyes are still closed, but he gets up to his elbows carefully, and he lets me grab his hand to help him sit up. I push and prod and heave until his back is propped up against the bathtub, and then I warn him not to move and not to sleep before running to the kitchen to call Rusty.

It goes straight to voicemail.

"NO!"

Who can I call? The nearest ER is twenty minutes from here, which would mean that emergency services would be thirty minutes out if they don't know the farm and the back roads to get here. I need to drive him there right now, but who can help? Anita? Booker? They couldn't help me pull him to a stand, let alone drag him to a car. I need someone who could bench press a horse.

Wait. No … I just need someone who can bench Tripp.

Duke! I grab Tripp's phone, but it's locked. I grumble a word not befitting a Southern Belle but very much befitting a freaked out Chicagoan and rush back into the bathroom.

"Smile," I tell Tripp, holding his phone in front of his face so that the facial recognition software unlocks the device. Then I pull up his contacts and look for his friend's number.

Nothing.

Huh?

"I need to call someone strong enough to lift you, Tripp. What's Duke's number?" I demand. But Tripp's eyes are closed again, so I lean down and tap his cheek. "Tripp," I say urgently. "Duke's number."

"Eight."

I type it in. "Okay, next number."

"No, eight." He sounds like he's barely hanging on, and the back of his head is swelling into a dinosaur egg. "Eight," he repeats. "Duke is number eight."

A light bulb goes off, and I find Duke's contact number under his jersey number. I hit dial.

"What's up, brother?" Duke asks.

"Duke, it's Jane. I don't have time to explain, but Tripp has a concussion, and I can't get him to stand up. How fast can you get here?"

"Ten minutes, tops." I hear commotion in the background and Duke mumbling something. A moment later, he's speaking quietly into the phone. "My sister's in town, so she'll stay with Lottie. Where are you?"

I tell him in time to see Tripp's head snap down and back up, like my sister used to when she was trying not to fall asleep. I sit on the tub's edge and lay his head in my lap so he won't injure himself again. And then, because I can't help myself, I run my hands through his light brown hair, a few shades darker than mine.

"Mmm. That's nice." He sounds so sleepy I almost stop, but the contentment in his voice pulls at me. Something tells me it's been a long time since someone took care of Tripp this way. His mom died when he was eight years old. In her present, affectionate moments, my mom would still play with my hair when I was twelve or thirteen. I missed out on a lot with a bitter, borderline criminally negligent mother, but he missed out on *everything*.

"Tell me about your parents," I say softly. He doesn't answer, so I scratch my fingernails playfully on his scalp and repeat the question.

He sighs. "Not much to tell. They were party seekers. Gone a lot. They left me with Nana and Papa." The fact that he's calling Tag "Papa" tells me he's not in his right mind as much as the knot on the back of his head. He's speaking differently, too. Like he's reserving his energy by only using independent clauses. "They loved fun. I got in the way. I held them back too much. Dad didn't want me on the plane. Couldn't even take me with them to crash."

Alarms go off inside of me. The accident his parents and grandmother died in was a plane crash? I don't know why this feels worse than a car accident. Maybe it's just the shock of it. The rarity.

"Papa didn't want me around any more than they did. He left as soon as I was gone. I came home from college to an empty house. I think he wished I was on the plane instead of Nana." His voice isn't emotional, but I feel wetness on my knee, and when I crane around his head to take a look, I see tears spilling from his cheeks. The sight makes me weepy as much as his story does. "Sometimes I feel the same way."

More tears fall onto my knee, and now I'm crying, too. I lean down to kiss the side of Tripp's head, whispering how sorry I am.

Tripp has never felt wanted. He's never felt like he was enough. Tag was so sweet to me, but I can't discount Tripp's years of experience with his own grandfather. Is there any chance Tag really didn't want him around, though? I can't imagine it, not with the way he made me promise to turn the farm into a place where Tripp would want to stay. It makes me wonder if Tag, himself, didn't feel like he was enough for Tripp. The way the people in town talked about him, the way he was so kind to me, so, respectful, so … proud, even.

But Tripp *never* felt that way? He never felt that ego boost that came from only a handful of words, a squeeze of the hand, and a delighted twinkle in his eye?

My grandpa always taught me to judge people based on my own experience with them, but ignoring the experience another person has is like describing an elephant as a tree trunk because I only felt its leg. An elephant leg is a lot like a tree trunk, but it doesn't take into account the rest of the animal and it doesn't paint the full picture. So while I can't dismiss my experience with Tag, I have to accept Tripp's, as well.

I think again of that final conversation with Tag. The urgency in his voice. The way he pleaded with me, made me swear to do everything in my power to make Tripp fall back in love with his home. The way he put all of his confidence and trust in *me*. Because he saw something in me that he was sure his grandson needed.

The memory is hard to reconcile with what Tripp has told me. I've built Mr. Carville up in my mind as this white knight whose goodness and love saved my company, saved me. But it turns out his suit of armor isn't white so much as shades of gray. It's ridiculous to be hurt by this when he wasn't my family, let alone when Tripp is concussed and dealing with his own painful memories of his grandpa every day just by being on this farm, but I can't stop it.

Not until Tripp mutters, "I want Jane."

My heart skips and stutters, and all other thoughts vanish. I kiss his temple again. "I'm here, Tripp."

* * *

Duke and I successfully get Tripp to the ER with only minimal grunting. When the hospital staff meets us with a gurney at the front doors, Duke hops out and helps them lift his giant friend. Everyone there knows Duke and Tripp, but when Duke insists I stay, they balk.

"It's late. Family only."

"She's his girlfriend," Duke insists. The burly nurse looks

unconvinced, hopefully because Tripp hasn't had a girlfriend in so long and not because he's had too many. "I'll give you an autographed football if you let us stay. Come on, Shane."

"Fine," the man says before letting us into the waiting area. "We'll get that x-ray and have the radiologist look it over quick as a hot knife through butter. We'll take good care of him," he tells me before he pushes past a pair of double doors and vanishes on the other side.

Duke grabs a cup of coffee and offers me one, but I decline in favor of an herbal tea. Coffee at night makes me jittery and anxious, and I already feel both of those things in strides. The adrenaline from the last hour is wearing off, leaving me cold and keenly aware that I'm wearing shorts and a wet tank top. I glance down and groan.

"Here," Duke says when he returns. He takes off his black t-shirt to reveal a white undershirt beneath. It's a testament to how concerned about—or maybe smitten with—Tripp that I don't ogle Duke's rippling display of chivalry.

I take the shirt and tea gratefully.

"Ready to talk about why you two were soaking wet with his head in your lap when I showed up?" I chuckle darkly and explain about the sink, leaving out all the flirting, but Duke reads me like a playbook. "So you two were getting frisky and broke the sink. I know players who've done the same to hotel rooms."

"Dude." I shoulder check him. I've run into him enough times over the past two months that Duke feels like an old friend already. Somehow, there is zero awkwardness or discomfort, in spite of his fame. But, then, maybe like Tripp did, he thinks I'm a *Harrington* Harrington.

"Be careful with his heart, Jane. I don't know someone who cares more deeply than he does or someone who tries to avoid caring more, either."

"What do you mean?" I curl my hands around the steaming cup.

"Tripp fancies himself an island all the while looking around desperately for a ship that's willing to dock in his port." He squints. "That sounds sexual."

"You think?"

"You get my point, though."

"That's not helping," I tease, earning a laugh. "But yes, I think so."

"Tripp's had a hard life. I haven't seen him open up with a woman the way he does with you."

"We're not dating—"

"Oh, he's been abundantly clear about that."

"That's flattering."

"It should be. The bard would say the gentleman doth protest too much."

I smile into my tea at the Shakespeare reference as Duke continues, telling me about how angry Tripp was in high school, how Tag had sky high standards and Tripp was always struggling to prove himself. "At least that's the way Tripp saw it. Rusty and I never interpreted it the same way."

"How did you see it?"

"We thought Tag was trying to show Tripp his own worth. Trying to let him prove to *himself* that he was good enough. Tripp was always so much bigger and stronger than everyone else—excluding yours truly, of course—that he got a bad rap. People expected too much too young. At twelve, he was already bigger than most teachers, so when he made a joke in class or hit someone too hard during Pee Wee football, or when he accidentally broke something with his Hulk strength, everyone treated him like a grown man picking on kids or intentionally destroying things. Older girls were always hitting on him, which made him all kinds of uncomfortable." I nod, knowing *exactly* what that feels like. "A couple of years of that, and he felt he didn't belong anywhere or with anyone but Rusty and me. The stress of it made him a bit of a hothead."

"In what way?"

"Oh, stupid stuff. Like when Tag put the three of us to work building a fence around the main house when we were maybe eleven or twelve. Tripp got his hands on a nail gun and was playin' with it like an extra in Scarface." I snort at the reference. "He ended up shooting a nail through his own foot. Tag about lost his mind. He was so angry rushing Tripp to the hospital that I think Tripp shut down."

"Why did Tag get so angry?"

"Because his wife, son, and daughter-in-law died in a stupid, totally avoidable accident. Tripp's dad flew that plane with a hangover. His nana went to try to keep him from doing anything idiotic. I think Tag was terrified, and like most Southern men of a certain age, his fear made him harder, not softer."

I stare at my tea, but not even its warmth can touch the chill that's crept inside of me. "Does Tripp know all of this?"

"Yes and no. He's heard it all. But I don't think he values himself enough yet to listen. You catch my drift?" I nod. He takes a slow drink of his coffee. "Hopefully that'll start changing here soon."

"I hope so, too."

CHAPTER SEVENTEEN

JANE

Three hours later, Tripp is alert, aware, and annoyed. The x-ray confirmed that his skull isn't fractured, and the doctor said he has a mild concussion. He should be back to his old self in a few days, but I'm given instructions to make sure he rests, avoids screens and overstimulation, and to check on him periodically when he sleeps for the first night. Duke sold me as Tripp's girlfriend, so I can hardly push back on the idea. And I wouldn't want to. I set up camp in the ancient floral-patterned rocking chair next to his grandparents' bed and watch over him like a mother hen.

He is not pleased.

"For the hundredth time, I'm fine." Duke and I put him in the master bedroom because his childhood bedroom—where he's been sleeping—is too cramped for me to set up shop comfortably. Tripp is propped up in the middle of the master bed, holding an ice pack to the back of his skull. "I got my bell rung. Now get out of here and let me sleep."

"Stop arguing," I snap. "I'm supposed to watch over you while you sleep. You need the rest."

"And I'm trying to explain that I *can't* rest with you watching over me like a creeper."

"A creeper? Really? I'm making sure you don't slip into a freaking coma, and you're calling me a creeper?" I clap twice, turning out the light. Tripp hasn't come into the room since his grandfather died, so it has all the trappings of a septuagenarian's haven, including a bedside table with the Bible, Icy Hot, and a photo of Tag and a young Tripp picking strawberries.

Also a clapper lamp.

He double claps the light back on. "Yes, I'm calling you a creeper. You're going to *watch me sleep.*"

"Yeah, as your nurse not your stalker, you weirdo. Go to bed." I double clap the light off.

He double claps it back on, again. And he looks mad. "Jane, I'm a full-grown man. I'm not being contrary when I say I will not be able to sleep with you watching me."

"Why?" I demand in frustration. Why can't he see that I *need* to help him? That I need to make sure he's okay? "Why can't you just let me help you?"

"Because I'm worried about *you.*" His eyes squeeze shut, as if the admission causes him pain. Physical or emotional, I'm not sure. "Since you've been here, you've worked from dusk to dawn on the Sugar Maple Farms account for me and for your company. Then into the night, you're renovating Strawberry Fields, a cottage that isn't even yours. You're still coordinating with your team on their other projects multiple times a week. I have it on good authority that you miss breakfast more often than not, and I've seen firsthand that you're subsisting on protein shakes and whatever produce Anita sends over."

"You're describing half of the businesswomen I know."

"No, I'm not. I'm describing you." I move to protest, but he says, "With all due respect to womankind, I don't care about them and I'm not saying you're *different than every other woman.* I'm saying you, Jane Harrington, are working yourself to the bone worrying about everyone else. It seems to me that you feel responsible for the success of everyone and everything around you. Who feels responsible for you? Who is worrying about you?"

Him asking this in pajamas from his alma matter while sitting in the center of what looks like two twin beds pushed together does all sorts of funny things to my insides. He looks so vulnerable, I'm desperate to help him. It's not a desire but a driving force. Tripp has picked up on this after knowing me for a couple of months when I haven't told him a sliver of my childhood. Not even Millie's therapist magic could do that.

"Is that why you've started helping me with the cottage?"

"It's not because I enjoy Property Brothers."

"They wish they were as tall as you."

"Yeah they do." He smiles. "Jane. Please."

There's so much to his *please.* He's not just asking me to not watch him sleep. He's asking me to let him in. To drop the walls preventing us from advancing past flirtation. To not fight or banter but communicate. Or at least that's how it feels.

"I can't help it," I tell him. "You know I'm not a *Harrington* Harrington. I grew up in a trailer park so far on the wrong side of Chicago's tracks, not even John Hughes would make a movie about it. My mom used movies as a babysitter for Meghan and me while she was 'daddy hunting.' Her only life lessons were about how to use my *assets* to get ahead and how to make a solid hangover cure. I hated it, but I had to be strong for Meghan." I inhale a shaky breath and then spill my guts. And spill and spill.

I tell him about my mom, about her relinquishing all parental duties without ever giving up custody. I tell him about my devastation when my grandpa died and how the burden of caring for my mom and sister fell solely on my shoulders. I tell him about Meghan, about paying for her education and how I'm still subsidizing her rent. I tell him I'm terrified that I'm turning her into a Mini Mom by taking care of her bills and sending her money when I'm at risk of defaulting on my own student loans. I tell him about blocking my mom's phone number and admit that I occasionally unblock it for a week or two at a time, hoping she'll text me to say she loves me, but instead, she hits me up for money if she communicates at all. I tell him about my friends in turn, the ups and downs they've had and how guilty I feel for pulling them from their careers—careers that could have been wildly successful if not for me. I tell him how close we were to going under and share my fear that I've taken away years of productivity for them, even now that things are going better for us

I tell him how I'm taking a fraction of the paycheck I should to make sure they get paid first.

And then I tell him the most embarrassing part of all: I'm living on credit card debt.

Every financial lesson I learned growing up by my mom's bad example, every lesson I learned in my major and in one of the top business schools in the world. I'm betraying them all. And the stress of it keeps me up at night.

I don't know when I started crying. I don't know when this became a confessional, but far from putting Tripp to sleep, as I'd hoped, he's listening raptly and without any judgment on his strong, impossibly appealing face. I've seen him in so many situations over the last several weeks, and not once has he looked sexier than he looks right now, patiently listening without giving me a scrap of advice or trying to fix it all for me.

And in this moment of being truly, completely, wonderfully heard, I think I fall in love with Tripp a little.

The glider is close enough to the bed that Tripp reaches his long arm out and takes my hand in his. Then he pulls me off the chair and on to the bed. I squeal and then laugh and then cry as he tucks me under his arm like a doll and smoothes my hair before resting his head against mine.

"Thanks for trusting me with this, Jane."

"Yeah, I did you a real favor, didn't I?"

"Yes," he says firmly. He's beneath the sheets and I'm on top of them, and the crack in the twin beds is right beneath me. It reminds me of the wedgie I had the day we met, and I laugh in spite of myself. "I'm serious," he says. "I want to know these things about you. I want to know everything."

"I'm not sure about that," I say, still laughing. Stress, exhaustion, and emotion have caught up with me, and I'm as punchy as Ash when she pulls an all-nighter working.

"I am," he says. "So why is that funny?"

"Oh, that's not what I'm laughing about," I say between giggles. "I'm laughing because I'm propped in between the crack between the beds, and it reminds me of the day we met."

"Um ..."

"When you picked me up, I had the biggest wedgie I've ever had in my life. And it rode up the entire way until we got to the farm."

A laugh explodes from Tripp's chest, the same stress, exhaustion, and emotion evidently working in him. His booming laugh makes me laugh harder, and we both laugh ourselves to tears.

* * *

I startle awake in the early hours of the morning, not sure where I am or who on earth is next to me. I almost scream until I remember last night. And then I almost scream again out of fear that Tripp is in a coma or worse. I hold my finger close to his nose, checking for breathing. And checking. A slow puff of warm breath blows gently against my finger, and I sigh in relief. I shift carefully away from him, but he pulls me closer, drawing me back into the nook of his arm. Clearly not in a coma, then.

I don't even remember falling asleep. I remember talking, laughing, crying, talking some more. We were both dead tired, but when did I curl up against him? I thought I closed my eyes on the pillow a few feet away. Did he roll toward me?

No, he's still in the middle of the bed, where he was when he pulled me on with him last night. Which means I rolled toward him, and he somehow made space for me, tucked into his side like I was made to fit.

I should wiggle free, should get back to the chair, should give us both space.

Should, should, should.

Instead, I close my eyes, drape my arm over his barrel chest, nuzzle my nose into his neck, and fall back asleep.

"I guess we know why Tripp isn't responding," a voice says minutes or maybe hours later. I throw myself up to see Duke and Rusty standing in the doorway, grinning like fools. My heart hammers frantically, the way being abruptly awakened always does. "Looks like he and the ol' *not-girlfriend* fell asleep. In bed. Together." Tripp groans and I look over to see him blocking the overhead light from his eyes.

"Whoops, sorry about that," Duke says, turning the light back off. A bit of sunlight peeks in from the curtains, but it's dark enough in the room that Duke flipping on the lights shattered some rods or cones or whatever it is in your eyes that abrupt light obliterates. "I forget how miserable lights are when you have a concussion."

The two men come traipsing into the room as I try to get away from Tripp, but he grabs my hand, stopping me.

"They can see that you're on top of the sheet and I'm underneath," he says in grunts. "They know nothing happened."

"I wouldn't call that nothing," Duke says, far too smiley. Rusty's holding a breakfast tray that smells of bacon and eggs.

"Yeah, yeah," Tripp says, sitting up gingerly.

As much as I want to bolt out of this room, I'm even more

worried about Tripp's head. The bump is still goose-egg sized. "How are you feeling?"

"I *was* feeling great." His eyes twinkle. "Comfy. Snuggly. Well-rested."

I elbow his ribs softer than I normally would, but he pretends I drilled him. "Oh, poor baby." I pet his head and then stand up next to Tripp's friends. "Seeing as they brought you breakfast, I should get going. I'll check on you later?"

"No, stay, Jane," Duke says. "We brought enough for both of you."

"How did you know I'd be here?"

"It's a total girlfriend move, and you and Tripp have established that you are decidedly *not* his girlfriend."

I look at Tripp. "Are you sure you're not twins? I didn't know it was possible for so much annoyance to exist in two bodies."

"I'm Schwarzenegger," Duke says a split second before Tripp can. "You're DeVito. Ha ha, sucker."

"Finally a movie you actually know," I tell Tripp.

"I know Schwarzenegger," he corrects. "The man's workouts are legendary."

"How do you put up with them?" I ask Rusty.

Rusty shrugs, and his dirty blond hair falls in front of his face. "I'm the cooler."

He says it more like a quote than an explanation. "Is that a *Roadhouse* reference?" I ask, remembering how my grandpa would stop on the Patrick Swayze movie every time he was channel surfing and it was on TV. Which was all the time. You don't soon forget a movie where Johnny from *Dirty Dancing* rips out a guy's throat.

Rusty looks to Tripp. "Marry her."

"I don't even believe in marriage," Duke says, "and I agree."

"I take it back. You're just as annoying. Triplets."

"You're DeVito," Tripp and Duke tell Rusty before yelling,

"Jinx!" The commotion makes Tripp wince, but he waves off my concern.

Rusty and Duke pull the matching gliders over, while Tripp and I sit up on the bed. After a few hours, Rusty's parents call him away. The fruit stand business is bigger than ever since Rusty and Ash put their marketing heads together. It's like a fire has been lit under Rusty, and he's motivated to use his education and experience to make more of it. He's been taking to social media, making funny graphics and even short videos, one of which recently went viral and caused all of the Sugar Maple Farms stalls throughout the state to sell out in record time.

If the rebrand goes as well as I hope it will, I'm of half a mind to offer him a job.

One more person you'll be responsible for, a voice in my head says.

Yet that spike of fear isn't as intense as it would have been even a day ago. Opening up to Tripp was like taking a deep breath after sipping air through a straw. The memory of Tripp's patient, listening ear last night makes my heart feel too big for my chest.

Duke takes off soon after Rusty does, leaving Tripp and me in his grandparents' bedroom. It's decorated in dark, rich colors, and it feels like the bedroom of an old man. I reach across the bed for the picture I saw earlier of Tag and Tripp in a strawberry patch. Tripp is maybe ten years old, but already tall and lanky. With the sun behind them, their faces are hard to make out, but they're each holding a basket of strawberries, and Tag has his arm around his grandson. When I hold the picture under the light, I spot a grin on Tripp's face and a thin but real smile on Tag's.

"This is cute. When was it?"

Tripp studies the picture with a furrowed brow. "Huh. I think I was nine here. Tag took me to pick strawberries and he told me about how strawberries grow." Tripp leans back into the headboard, and I sink beside him, staring at the picture.

"He was passing on tricks of the trade?"

Tripp doesn't answer. He stares at the picture, the V between his brows deepening. "I guess so. I don't really remember." He closes his eyes and I take the picture from him and set it on the side table. I'm about to leave when Tripp slides down the headboard and pulls me beside him.

"Oh, so that's how it's going to be, is it?" I fake protest as I nestle into his side. He tucks me under his arm in what is fast becoming my nook.

"Did you sleep well last night?"

"Like a baby."

"Me too."

I take a deep breath, close my eyes, and stay there, perfectly contented, until we both fall back asleep.

CHAPTER EIGHTEEN

JANE

That afternoon, I take a break from looking after Tripp to clean up my wreck of a wet cottage and shower. The floor is a mess, and the laminate in the bathroom will have to go, but fortunately, the worst of it stayed in the bathroom. Good thing Anita insisted on giving me a cottage-renovation budget that includes the bathroom floor.

I grab some supplies to head back to the main house when I get a phone call. I answer it without thinking.

"Hello?"

"Big sis!" Meghan says. "You've been impossible to reach. How's North Carolina?"

"South Carolina," I correct her, "and it's great. You should come out and see this place. It's like something out of a movie."

"So tempting," she says, her voice shifting in a way that I've heard countless times before. My stomach drops. "But I have a lot going on here. That's why I called."

"Meghan,"

"I was in a car accident, Jane," she says as if she has stage four cancer. "The repairs are almost $2500."

"Which is why you have insurance. I send you money every month for it, remember?"

"About that … "

Anger rushes over me like a Chicago wind. "Do not tell me you canceled the insurance and have been pocketing that money."

"I had to! Marnie found this super cute loft, and the rent was just a bit more than I could afford."

The unjustness of what's going on is so intense, I feel physically ill. After the years I've spent taking care of her, for her to throw my generosity in my face so she can have a more glamorous lifestyle while I'm living off of credit cards is too much. "No."

"You haven't even heard what I'm asking."

"I can't talk about this right now, Meghan. I have to go meet my client. I'll call you tomorrow." I hang up before her protests can get too vicious. She's always had a way of cutting to my core. I've never stopped feeling protective of her, but by being so protective, I've taken her growing pains away entirely. Which means she hasn't grown.

Everything she's become is my fault.

I sit in the truck in front of the house and rest my forehead on the steering wheel. "You failure," I whisper to myself. "Look at you. Look at the mess you've made." For years, I've taken the weight of everyone else's burdens on myself. I've tried so hard to be as different from my mom as possible, to prove that I'm not some opportunistic pretty face, but I haven't helped anyone. I'm a liability. The King Midas of Dumpster Fires.

Things with my friends still aren't the same, at least not with Parker. She may give advice or talk to me in a professional capacity, but we're not *talking* like we used to. Each of the Janes are the best of besties, but Parker and I have always understood each other in ways the others haven't. Maybe it's because we went to business school together and experienced so many of the same difficulties being taken seriously, although for different reasons. Her distance is a wound that won't close. She clearly hasn't forgiven me for trying my hardest to help, and when I try to broach the subject, she shuts off. Goes all business on me. I don't know how to make it right.

And look at the cottage! I should have left the renovation to professionals. It was selfish and self-aggrandizing of me to think that I could do something so ambitious. The DIY shows make everything look manageable, but I'm the idiot who thought I could actually do it all. Painting and scraping walls are one thing. Showers? Plumbing? What was I thinking?

If I hadn't taken this job, Tripp wouldn't have gotten hurt.

If I hadn't taken this job, we wouldn't have—

The thought stops me short.

I can regret renovating the cottage. I can regret every time I've bailed Meghan out. I can regret taking the job before consulting my friends. But I can never, ever regret taking this job.

And there's one enormous reason for that.

Tripp.

My staggering mental load shifts as I think about every interaction with him. Every joke, every fight, every heart-stop-ping smile, every moment of hair-pulling vexation.

Ash was right. He's absolutely vexy.

I don't regret knowing him for a second. Not for a single second.

I pull down the truck's vizor and give myself a pep talk.

"You got this, Jane. Tonight's going to be big. You're not a mess. You're *not* the King Midas of Dumpster Fires. Your company is solid. Parker will forgive you one day. The doctor said Tripp's going to be okay. Meghan … okay, she's a dumpster fire, but one thing at a time. Your mascara looks good, your granny undies are sitting right and tight, your friends and Tripp are okay, and you got this. Okay? Okay."

I hop out of the truck and make my way toward the house. I spot Anita and Booker over in the expansive yard and they grin and give me a thumbs up, confirming everything is in place. Booker gives me a wink before I head inside and upstairs, and that vote of confidence pushes me over the edge.

I got this.

Outside of Tripp's room, I take a deep, slightly shaky breath, but it's not self-pitying. It's eager. After four hours away, I can't wait to see Tripp.

"I'm back!" I say when I open the door.

Tripp's head raises from his phone and his eyes rove over me. He's not sitting in bed anymore but rather on the glider in the corner. "I know it's only been a few hours, but you are a sight for sore eyes."

I fake a curtsy. "Thank you."

"Also for a sore head. Can you toss me a couple of ibuprofens?"

I bring him a glass and two pills as doubt sets in over my plans for the evening. He suffered a serious injury and I'm acting like it's a flesh wound. "You shouldn't have gotten up. You need to rest!"

He swallows the pills and sets the glass down on the table beside him. I stand in front of him, waiting for an answer. Sitting, he's closer to my height than he is standing. "No, I needed to shower. I have a mild concussion. I'm not overexerting myself by showering or grabbing—" His mouth slams shut.

"Grabbing what? Tell me you didn't walk downstairs alone!"

He doesn't even have the sense to look guilty, although his answer says otherwise. "Sort of."

"Tripp! You should have someone with you if you're walking around. What if something had happened to you?"

The look on his face changes from irascible to tender. "Jane, you know my fall wasn't your fault, right? You're not responsible for my choices, even if you're there when I make them. And you're certainly not responsible for acts of God."

He takes my hands in his, and the feel of them is a weight anchoring me. "*Acts of God* are natural disasters like trees falling, not men."

"I'm bigger than some trees." As if to illustrate this, he shows how his hands engulf mine. They're so big and strong, yet so gentle. I'm really starting to enjoy holding hands with this man. And by starting, I mean there hasn't been a second since we met that I haven't loved his touch, even if I've tried to tell myself otherwise.

I slide my fingers in between his. The movement is so intimate that my face heats, but I don't stop or retreat. I don't want to. "It's hard for me not to carry the weight of everyone else's decisions."

"Then practice. Say, 'Tripp, you handsome devil, I am not the boss of you.'"

"No. I *am* the boss of you."

His eyebrows raise, and suddenly he lets go of my hands and puts his on my hips. He pulls me closer so I'm standing between his knees. "I'm pretty sure I'm the boss of *you.*"

My face is so close to his. I could trace the curve of his lips with my finger if I wanted to.

I want to.

"You're my client, not my boss." He's still pulling me closer, and I'm still absolutely, positively letting him. Our faces are breathing distance apart now. When he gives me another tug, I squeal and let him pull me onto his knee.

"The customer is king." His words are so low, they reverberate in my chest. Our mouths are equal now, and our heads are both tipping in the universal signal for "KISS ME NOW."

"Hail to the king," I whisper, closing my eyes. The distance between our mouths is measured both in fractions and universes. We are millimeters apart, yet the space between those millimeters constitutes infinities. Each tiny movement to get closer feels like an eternity, and the anticipation builds in my chest until my cells are buzzing with need.

And when we kiss, worlds collide.

Our lips are hot and hungry, and our hands are equally so, grabbing, feeling, caressing. He puts his hand in my hair, making my skin erupt in tingles. I slide my hands around his back and dig my fingers into the muscles surrounding his spine. How have I ignored this part of his body for so long? The muscles in his back deserve to be sculpted. The full artist community needs to see this man's back and sculpt and paint and write sonnets to it. Heck, even a paint by number would be fine. How is it possible that his spine is tucked in a valley of muscles like this?

"I love how big you are," I tell him, my teeth around his bottom lip, my hands digging into muscles I didn't even know existed. "I love it." He moans, and the sound makes every cell in my body shiver.

When I was a kid, I missed more breakfasts than I got. Occasionally when the hunger carved too deep a pit in my stomach, I'd drag Meghan to school early enough that we could get the free breakfast. Sinking my teeth into that first bite of a muffin or hard-boiled egg was almost painful for how good it felt.

Kissing Tripp is like that.

How is his mouth real? It's agony thinking of how I've lived so long without this, without him, without his lips on mine. I've been so hungry for so long, I didn't realize how badly I was starving, how desperately I needed sustenance.

And something tells me Tripp could sustain me for a long time.

I shift on his knee, but he seems to misinterpret as me trying to leave—as if!—and he drops his hands to my hips. His grip is firm, but not controlling. Steadying. Entreating. The press of his thumbs in my waist sends a thrill through me. "Don't go." It's barely a whisper, but the words carry all the way to my heart, and the urgency leaves me, replaced with something solemn. Binding.

"I won't," I promise.

"It's okay, y'all," a voice calls out. We fly apart, but before I can fall from Tripp's lap, he grabs me back to him. I put an arm around his shoulders. You know, for balance, not caressing, or anything. "Tripp and his not-girlfriend are not-kissing!"

"Good grief, Ogden," Tripp complains into my neck. A wave of heat rushes over my face—a mix of embarrassment and desire—but I don't let go. "Are you ever not here?"

"I'm like a bad penny." Duke gives us his signature wolfish grin, and I want to wipe the smugness from his face.

"You know pennies don't exist in Canada. Those Canucks are doing something right," Tripp says. His breath puffs against my neck when he speaks, and it's a struggle to keep my eyes open and my hands out of his hair.

Duke just laughs and looks at me. "Apologies for the interruption, but I thought Jane would appreciate the *surprise.*"

My surprise!

I pull myself reluctantly from Tripp's lap, grab his hand, and help him up. Well, not help, but exert a considerable amount of force that barely budges him. He does the rest. "Come with me."

"With *us,*" Duke corrects, standing to Tripp's side to help him walk.

Tripp elbows his friend in the gut. "If you try to help me down the stairs, I will murder you in your sleep."

"Worth it."

In the end, the two tree-sized men can't fit side-by-side down the stairs. Tripp is steady enough on his feet, but Duke walks in front of him, just in case, and I find myself grateful for the man, if not for his abysmal timing.

At the bottom of the stairs, I take Tripp's hand. "What are you two up to?" he asks with narrowed eyes.

"Co-conspiring." I lead him through the house, outdoors, and over to the side of the house.

Where his friends and plenty of the staff are waiting, some with their families. A handful of kids run in between lawn chairs, picnic blankets, and the popcorn and cotton candy stands I borrowed from the factory.

"What is this?" Tripp asks. Is it my imagination, or is he swaying? I slip beneath his arm to hold him steady, fully aware that if he falls, I'll fall with him.

There's a metaphor in there somewhere.

"Uh, well, I invited them. Anita and I did," I say. I thought it would be a way to bond him further to the farm, although now I wish I'd chosen any other time. The memory of his mouth and hands and back muscles have scattered my thoughts on the wind. "We thought a monthly movie night could be a fun way to strengthen a sense of community with the farm employees and their families. Anita spread the word, but I think if we can make this monthly, it'll get a bigger crowd than two hours notice can do."

Still, there are maybe forty people here. More than either Anita or I expected. She and Booker sit with Lottie and a woman who must be Duke's sister, considering her height and blondeness. Lottie keeps climbing in Booker's wheelchair with him, and Duke's sister looks visibly stressed. Booker, on the other hand, seems happy as a clam.

"I'm going to go save my sister from a coronary," Duke says, patting Tripp's back. "We have camping chairs for y'all."

We follow Duke, and Tripp grabs my hand and grumbles. "Couldn't you have scheduled this for another night?"

I lean into him and clutch his rock-hard forearm with my free hand. "Believe me, I've never been angrier about one of my brilliant ideas."

He flashes me a smile that makes my toes curl. "Later?"

"It's a date."

We're about to settle in when people swarm Tripp, thanking him for the movie and asking after his health. Tripp reaches his arm around me, gluing me to his side as he speaks. He's only recently made effort to get to know his employees, and what little effort he's made has been at arm's length. He looks bewildered by the attention, gives me all the credit, and tells them that his concussion will be fine.

Soon, the family-friendly movie is in full swing, and the crowd around Tripp has been moved to the side of the projector, as too many kids were complaining. Lottie broke into tears when she heard that Tripp got hurt, and now she's in Tripp's arms with Duke standing next to them, rubbing her back. They look like the insanely hot stars of a buddy comedy movie about brothers having to raise their sister's kid, or something.

It's possible I think in terms of movie plots too much.

At any rate, I sneaked away when Tripp grabbed Lottie so that I could mingle and observe unnoticed. Tripp is now fully engaged with whomever he's speaking to, and his personality has come alive. It's perplexing that he's held himself back when he so clearly enjoys being around and getting to know these people. *His* people.

Which makes me miss *my* people.

I take a video and send it to my friends with a *wish you were here* text.

Their responses come in quickly.

LOU: You are making me homesick, girl. More pics!

MILLIE: Are you on the set of *Sweet Home Alabama*? How is that real?

. . .

ASH: Why are you taking videos of THINGS when you could take clandestine videos of TRIPP'S ARMS? Also his butt. I think I could bounce quarters off his glutes. Glutes? Did I use that word right?

PARKER: Looks like a great event.

My jaw falls open.

Excuse me? That's it? Parker Jane Emerson, the girl who spits sass, the girl who lives and breathes events, the girl with opinions on everything is saying *that*? I storm around to the other side of the yard, where the cell service is better. Calls drop on the farm all the time, and no way am I letting her off the hook that easily.

She picks up on the third ring. "Hi."

"*Looks like a great event?'* Seriously, Parker? Seriously?"

"What? It does!" Her defensiveness further incenses me.

"You are my best friend, and I get that you're mad that I took the account without talking to you, and I know that was a jerk move, okay? I get it, and I'm sorry. But you have no idea how much pressure I've been under."

"*I* have no idea the pressure? Me? I'm the CFO! Finance is literally my middle name! Title. Whatever! You don't think I know how bad our finances were before Sugar Maple Farms? You don't think I've been scrambling to cut costs for the last year? I knew exactly what was going on, and that was before you *insisted* that you take over employee compensation." Guilt makes my neck feel itchy and splotchy. I'd hoped she wouldn't question that, but only my own hubris could have hoped something so stupid. "All this time, you thought I was mad about this account, and yes, I was mad in the moment. But you didn't even notice that it started before then. I've been angry since the minute the rest of us got 'raises.' You know, when we were all somehow getting bigger cuts of each account, despite not increasing our rates?"

My ears start to feel hot. "Parker, I—"

"You slashed your salary to give us raises, and you didn't even *ask* me, Jane. You're the CEO, not the dictator. Jane & Co. was *our* idea. Yours and mine. You should have told me what was going on instead of treating me like a little kid who needed protecting. You have no idea how much that hurt me."

If the guilt weren't already bad enough, now it's suffocating. "But after everything with your last job, it was my fault—"

"*No.*" Her words slice the air, cutting me off. "It's *because* of what happened with them that you should have kept me looped in. I made my choice to leave money on the table because I wanted to start something that mattered, something where I would have a voice and be seen as an equal partner. And you took that from me."

A chorus of cicadas swells around me. I open my mouth to protest, but no words come out.

She's right.

She's absolutely right.

I was so busy trying to take care of everyone in a way that meant something for *me* that I didn't consider how to care in a way that meant something to *them*. Parker's size has meant that she's been overlooked and underestimated her whole life. That may sound silly, but I saw it firsthand in grad school. We both got our fair share of comments over our looks. But not everyone assumed that either of us curried special favor by being attractive. Many knew our merits. Whether they knew it or not, though, some of our peers and instructors took me more seriously because of my height, both males and females.

They took Parker less seriously for the same reason.

I watched her get demeaned and condescended to. When she graduated top in our class at Northwestern, it was no surprise to anyone who'd ever listened to her, but it was a surprise to everyone who hadn't. It sounds stupid, doesn't it? It doesn't make it untrue. She got her dream job coming out of our MBA, and it ended up being more of the same, with an entire VP team not taking her as seriously as she deserved.

And I've done the same thing to her by ignoring her actual needs in favor of my perception of her needs. My *projection* of her needs.

For a long moment, shame eats away at my stomach, and I can't speak.

"Are you still there?" she asks.

"I'm here," I whisper. "I screwed up, Parker. I'm sorry. I silenced you by boxing you out, and I didn't treat you with the respect you deserved. It was condescending and stupid of me, and I should have known better. I'm really sorry."

"Thanks for getting it," she says simply. "Now, will you talk to me? Like I'm your best friend and not someone you need to coddle?"

So I do. I tell her what I told Tripp last night, and with every word, I feel my burden easing, getting lighter. I feel the weight of responsibility balancing into something more manageable just by having it known. Our financial woes are hardly what they used to be, but marketing is a fickle business, and this account and the ones coming in won't last us forever. If we're going to survive, I need to be open with my friends, and I need to let them help.

And yes, obviously I'm crying.

"So let me get this straight," Ash says into the phone, and my mouth falls open in horror. "You thought we were all looking a bit ratty so you gave us a raise from your paycheck?"

"No! PJ, did you put me on speaker?" I demand.

I hear a scuffle and then Parker's voice. "No, I did not. A

certain nosy friend of ours heard me lecturing you, which means that two other nosy friends came into my room before I could lock the door."

"So they know everything?" I wish I could fall into a pit and be buried by cold earth with how stupid I feel.

"I didn't put you on speaker," she says, and I understand the subtext: they only know what Parker said, her comments back to me. They didn't hear me unload about my life and childhood. They don't know that my fears for their wellbeing are so deeply rooted that I couldn't sleep for months. They don't know about Meghan or my credit card debt. That will stay between Parker and me.

Maybe I'll be able to tell them all of it someday, but for now it's enough that I've told my two best friends—

I stop.

Two best friends? Do I really see Tripp as my best friend? As someone so important, so essential to me that he's reached the top tier?

Yes.

I am falling for Tripp.

Hard, fast, and headfirst.

CHAPTER NINETEEN

TRIPP

"Jane?"

The movie is over and the majority of the crowd his dispersed. Most people cleaned up their own spaces, so the remaining work is minimal. I would get up to help Rusty and Anita, but my arm is around a sleeping Jane, and I can't move without waking her up.

I never want to move.

But we have to move.

"Jane?" I repeat.

She's like Lottie. She fell asleep to sound, so sound isn't waking her up now. I trace a letter on her cheek, reveling in the feel of her skin. Jane's skin is softer than a pillow. I trail my fingers across her jaw line and down her neck to her collarbone. A wave of heat roars in my gut like a furnace.

How can anyone be so beautiful?

How am I sitting here with the most spectacular woman I've ever known and the rest of the world is just moving like nothing has changed? How are planets still on course in the sky? How is the earth still rotating on its axis when someone like Jane is in the world, in *my* world?

She fell asleep halfway through the movie, nestled under my arm with a bag of cotton candy in her lap. I still can't believe she did, after insisting that she's never once fallen asleep during a movie. From last night's conversation, I suspect Jane was always too worried about taking care of her little sister to fall asleep. She was constantly on guard duty but with no one to relieve her. The fact that she's fallen asleep now, does that mean *I'm* her relief? I want it to mean that. I've never been so crazy about a woman in my life. Not even close.

My friends would say that I've fallen quickly for women before, but I've always fallen out even quicker. Or maybe they have. I'm not the easiest guy to put up with. But Jane learned to put up with me before she even liked me. That has to be a good sign, right? These last couple of days have felt like a fast forward in our relationship. We finally got onto a good road together, and then—BAM!—we're on that same road, fifty miles ahead.

I want to be on this same road with her a thousand miles ahead.

Patience, Tripp.

Something about Jane makes patience a chore. From the moment I met her, I wanted all gas, no brakes. Her becoming my short-term enemy is the best thing that could have happened to me. We got to know the worst parts of each other and managed to build a relationship in spite of those unattractive traits.

Not that Jane's were unattractive. She makes being a white knight look good. She makes drooling in her sleep look good, too.

"Jane," I say louder. I tickle her face again with no response, so I squeeze her thigh.

She jumps like a cat in water.

Her forehead cracks into my nose, her elbow jabs my gut, her limbs splay all over.

"Ooh!" I grab my nose.

"I'm so sorry! Did I hurt you?"

She sits stark upright and inspects my nose as crickets and katydids serenade us and the stars in the heavens twinkle in laughter at us. I insist that I'm fine, but that doesn't stop her from doting on me. Once she's assured that all is well, she leans back and drops her head on my shoulder. We're more than straining the weight limit of the inflatable camping couch, but it holds.

"I fell asleep?"

"Yes." Her head shakes. I peek down to see her touching her lips and chin. "Did I *drool?*"

"Yes. Do you normally do that?"

She groans and hides her face against my chest. "I certainly hope not," she mumbles. "I can't believe I fell asleep. I *never* fall asleep in movies. I mean *never.*"

"I was hoping I would have that effect on you," I say.

"What effect?" She tilts her head back to peer up at me.

I could make a joke, but I want my words to mean something. "Letting you know you're safe to be human."

Her eyes are pools of vulnerability in the moonlight. She puts her hands on either side of my face. Her fingernails lightly scratch at the stubble, a move that would make my legs weak if we were standing. I wrap an arm around her waist while my other hand draws on her back. The inflatable couch creaks, but we pay it no mind.

We're too busy staring in each other's eyes.

"You do have that effect on me," she whispers, her dark blue eyes drawing me in. Her breath smells like cotton candy, and I want to taste it to see if it's blue or pink.

"Mmm." I don't even know what I'm trying to say. Am I agreeing with her? Am I asking her to tell me more? Am I grunting like a caveman because that's what I feel like?

Jane pretty. Me kiss Jane.

Her lips part, and they're the only things that exist in the world. There is Jane's mouth and my burning need to kiss it again, and that's it. Everything else has ceased to be.

ME KISS JANE.

Her lids slowly shut, and mine go with them as our faces get closer. Our noses brush, sending a shock straight through me. Her lips sweep lightly over mine, and the sensation travels all over my body, electrifying me. I put my hand in her hair and quickly deepen the kiss, and she complies willingly.

Our first kiss was all heat and hands. I was too greedy for her mouth. This time, I'm intent on taking it slower, showing her my range.

As we kiss, I feel like we're on a boat, floating out to sea. I know there are people around us still, even if they're too polite to pay us any mind, but it's all going quiet. Even the creaky protests of the camping couch fade away until it feels like the floor is falling out beneath us.

Wait—

A loud POP sounds, and then ...

CRASH.

My butt hits the ground hard, and Jane and I tip backwards. I manage to hold us up with my core, but Jane collapses into a fit of giggles and I lean the rest of the way back on the destroyed inflatable.

"I bruise my tailbone and all you can do is laugh? Real classy," I say.

"No way did that hurt. You have muscles on top of muscles protecting that thing." Jane twists so that her upper body is on top of my chest, while her legs rest on the grass. She stretches up to kiss my temple. "But I'm sorry if your head got bumped."

"And butt."

"I'm not kissing your butt."

I shake with laughter, and Jane's nose presses against my cheek. "You could at least check it for injury."

She's still giggling when she kisses me. Her fingers rake through my hair, and I react audibly.

"Did you just make a yummy sound?" The apple of her cheeks push against mine in a smile that makes it impossible not to mirror.

"Mm-hm." Caveman Tripp is too happy to think. I roll onto my side so we're facing each other, and I draw letters all over her back. "Kissing good."

Jane laughs again. I wonder if or when she'll notice that my doodling on her back is intentional. I'm staking my claim. Marking my territory with every motion. Signing my name.

T.

R.

I.

P.

P.

I'm in this with her. And now I need to find a way to keep her in it with me, too.

* * *

Refinishing the bathroom in Strawberry Fields takes us a couple of days, so Jane stays in the B&B with Anita and Booker so she has access to a real bathroom. The entire floor has to be replaced, as do the old pipes. We hire a plumber rather than risk it on our own, but we tile the floor and the bathroom. Working projects together at night after overhauling the farm during the day gives us constant together time.

I cherish every minute. Is that an old-man thing to say? Don't care. I cherish it. Take that, hipsters.

"Tripp Carville, if you don't get off your phone and finish laying that tile, so help me, I will shave your head in your sleep."

"Ooh, kinky," I say, putting down my phone. Uncle Lawson is impressed by the progress on the farm. More than impressed. Jane managed to get a meeting with South Carolina royalty, Evan Beauchamps, and his influencer fiancée, and they're considering having their wedding at the farm this fall. This gives us a hard deadline. Several hard deadlines.

The famous sugar maple sits right by our equally famous white barn. The leaves turn yellow and orange throughout October and reach a vibrant, brilliant red by Halloween, staying that way until Thanksgiving. So we have our work cut out for us to have a tourist-drawing pumpkin patch *and* a celebrity wedding before Thanksgiving.

Building, landscaping, animal therapy, events...

Without Jane, I would think it impossible. With Jane, I think it could be done by September. An idea strikes me.

"Hey, we should do something for Labor Day," I tell her as we scrape.

"Good idea. The industrial kitchen should be up by then, so we'll—"

"I meant you and me. Maybe we could ... go somewhere."

The tentative note in her voice draws me closer. "You and me?"

"Yeah. Maybe we could go visit your friends in Chicago."

She seems to glow from within. "Really? You don't think you'll be sick of me by then?"

"Good question." I push her away just to pull her back. "No."

The floor is officially scraped, and Jane gives me a sweaty, salty kiss that shouldn't be as tantalizing as it is.

After a bit of making out, Jane puts on a Clint Eastwood movie and we cuddle up on the loveseat, her back to my chest. When Clint first comes onscreen wearing his flat brim cowboy hat, squinting that angry squint, Jane sighs.

"Why does he always look like the sun is giving him a headache?" I say to rile her up. "He looks stupid."

Jane spins around on the couch, her mouth open in an amused O.

"*You* think his steely gaze looks stupid?" Why does she sound so sassy, and why do I like it so much? "*You*, Tag Carville III, think that Clint Eastwood's grumpy, steely gaze is over the top?"

"Yes! Look at him!"

She tips her head back and laughs, exposing her long, lean neck. "You know you look like him, right?"

"What? I do not." Do I?

"Have you never looked in the mirror? My literal first impression of you was that you have Clint Eastwood's face on Jack Reacher's body."

I grin wider than the Cheshire cat. I don't know pop culture that well, but Clint Eastwood is the man, and I've read every Jack Reacher book. There couldn't be a cooler combination, and she knows it. "You are so obsessed with me. I'm your dream man."

She pushes me. "Shut it."

"No, you are! It's okay, admit it. I'm gorgeous and you looo —" *Too much! Reel it in, Carville!* "—oove my pretty face and body." I bat my eyelashes.

She plants a big, soft kiss on my mouth, and I lean back against the couch, enjoying the feel of her against me. "You are tolerable, I suppose." She kisses me again, and I nibble on her lip, keeping her close. I can't get enough of the taste of Jane. Even after she's eaten, there's always something distinctly her. I don't know if it's lip gloss or toothpaste or what, but if Jane's mouth were an ice cream flavor, it would sell out immediately.

Jane's phone rings, and because we're fully into making out now, she silences it and throws it on the coffee table. A moment later, it rings again. She digs her fingers into the muscles on my back and lets it go to voicemail. Only when it rings a third time does she groan and check it.

Meghan Harrington.

Her sister? The same sister who is asking her for more money? The same sister she's been avoiding for the last couple of weeks since Jane told her she wouldn't keep bailing her out?

Obviously it's the same sister. She only has the one. But my surprise at her persistence dumbfounds me.

"Is that your sister?" *Duh, Tripp. You've already established this.*

The color drains from Jane's face. "I can't believe she's calling me again." She seems to physically shrink in on herself. Her shoulders hunch down and her spine curves. The sight lights a fire in me.

"That's it. I'm giving her a piece of my mind."

I reach for the phone, ready to cuss her out, when Jane grabs it out of my hand. She looks madder than a hornet. "I can stand up for myself, thank you very much."

"Good! Then do it." I sit back and put an ankle on the opposite knee, pretending to be cool. I wouldn't mind giving her sister what for, but Jane's right to be annoyed. I don't get to insert myself into their situation. Hopefully she can take some of her annoyance with me and dump it all over her sister, though. "Go on."

She stabs at her screen and glares at me. "Hello?"

I don't hear what her sister says, but I catch a placating, even desperate tone. Jane's face quickly morphs from angry to wary to concerned. I lift my eyebrows at her, and she moves her face's threat level back to wary.

"Meghan, I know that you're upset, but it's not fair—"

"You want to talk about fair?" Her sister's shrill voice reaches me across the couch. "You left me! I didn't see you for three years. You *abandoned* me with *her!*"

Jane starts to cry, and it is everything I can do not to rip the phone from her hand and give this girl a talking to, Anita style. Instead, I sit up and trace my name on Jane's back, letting her borrow my strength if she doesn't have it in her right now. Sitting so close, I can hear both sides of the conversation now, although Jane's side is mostly interjections of how she left for college, how she couldn't defer her scholarship, how if she'd stayed at the house, she wouldn't have been able to say no to their mom, who wanted Jane to drop out and go into modeling.

Her sister is a master manipulator. She uses the right blend of cajoling, hurt, anger, and understanding to chip away at Jane. "Isn't it strange that you got the same scholarship that the old man at the golf course was always talking to you about? What did you have to give him in exchange for it?" Jane's face turns a dark shade of red as she protests, but her sister continues, "I don't blame you, sis. Us Harrington girls have always had to survive. You were surviving!"

"I *never.*" Jane spits the word out. "He worked in administration and helped me with my essay. He wasn't even on the scholarship committee—"

"Of course. Of course," she soothes, succeeding in taking away Jane's confidence entirely. I cover Jane's hand with mine, and she whips her head around, looking like a wounded rabbit caught in a fence.

I pull the phone down from her face. She strains against me, but she stops fighting the farther the phone gets, as if her sister's hold is lessening. "You don't owe her an explanation, Jane. You were a kid, too. You were allowed to protect yourself from your mom. You did the best you could for yourself and Meghan, but it was never your job to protect her, only to love her."

Jane drops the phone and buries her face in my shoulder. "If you want, I'll hang up and block your sister now."

She pushes back. "No, I can do this." She takes a deep, steadying breath. "Keep writing your name on my back, okay?"

She knows? My cheeks feel as warm as my heart. But I comply.

"Meghan, it's time for you to stop talking and listen. I have worked my butt off for everything I've ever gotten, yet you live in more luxury than I ever have. I looked after you the best I could after Grandpa died, but at some point, it changed from me helping you to you taking advantage of me. This has to stop." She takes another big breath and looks at me. "I will continue to pay your bills for one more month if and only if you make a budget, break your lease and find a cheaper place to live, sell your car, and use public transportation like *I* do. You have two weeks to make your plan—" I lift my brows. "Scratch that. You have one week to make your plan and two weeks to execute it. I love you too much to let you become Mom."

She hangs up. Then she jumps off the couch and into the air as if the Bears just won the Super Bowl. "Yes! That felt amazing!"

I stand and she jumps into my arms. "*You* are amazing! And she sucks."

"You know, she kind of does. But I hope this'll help her stop sucking." I lower her back down and put my hands on her waist. The feel of her intoxicates me. She lays her head on my chest. "I feel like a superhero. Like I'm invincible! I still can't believe it. I've wanted to say something for years, but I never felt strong enough." She looks up at me, and her eyes glisten like a starlight sky. "Not until you."

"Me?" I ask, not because I want her to butter my biscuit but because it's hard to believe that I did anything but threaten to chew out and block her loser sister.

"Yes, you big knucklehead! I know you wanted me to feel safe being human around you, but it turns out you also bring out my inner superhuman." Her head tilts as she looks at me. "Knowing you cared enough to be upset and to want to help meant a lot to me. Maybe it sounds stupid, but I couldn't have done it without you."

"It doesn't sound stupid." I pull her close. "I'm proud of you. And you should be proud of yourself."

"Thanks," she whispers.

We sit back down to watch the rest of the movie, but my head is somewhere else.

Jane keeps letting me in, letting me be her moral support, and I still haven't made a single meaningful confession when I wasn't concussed.

Why?

Being on the farm isn't as hard as it used to be. Bad memories are being replaced with good ones every day. Yet the memory of my final conversation with Tag haunts me. He seemed proud, but then he talked about picking strawberries and shut down my offer to come see him. Did he hang up right after to hire Jane or did he hire her first and call me to get in my head? He wasn't really proud, was he? And that enigmatic note in the will—*Sugar Maple Farms is yours, free and clear. I trust you'll know what to do*—mocks me. Life with him wasn't always bad, but the older I got, the more it felt like a constant quest to prove I was worthy of being a Carville. In death, he ensured that I would be tied to the only family business that didn't have his name on it.

I want nothing of this final test of his, but thanks to his will, I can't give it up, either.

If I can sell Sugar Maple Farms back to Carville Industries, will the lifelong struggle end? Will that erase my self-doubt? My hunger to prove myself?

I should tell Jane about Tag and the will and why I need to sell the farm when we're done. Businesses rebrand all the time in order to sell to a larger company. She's a businesswoman. She'll understand. She may even have ideas on how to make the farm more desirable to potential buyers.

Or she may decide she's not interested in investing so much personal attention to a farm that's going to be sold off to another company.

No, that's not fair. Jane's my partner in all of this. My ally. I should let her in.

But I'm afraid.

If I don't let her in, what if I can never give her enough to want to be with me?

If I let her in completely, what if she doesn't like what she sees?

What if she rejects me like Tag did? What if I'm not enough for yet another person I love? What if I come home to find that —like Tag—she's just *gone*?

My head and my heart fight a vicious war for the rest of the night while the woman of my dreams rests under the crook of my arm.

At the end of the movie, Jane walks me to her door, stands on her tiptoes, and pulls me in for a goodnight kiss.

Tomorrow, I tell myself. *Tomorrow.*

CHAPTER TWENTY

JANE

"*Y*ou're jostling too much, Jane. Walk more steadily," Parker says through the phone.

"You try avoiding potholes on country roads without jostling," I grumble.

Because Parker's the only one of us who hasn't spent time in the South, she wants me to take her on the same "tour" I took Millie and Ash on.

By phone.

"Okay, pause. Look at that charming storefront! What does the general commercial district say about colors? This town needs to stick with a theme if they want to be a viable tourist destination."

I agree. Like I agree the next time she gives me feedback for the town, as if the mayor is taking notes. The signs are outdated and in varying states of disrepair. Landscaping is pretty but not kept well enough. The school needs a facelift. The potholes need filling. The shops are quaint and appealing, she says, and the Riverwalk we're overlooking is picture perfect.

From my bench, I sigh.

"You seem happy," Parker says. She's used a lighter palette today, and it makes her look younger. Not that she isn't young, but the makeup she typically wears makes her more of a fortress than an age. An indeterminate wall of strength and genius.

"I like it here. The people are kind, and they go out of their way to help each other."

"So just like Chicago, then?"

"Ha! Oh yeah. Just like it." Jadyn and Dominic from the factory walk by and thank me for the movie night last week. I brush off the compliment, telling them it was all Anita, and they thank me, anyway. As Parker and I talk, another half dozen people I know pass by, and I wave and introduce them all.

"Wow, so you didn't tell me that you're basically a celebrity now."

"No, the people are really that friendly."

"Mm-hm. Right."

We talk work for a bit, and Parker mentions some consumer behavior insights Millie recently gathered for one of our new accounts.

"What happened when Millie came down, by the way?" Parker asks. "I keep catching her looking at pictures on her phone or even looking the town up on her laptop while she's working. It's like she left Sugar Maple but Sugar Maple hasn't left her."

I mention how she connected with Lottie, and I leave it at that. We both know enough of Millie's history to connect the dots.

"Well, between you and me, I wouldn't be surprised if she contacts your boy Tripp about taking over the animal therapy practice you guys are working on. She's seemed distant."

The pang in my heart is both for Millie and me. The idea of

going back to Chicago now seems less appealing than it did a few months ago, even as the full heat and humidity of summer bears down on me. I love my hometown, but it lacks warmth. If you say hi to someone on the street, they assume you're a mugger or a Canadian tourist. I don't know if anyone has ever been mugged here. Tripp doesn't even lock his truck when he parks it on the street.

Small town life isn't for everyone, and big city life isn't any better or worse. There's a give and take to every place you live. But the city you live in is like a relationship. I've been giving to Chicago for a long time, and I'm getting tired of our one-sided relationship.

"I sent you the information on our lease, too. We need to decide if we want to renew the contract in October or look elsewhere."

Normally, this is the time where I would make a decisive answer. "What do you think we should do?"

Parker's immaculate eyebrows barely quiver. "Find somewhere cheaper. We're developing a reputation for being savvy. And savvy people don't renew a lease in the Loop just to look cool."

"It doesn't even have to be in Chicago," I say.

"Going out to the 'burbs will hardly save us money."

"You're right." I wasn't thinking of moving out to Oak Park or Naperville, though. I was thinking about relocating a thousand or so miles south. "How would you feel about researching office space?"

If this unexpected sharing of responsibility fazes her, she doesn't show it. "You got it, boss."

"You mean partner."

She feigns a gasp. "What would Tripp say?" I stick out my tongue at her. "Have you guys talked about what happens when the contract is up? When the rebrand is officially done and it's time for you to go back home?"

Home.

The word has never felt so foreign. What makes something home? Geography? The city you were raised in or live in? The people you're with? My friends have been my family for so long, but as badly as I miss them, I would leave a piece of myself here going back to Chicago. I've come to love the farm and town. I've found myself here, especially these last couple of months since dating Tripp. "Jaaaane. What is that face?"

I blink and come back to myself. "Um … "

"Are you thinking of uprooting your life for him? Giving up your career? Have you guys even talked long term?"

Parker's trying her best to keep the judgment out of her voice, but she can't keep it out of her eyebrows. They're so dark and striking that I catch the tiniest twitch. "I'm absolutely not giving up my career, and no, we haven't talked long term."

"But you're still thinking of uprooting your life?"

I don't answer right away. I take my eyes off hers and look at the river. The water babbles and whispers a quiet serenade. "I don't know. I'll really miss this place. Maybe I'll get a winter home here."

"Maybe we need a Jane & Co. retreat."

My laugh cuts before it can even start, because a big, flashing light bulb goes off in my head. "Parker Jane, that is brilliant! Can you imagine how much the CEOs and HR officers of the world would love a corporate retreat on a farm? On a working orchard?"

Excitement writes itself on Parker's face. She majored in hospitality management for undergrad, and although she's more than adept at finance as our CFO, we all do double and triple duty. Parker's events alone are worth our fee. We start brainstorming, and as I kick out an idea, Parker drills it down. My friends and I work well together because we feed off of each other like this. I'm the visionary, the big picture thinker. Parker is the executor. She looks at that 30,000-foot view and sees exactly where the homes and streets, the trees and stoplights go. She translates vision into action. The same balance exists with each of my friends. There would be no Jane & Co. without *all* of the Janes.

"This is reason 412 why I wish you guys were here," I say, a hollow longing in my chest. "There's nothing like the energy we get from working together."

"I know." She says this with a sigh that tells me she misses me, too. "It'll be good to have you back home when the job is done."

I think about her words for a long time after we hang up.

* * *

"Keep your hands to yourself, Janie Jane," Tripp says to me when I try to kiss him for the sixth time tonight. "Jack is about to do some serious damage to the group of people stupid enough to pile up on him."

"I've created a monster." I huff and lean back onto the couch, slinging my legs over his.

Tripp is now as obsessed with action movies and series as I am, and he insists on watching something every night after we finish whatever project we're working on in the cottage.

Honestly, I'm making them up at this point. Changing out fixtures. Replacing baseboards that were already fine. I should feel guilty about the cost, but Anita doesn't mind. Besides, our fortune is changing. With the response to the Sugar Maple Farm's label and the direct business-to-business campaign we've already implemented, demand for the products are at an all-time high. Tripp is talking about expanding the factory to keep up with new orders, which means hiring more people, which further means expansion for the town.

It also means that Jane & Co. is officially turning away business. We have more accounts than we can cover as is, and thankfully, Rusty has agreed to help out on the sly. If his parents find out, I think they'd throw a conniption over Rusty splitting his focus, harming the family business, whatever. They seem intent on growing the fruit stands as much as possible now that things are really booming. I would feel guilty taking Rusty's time if he hadn't looked like I'd saved him from a burning building when I asked for his help.

I've also cut off my sister, officially. She refused to even make a budget, so I told her that I love her and will always be there for her in every way but financially. She cried and accused me of abandoning her, blamed me for everything, and it was only Tripp's presence that gave me the strength to hang up and block her number. I'll unblock her in a few months. Maybe. I need to get comfortable having walls before I consider opening doors to visitors.

Lastly, with this account and all the new business we're taking in, my personal finances are shifting. With a steady paycheck, I've managed to pay off my credit card debt and can finally start on my student loans. Millie is back to vintage shopping and making payments on her medical debt. Parker's savings are being replenished. Ash has electric blue streaks in the front of her hair again.

Lou, well, she probably donated her cut to her favorite charity.

The freedom makes me feel almost dizzy. Playful, too. And handsy.

I go in for another kiss, and Tripp puts a finger in front of my mouth and pushes me back. "Down, girl." I pinch his knee, and he squeals like a baby pig.

"No. Bad Jane. Bad."

"I'm not a dog!" I feign outrage.

Tripp's voice drops, and his accent kicks up a notch. A sexy one. "I'll give you twenty minutes of make out time, and then I *will* finish this show. It's the last episode, and you made me watch it in the first place, need I remind you."

"Details, details."

Many super smoochy, swoony, delightful minutes later, Tripp has forgotten all about the TV. We are a tangle of lips and limbs. "A guy could get used to this."

My conversation with Parker rings in my ears. I force myself to keep my voice light. "How would that work, exactly?"

He kisses the tip of my nose. "Maybe we could use that weird chamber that Han Solo gets trapped in. We could have them freeze us in mid-kiss." I sniff a laugh. "Or … " His voice changes, but his face remains neutral. "Maybe we could … keep this going. After the job ends, I mean."

My insides throw a party with streamers and noisemakers and confetti cannons. "You'd want to try things out long distance?"

"Definitely. Or shorter distance, too. I'm not married to Sugar Maple, South Carolina, you know."

I sit back. This isn't what I expected. I don't know why it bugs me that he would even consider leaving the home his family worked so hard to provide for him. This isn't what his grandfather wanted. I was supposed to help his grandson fall back in love with his home not be the reason he would want to leave it. "You would leave all this behind?"

My shock clearly wasn't conveyed because he looks relieved that I would ask him. His brow is clear and his face wide open. "In a heartbeat. I don't care about Sugar Maple, Jane. Not the town, not the farm."

Why does it feel like he threw a glass of ice water on me? Why does the back of my throat ache at his words? All I've ever wanted was a place where I felt safe and cared for. He has that and couldn't care less. "Why?"

If my last question opened him up, this one stops the door abruptly. "I don't have the best memories of this place. Tag wasn't like your grandpa. He didn't make me feel safe and special, he made me feel like I would never be good enough. You can't understand."

"Then help me understand," I say. I hope it's an invitation that he wants to accept. Because I want him so badly, I want *us* so badly, I'm having trouble sleeping again. When I'm not with him, it's nearly impossible to rest my mind.

I hope Tripp will give. I hold my breath, hoping he'll bend and expose the broken parts of him that he tries so hard to keep hidden.

He doesn't. "Tag was cold and demanding. There's not much more to say." His face softens then, and he puts a hand in my hair. "But that doesn't change anything. I'm all in with you, Jane. I want this to work."

"I do, too."

But if he can't even open up to me, how will that happen? How can I be true to Tag's memory and to Tripp's heart?

How can I be true to mine?

CHAPTER TWENTY-ONE

TRIPP

"So what did you tell her?" Duke asks. We're in the box —his home gym—doing Preacher curls with a stupid amount of weight, but we always push the limits when we work out together. We're competitive like that. Meanwhile, Rusty is doing pull ups with a weight vest. We pretend not to be impressed, but Rusty can do more pull ups than anyone I've ever known. He's got a leaner build than we have, but the dude is still stacked. Duke would never let him in the box otherwise, best friend or not.

"I told her she wouldn't understand."

Duke snorts. Rusty actually drops from the bar with laughter and doubles over. "Classic Tripp."

"What? She wouldn't! Her grandpa was a saint!"

"You said her dad split when her sister was born," Duke says. "She hasn't seen him since. Her mom was probably criminally neglectful and Jane paid her family's bills through high school and college. The saintly grandpa she loved—the only grandparent she ever knew—died when she was barely a teenager. And now her sister has been manipulating her for money? I'm not saying it's a 'who's had it harder' contest between the two of you, but if it is, she ain't exactly losing." Duke hefts a barbell up and down, sweat dripping down his face as fast as my stomach feels like it's dropping.

"What did she say?" Rusty asks. He wipes sweat from his face, but I swear, there are tears from his laughter there, too. My boy is a generous laugher.

"Please tell me she tanned your hide," Duke begs.

"She wasn't upset at all. She asked me to help her understand."

Rusty and Duke share a look of surprise. "Marry her," Rusty says. He flips down into a handstand against the wall and starts doing push ups.

"Never get married," Duke says. He drops his barbells and starts doing box squats.

"You got married," I say, jumping on the box next to him.

"And we all know how that turned out. Lottie aside."

"Jane's not Carlie," Rusty argues.

"I didn't know *Carlie* was Carlie."

We both raise our brows to that. "Don't listen to him." Rusty tells me. "He got sloppy drunk in Vegas and married an emotional vampire against his better judgment. He managed to cast her out, but she got a nibble in before she left. It's not his fault he turned."

Duke looks like he wants to do violence to Rusty, but as quick as Duke is for an almost six-four, 225 pound quarterback, Rusty ran a 4.4 second forty-yard dash in college. Duke would lose the chase. Fast.

"I miss Miwwie," Lottie says, not looking up from the alphabet game on her tablet. She's dragging a letter "l" into its outline, and the creepy talking letter keeps saying, "L is for love, l is for love."

Duke closes his eyes in a "give me strength" look. "I know, pumpkin. But we're not talking about Millie, we're talking about Jane."

"I like Jane. Her's my friend. I don't want her to be a vampire. What's a vampire?"

"'*She's*' my friend," he gently corrects. "And a vampire is a pretend monster."

Lottie accepts this and returns to her game. I drop onto the weight bench as Duke spots me. "So what's the plan with the farm? Are you going to sell it to Lawson? Are you hoping to work for him or … ?"

I haven't told my friends that I'll be on the first plane out of here when I sell the farm. I grunt. "Maybe if I did, I'd finally prove to Tag that I'm a Carville."

"Not this again," Rusty says. I almost lose hold on the weights, but Duke steadies them, helping me rack them. I sit up.

"What?"

He holds up his hands in a peace gesture. "Nothing. Forget I spoke."

"No, if you have something to say, say it."

"It's nothin' you haven't heard before," he warns. I nod, so he continues. "You didn't see Tag accurately. Before you say it, I know I didn't see Tag when it was just the two of you at home. But I practically lived with y'all during the summer. I heard him give you his *Carville tests*. I never saw them the way you did. You viewed everything as Tag threatening or taunting you. But Tag was an old cowboy. A John Wayne, Clint Eastwood type. He was a man of few words, and he used them to motivate you the only way he knew how."

I drop back down to the bench, annoyed. Rusty's right about one thing: we *have* had this conversation before, and I wasn't feeling it any more last time than I am now. "Easy for you to say," I say, grunting between reps.

"Maybe." He hangs his legs over the bar near us and starts

doing crunches. "Those projects in his workshop saved me." He huffs. "So maybe I didn't see him accurately, either."

Rusty isn't kidding. He went through a bad bout of depression when he was in high school after his younger sister died. Tag had already let Rusty into his sacred space before then, but after, they were practically inseparable. I envied Rusty more than I can say, even now. My throat hurts thinking about it. Tag and Rusty fixing a fence. Tag and Rusty making a bird feeder. Tag and Rusty, Tag and Rusty, Tag and Rusty.

"You two were a team that I wasn't allowed to join," I say. The knot in the back of my throat grows, and my nose stings.

"You were always sloppy in there, Tripp. Even before you shot a nail through your foot. You would grab a tool and pretend you were an ax murderer, try to chuck nails like they were throwing stars. He was too afraid of you being in the workshop with us," Rusty says. "But you're the one who refused to help when we stepped out of it."

An uncomfortable memory surfaces of exactly what Rusty is describing. I was ten or eleven, maybe. Tag was building me a new set of dressers, and I went out to watch him. At first, I sat on a stool and watched with my safety goggles on, mesmerized by the process of him cutting wood. And then, when he was finished with the table saw and was moving on to the next stage, I went over to the saw, flipped it on before he could stop me, and sawed my safety glasses in half. And nearly my arm. I was reaching across it rather than keeping my hands on either side. Tag saw it and barked at me "Hands up!" just in time. The saw grazed my arm, but even now, thinking how bad it could have been makes my stomach turn. I flip my right arm over and spot the long, thick, shimmery scar I'd forgotten about.

I think about Little Tripp. About how desperate I was to be noticed, to be cared about. In my honest moments, I can admit that I was as reckless as Rusty says. I was a lost, abandoned, dumb kid who would have cut off my own hand if it meant that someone would have paid me attention.

But Tag was still the grown up. And my being stupid doesn't make up for him ignoring me.

"I was never asked."

"You were. Constantly. The second we stepped out of the workshop, he'd call you over from wherever you were in the fields or in the house. You wouldn't come."

"No. Never happened," I insist.

"It happened," Duke says. "Not always, but definitely in the early days. The corral when he got the pigs? The tire swing?"

I don't remember the corral, but the tire swing pricks at my memory. Tag knocking on my bedroom door and asking if I wanted to help him put up a tire swing. Me saying no. Coming out to the reservoir an hour later to see Rusty and Duke swinging, Tag nowhere in sight. The jealousy of knowing, once again, he'd chosen Rusty over me.

Or had he?

"I always wondered why you ignored him," Duke says.

"You don't understand—"

"No one does," Duke says, flaring his nostrils.

"It wasn't like that!" I bellow.

"Use your inside voice," Lottie says, holding a finger up to me.

My chest heaves and I rack the weights, not sure I can handle any more. How can my best friends gang up on me like this? Don't they understand how badly just talking about this hurts? Why can't they have my back instead of always defending Tag? They weren't there when I came home to an empty house, knowing that, yet again, I wasn't enough for someone to stay.

I was supposed to be enough for him to stay.

"Have either of you considered that you both saw him accurately and he simply had more than one side, like all of us? Maybe you're both reducing Tag to a hero or a villain and aren't willing to consider the fact that he was shades of both." Duke shoos me off the bench, and thèn because he's a showoff, he adds twenty pounds.

The only thing he could ever beat me at: bench pressing. He gives me a minute to stretch out before I spot him, and then he gets to work. He doesn't talk until he's done one more press than I did. He racks the weights and sits up, panting as he talks, but that doesn't stop him from talking. And talking.

"The Tag I saw was closer to Rusty's. Old school motivation techniques with a good heart. It was weird that he stopped having you in the workshop with him, but I assumed he thought Rusty needed to talk."

Rusty's cheeks are already red, but his neck flushes.

"Tripp, you saw a petty puppet master. I bet that's how your dad talked about him, even if you don't remember it. But your uncle and aunt were talking about it at Tag's funeral, how it broke Tag's heart that his relationship with your dad was so strained before the accident. Tag told them it was his greatest regret that they hadn't been closer. He couldn't figure out how he'd raised a son who cared more about chasing thrills than his family and duty."

"I didn't know he said that," I admit. But Duke is absolutely right about how my dad talked about Tag.

The first time I ever heard Dad talking about Tag's Carville test was the day he bought the plane. When he hung up the phone, he complained to my mom. I was playing Mario Kart past my bedtime in the other room and heard every word.

"He told me that deciding what sort of man I'm going to be is the ultimate Carville test: am I the sort of man who always chases whatever is over the next horizon or am I the sort who can find adventure wherever I am. He said he wanted *to trust that I'd figure out, but he wasn't so sure he could. What does that even mean?"*

Tag told my dad he *wanted* to trust but wasn't sure ...

Yet Tag always told me he trusted I'd know what to do next.

Did he mean it all those years?

Did my dad's words poison me against Tag without me realizing it?

Or am I just exhausted from the workout?

"I didn't realize I was gettin' a therapy session today, boys. Who should I pay?" I ask.

"Me," Lottie says.

* * *

I give Lottie a high five and a sweaty kiss on her cheek as we leave.

Rusty walks beside me. When I glance over at him, the same old jealousy burns for what he had with Tag. But now there's something new, something that quenches the heat of jealousy and fills me with regret.

What if my friends are right?

Being orphaned at a young age is the stuff of Roald Dahl books. Have I been oblivious to the pain of those around me? *Oh, your dad's a mean drunk? Well, mine's dead, so take that.* Duke's right: pain isn't a competition. Yet I've made Rusty feel like he was losing for a long time.

Guilt gnaws at my chest, clawing up my throat.

"Rusty, I owe you an apology," I say as we pull out onto the main road. Duke's place sits on a dozen or so acres next to Tag's estate on the other side of town.. "I was jealous of you and Tag. I felt so alone at home." The back of my throat itches. "I resented that you got something that I felt should have been mine. If I'd been a better friend, I would have been happy you had someone you felt safe with. I'm sorry."

I've never known the whole story with Rusty's parents. I know his dad was awful before he went to AA, but I'm starting to think it was a lot worse than I knew. The thought turns the guilt from painful to sickening.

"I'm sorry you felt left out," Rusty says. "Tag taught me how to be a man, Tripp. I know he wasn't perfect, but he's the first man in my life who taught me that a father's duty is to protect and care for his family. He showed me that family is a privilege, not a burden. I feel bad that you didn't get the same thing from him. You missed out on a lot, but it's hard not to feel disloyal to him when he's the one who took me to the eme—" Rusty's words stop so abruptly, I could think he was choking. From the driver's seat, I steal a glance at my friend. He's looking out the window at the countryside, but I catch a glimpse of his mouth pulled down in a frown. The shake of his head tells me he's done talking, even if I wish he'd continue.

"You don't have to defend him to me, Rusty." I pat his shoulder. "Tag did the best he could. I'm beginning to think his best was better than I thought."

Rusty nods but he doesn't answer. We're both mourning the passing of the most important father figure in our lives, but in different ways. Rusty's mourning the loss of what he had. I'm mourning the loss of what I didn't know I had. What I could have had.

We both lost a lot.

Maybe we can bring a bit of it back.

"What's your favorite memory with him?"

From the corner of my eye, I see Rusty's frown flip. "Inviting him to our Eight Grade Promotion."

"Huh?"

"The three of us came over after school and each gave him an invitation. He was sittin' at his regular spot at the kitchen table, eating his afternoon peach cobbler. Do you remember how he always used to eat it during peach season? He took a bite, ripped one of the invitations open, then said, 'Y'all are getting promoted, huh? I hope it comes with a big raise.' And then he laughed." Rusty starts chuckling at the memory, pausing the story. Or at least I hope he's pausing the story, because while that's sort of funny, I don't think it warrants this big a reaction. "And then—" more laughter. "And then—" Rusty's laughing so hard, he's in tears. His laughing makes me laugh to watch him. "And then he tried to swallow his bite of cobbler, but he started laughing again and he—he—he spit it everywhere!" Our laughter roars in the cab. "Once it started, Tag couldn't stop!" Rusty's wiping his face. "He was spluttering cobbler all over the table, all over our nice invitations with the RSVP cards. The cobbler was coming out his nose, his mouth. He was crying with laughter. He was this wet, peachy mess, and the worse it got, the more he couldn't quit laughing." Rusty takes a minute to get over his own laughing fit and he sighs. "The three of us busted up, too. We were all just laughing in the kitchen together. Then Tag finally got a hold of himself, wiped his face off, and stood up. Do you remember what he said?"

I lower my voice and up my twang in my best Tag imperson-ation. "'I trust that you chuckleheads can clean this up.' Then he dropped his napkin like a mic."

"Oh man. It was so John Wayne."

"Right. Ain't nothing more John Wayne than peach cobbler coming out your nose."

We both crack up again.

CHAPTER TWENTY-TWO

JANE

J have a new mission. I'm calling it Operation Make Tripp Fall in Love with Sugar Maple.

It's going so well.

And by "so well" I mean not at all.

I keep sending my friends videos of the town and of the farm as if somehow convincing them will convince Tripp. We've come so far and have so much to be proud of. The farm has, I mean.

As much as I love this job, I'm tired of the mental gymnastics involved with it. I don't know where my job begins and Sugar Maple ends anymore. And with Tripp and I dating and him somehow considering relocating while being CEO? Ugh. I can't wrap my head around the idea of him managing the farm from some penthouse loft in Chicago, wearing a turtleneck or something.

Okay, that's not true. He would look dead sexy in a turtleneck. And I would kiss his face off in a loft in Chicago, or in a barn, in—

Uh oh. I'm going full Sam-I-Am. What would Tripp say? I sniff at the thought.

"I would kiss him in a loft, and I would kiss him with no socks. I would kiss him here and there. I would kiss him anywhere," I whisper to myself.

Is it obvious that I'm buckling under the stress of all this?

At any rate, Parker and I are currently coordinating events.

Food truck Fridays with vendors from all over the Low Country.

Monthly drive-in movie for the community.

Fall Festival.

Christmas Lights at the Farm.

Bunnyville.

The best part? Tripp has finally agreed to pave the dang roads on the farm. Well, at least the ones the tourists will use. The ones just for employees will remain firmly—or rather, *loosely* gravel.

As I walk around this place, it's so different than it was six months ago. Where it once felt like the farm that time forgot, now it's vibrant, alive, and teeming with tourists and customers, even with dark clouds threatening rain. Two buses from local childcare centers are parked in the lot, telling me that somewhere, little kids are having the time of their lives. The summer programs are coming to an end, but school field trips start next week. The Pay What You Can stand is in full swing, and I see families walking with baskets full of produce toward it. Ash designed a handful of cutouts, which Booker and Rusty made, and I can't help but snap a few shots as I see moms coax their kids behind the cutouts.

I send one of the pictures to Tripp with heart eye emojis.

. . .

JANE: The fruit of our labors.

TRIPP: The fruit of YOUR labors. The farm would be lifeless without you. You're amazing.

I grumble. I'm trying to get him to fall in love with the farm, not with … okay, I'm also more than fine if he's falling for me. But I'm offering a two-for-one special right now! Love the farm, love me!

Next, I send the pictures to my friends.

JANE: The cutouts are a huge success, Ash!

Ash responds with a GIF of a woman crying happily.

ASH: This warms my cold, dead heart.

PARKER: You don't give yourself enough credit. Your heart is undead, at least.

LOU: You have the warmest, undead-est heart of us all.

ASH: Are we talking Spike undead or Angel undead?

. . .

PARKER: Neither. Drusilla, obvi.

Laughing, vomiting, and sobbing emojis pop into the thread.

MILLIE: Stop it, vamps. That boy is missing his two front teeth! If that doesn't thaw y'all's frosty souls, you're deader than undead.

LOU: As the only bona fide Southerner here, let me congratulate you on your excellent use of the word y'all. I'll make Southerners of all y'all yet.

ASH: Uh, do you see Jane? Cutoff jeans, cowgirl boots, and working on a farm? My girl's already gone full Southern. She's not leaving Sugar Maple without a fight. Or a ring.

Cue the Beyoncé memes.

JANE: Ha-ha! Real original y'all. Aaaall y'all.

Smoochy face gifs, "She said yes!" gifs, and wedding day gifs flood my phone.

JANE: Please. I wouldn't plan a wedding if my life depended on it.

. . .

ASH: Talk about a cold, undead heart …

JANE: Get back to work or you're all fired.

PARKER: You heard what the boss said. Get to work, slackerzzz.

LOU: Jane, can you fire PJ for the zzz thing already? It's older than the cookies in my meemaw's cookie jar. And she died ten years ago.

PARKER: You mean ten yearzzz ago.

LOU: I quit.

I stow my phone with a laugh and start walking before I've even looked up. Which is how I walk straight into Tripp. He stops my shoulders right before my face smacks into his pecs. "Oof! Nice save."

He bends down and kisses me, and things get interesting fast. What I expect to be a short kiss, seeing as we're in the middle of his farm, is filled with intensity. His generous mouth is hot and demanding. I'm tingling all over as I put my hands on his chest and push him away. "Tripp." I feel breathless. "We have an audience."

Tripp growls and takes in the families and field tripping kids with a glance. A mom is actually covering her son's eyes, as if we're half-naked instead of simply kissing.

Really, really good kissing.

"Excuse us," I tell the families with a wave. "He just got back from … "

"The war," he says, and before I can elbow him, he continues, "with weeds."

I roll my eyes so far, they could see heaven through the top of my head. Then I squeak with surprise as Tripp pulls me up onto his back and starts giving me a piggyback ride over to his truck.

Like any brilliant CEO, I capitalize on the opportunity. Mostly because I want to stay attached at the literal hip to my hot boyfriend.

"Whoa there, horsey. Where do you think you're going?" My legs are wrapped around his back and dangle at his waist. As always, I'm struck by how I can feel so many individual muscles even with my legs. He's locked my thighs in with his massive arms, and his hands are gripped around my calves, just above my leather cowgirl boots, holding on softly but firmly. Boy, am I glad I shaved this morning. Tripp seems to be too, as his fingers lightly glide over the smooth skin. The touch makes my eyes flutter closed.

"I'm taking you to my truck."

"No way. I'm in charge here, and I want a tour."

With my arms draped over his shoulders, I leverage myself against him so that I can see his face. I plant a kiss on his cheek and then nibble on his ear.

Have I mentioned before how sexy his ears are? Ears are sexy, it turns out. Little known secret of life. "Jane!" Tripp's face scrunches and he nearly stumbles. "Ticklish, remember?"

"My bad."

"Apology accepted. Now what sort of tour you lookin' for, li'l darlin'?" He heaps on the accent.

I make a biting sound right by his ear but stop myself from

following through. Barely. There is nothing in the world that smells as good as Tripp does. He smells like fruit, unsurprisingly, and soil and freshly mowed grass. His deodorant is an all-natural kind, I learned after his concussion. Blue Tansy, or something. I don't know what that is, but it pairs exceptionally well with the rest, making Tripp irresistible. I'm smelling his neck before I know it.

His face bumps against mine, and when he talks, his voice is low and sparks something primal deep inside of me. "Easy now. You're the one who said no making out in public, remember?"

"What?" I let my lips touch his ear again. The teensy hairs on his earlobe tickle my lips, shooting sensation through my mouth and down to my toes. "That can't be true. I would never make such a dumb rule."

His hands clench on my knees, and I know he's trying hard not to flinch out of control. I should probably stop messing with his ears but torturing him is too delicious. Tripp growls again, and before I can even squeal, he spins me around so that my legs are wrapped around his waist instead of his back. He holds me up so easily, like my weight is barely worth noticing.

I love it.

I love how he holds me like I'm precious but not breakable. I love the way he looks in my eyes like they hold the secret to his happiness. I love arguing with him and I love how he argues right back. I love his touch and his laugh and his growl. I love how tender he is with Lottie and how respectful he is toward Anita. I love how he's making the effort to learn people's names and how he smiles at people as they go by now instead of ignoring them or glaring. I love that he made the appointment to pave the roads all by himself, the first sign he's given me that maybe, just maybe, he would stick around. I love …

I love him.

The revelation isn't earth shattering, yet it rocks my world.

I'm so far past pretending that what he thinks and feels doesn't matter to me. His opinion has come to mean more than any other. I text him before I text my friends! I'm fantasizing about a world where he wants to keep me here, where I work remotely and travel to Chicago once or twice a month for meetings and to catch up with my friends. The idea of not being with them anymore is brutal. Heart-wrenching.

But the idea of not being with Tripp anymore is unbearable. I don't want to be without him. I don't want to be away from him. I don't want to wake up and go into an office building instead of what has become our shared office. I want to make plans with and for him.

"What is going through that big, beautiful brain of yours?" he asks. Even perched on his waist, I'm barely eye level with him. I shift, but his grip on my thighs doesn't falter.

How do I answer this? We both obviously care for each other. He's told me how serious he is about me. But do I really want to be the one to push for more? The weight of the promise I made his grandfather pushes down on me, shoving the air right out of my lungs. I promised Tag that I'd make Tripp want to grow old here, and all I've managed to do is become his excuse, his reason to leave.

He wouldn't actually leave, though, would he?

Tripp looks at me expectantly, like he's waiting for the answer to his question. "I was thinking about how much trouble a young Tripp must have gotten into on this farm. Your puppy dog eyes could get you out of anything, I bet." Will reminding him of his happy times here work? Will it make him want to stay on the farm? My own hypocrisy strangles me, even as I plant the seeds of manipulation. I'm fully considering ways to work remotely at my job so I can be with him. Why do I begrudge him so much for doing the same with me? He cares so much about me that he would relocate so I can do *my* job. What woman doesn't want a man who cares that much? What woman doesn't want to be the one to be sacrificed *for*, for a change?

Although, isn't that precisely what I'm hoping for? That he'll sacrifice whatever dreams he has of going elsewhere to be where I want?

He tips me forward until our lips are touching. "Come on. Let me give you the tour."

CHAPTER TWENTY-THREE

TRIPP

$\mathcal{J}$ can't shake the feeling that Jane's keeping something from me. She jumped down from my arms so quickly, I thought she was going to run. But then she took my hand and pointed at various places, asking, "What happened there?" I worry that she's asking because she's trying to soak in as many memories as she can. The rebrand has come far enough that she could do the rest from Chicago. She could leave whenever she wants.

Does she want to leave?

"How is this humidity real?" a passing tourist asks. The man is sweating bullets.

"It's like a steam bath," a man with him says.

"It's hotter than the gates in Hell!" another says.

Jane chuckles. "I think that one's my new favorite."

"It really is like walking through soup," I agree.

She gapes like I've just found gold. "No, that's my new

favorite." She wipes her forehead under her hat and we keep walking.

When you live on a farm through your teenage years, something exciting (or embarrassing) has happened just about everywhere. So I tell her everything, partly because I'm a sucker for her deep blue eyes, and partly because I want to delay whatever it is that's starting to feel inevitable. I show her where I first learned to drive and where I first crashed (into the peach grove). I point out Tag's shed, the fence I roped Duke into helping me paint, the corral where I ran an impromptu petting zoo to get the attention of a girl in school.

"Wait, you didn't have animals on a farm?"

"It's technically more of an orchard, but Sugar Maple Farms sounded homier to my grandparents."

"So how did you manage to set up a petting zoo?"

"The art of the hustle, little lady," I say, tipping an imaginary hat. "A few kids at school grew up on ranches or farms with actual animals, so we decided to do a swap."

Her laugh makes my cheeks hurt from smiling. "What on earth did they get in return?"

"Oh, all sorts of things. Money, chores, money, rides in the side-by-side. Money."

"But did you try money?"

I cluck my tongue and feign surprise. "Why didn't I think of that?"

She swats at me, and I make sure to flex, because I love how she looks at me like she can't believe my muscles are real. If I didn't already spend five days a week lifting at Duke's, I would start just to keep seeing that look on her face. "What did your grandpa do?"

"He gave me the blueprints to build the pens the animals would need and said, 'Have at it. I trust you'll do right by them.'"

"I thought he never let you in his shed. Was this a Carville test?"

I reach back into my memory. He said *trust*, like he always did with his tests, but looking back, I see this one differently. "I think it was, but it didn't feel negative like the other ones did," I say. "I took him at his word. He trusted me to do right by the animals."

"What made you believe him instead of reading into it?"

"I honestly don't know." Our hands swing in between us, and I let them swing bigger and bigger while I think. I caught a glimpse of Tag smiling when he drove by in his truck. Was that all it took? Knowing that he'd been amused by the display? Or had I suspected deep down that my happiness had made him happy? The older I got, the more I ascribed ulterior motives to Tag. I'm starting to wonder how much of that was real and how much of it was the story I told myself to justify my own behavior or feelings.

Either way, his parade of women during my college years wasn't a story I told myself. But what *was* the story? He'd started dating when I left for college, as if he'd been waiting for me to leave. The first couple of women had been in their sixties. Very age appropriate. The last woman had been in her thirties. Very not. In the last ten years of his life, he spent less and less time at the farm and more and more time at his beach house on the Isle of Palms or at Uncle Lawson's place in Atlanta.

Coming home for a long weekend just to find the place empty was enough to make me feel orphaned all over again. I'd thought he'd be so happy to see me. I couldn't wait to see his face, hear his booming, "Tripp, my boy!" Get one of the hugs he gave out so rarely but always seemed to have when I needed it most.

I hadn't realized how much I'd come to count on Tag until he wasn't there.

My pause has reached non-answer territory, but I clear my throat. "I don't think I know what a Carville test really was anymore." I have so much more I want to say, but I don't know how. I don't know *what*.

If I keep talking, keep trying to process through some of these emotions, will I scare her off? When I mentioned possibly following her back to Chicago or both of us going elsewhere, her energy shifted completely. Am I a fling? Is that all she's interested in? My throat goes dry, and my pulse speeds up like I'm doing box squats.

If I try to let her in further and she runs …

"Enough of the heavy stuff," I say. "Let me show you where I found out I'm allergic to fire ants."

Jane's smile doesn't reach her eyes, but she keeps a tight hold on my hand and walks with me. Storm clouds roll in overhead, and when the rain comes, I'm glad of it.

Jane squeals and we run for the main house.

While we make dinner, familiar self-loathing bubbles in my gut, turning my stomach sour. "You okay?" she asks as she cuts tomatoes for a salad.

"It's nothing. A headache," I say.

"Oh no! Sit down. Let me get you something."

"It's fine, Jane, I just need water," I say. And to prove that I won't be one more burden on her, I stand and get the water myself.

She eyes me funny, but she lets it go. She does, however, insist that I sit while she makes dinner.

"You're not some housewife who needs to cook for me," I grumble.

She throws the tomatoes into the salad and then wipes her hands on the apron. "No, and you're not some spoiled rich boy who can't do it for himself. You have a headache, and dinner is a salad and steaks on the grill. I don't exactly need help."

She doesn't. She doesn't need anything.

Not even me.

"And I don't need you to worry about me, Jane. A headache

shouldn't stop me from making dinner. I've been doing it by myself for years."

Her expression turns wry, and she opens a cupboard to grab the oil and vinegar. "Do you want a hero cookie for that? For being a grown man who can power through a headache?"

"No, I want you to stop treating me like one more weight on your shoulders."

"What?" A deep line forms between her brows. "I've never treated you like that. I don't *see* you like that."

"You're treating me like that right now. The last thing I wanted was to become another burden to you."

"Tripp, you're my boyfriend. I'm making you dinner because you have a headache. I would do this for anyone—"

"So I'm just *anyone*, huh? Even better." I sound so bitter that I want to bite my own tongue. But it's like I'm watching the nastiest part of me creep out from deep inside and I'm powerless to stop it. Rational Me is yelling at Ugly Me to calm down; everything is fine. Ugly Me just flips Rational Me the bird.

Jane puts her hands on the counter and takes a deep breath, and then another. Shame coats my insides.

"Tripp, what's going on right now?"

"You've been off, but even without that, we need to face the facts: this job has an expiration date, and you evidently don't want me following you to Chicago when this is all over."

"Because your whole life is *here*!"

"And your whole life is there! Your whole life except for me. Which—let's face it—means you don't want me there."

"That's not what that means!" Her mouth opens and closes and opens again. She's holding something back, and it hurts. But aren't I doing the same? Why can't I let her in? "Tripp, I care about you, and I want to be with you. Do you want to be with me?"

"Yes." More than anything.

"Then why are you picking a fight with me?" Tears shimmer

in her eyes, but they don't fall. They don't fall from mine either. I cry sometimes. I'm not a robot. But I haven't cried like I want to now in ages. Not since that first time I came home to the empty house freshman year, come to think of it. I cried so hard that I felt like my soul was raw and exposed, and no one was even there to see it.

It was a long weekend—Columbus Day, maybe—and I was deep into my Intro to Psychology class. For the first time in years, I was ready to talk to Tag. I wanted to talk about my grief and tell him about how I never felt good enough for him. I wanted to make him talk, for once. I'd texted him a couple of weeks earlier about maybe coming home for the long weekend.

I said I missed him.

He said, "Me too."

That "me too" carried me the whole drive home. I was nervous but excited. I had a need for parental approval that I was finally going to ask to be met, and he finally seemed willing to meet it.

Except when I showed up, he wasn't there.

Jane asked me why I'm picking a fight. "I don't know," I tell her. "But I'm sorry."

She hugs me and lets me hug her back. The pain retreats for the moment. But I've seen behind the curtain now, and I'm afraid that these demons are just going to keep coming back.

I have to fix this or I'll risk losing Jane forever.

* * *

"You told me a few months ago that you've never felt like you're enough, do you remember that?"

Millie's face on my phone's screen is what I would describe as concerned neutral. When I called her, I thought I was just going to ask her for advice on how to find a good therapist. But when she asked me how I was feeling, the dam broke, and I couldn't stop talking. I accidentally face-timed her with my cheek a couple of minutes in, and the call switched over. She was on a treadmill at the time, and while she offered to stop, I insisted that I didn't want to disturb her and would only take a minute of her time.

A half an hour later, she got off the treadmill. At ninety minutes, we're still going strong. Millie explained that she couldn't be my therapist because she knows me but that she'd be happy to talk me through some helpful exercises I could do on my own.

Only it turns out that I don't understand how to do them on my own, so she's doing them with me.

"I remember," I say.

"And when I asked you 'enough for what,' what did you say?"

"Enough to stay."

"Exactly. Now, walk me through again what was going on tonight?"

"She was acting off, and I was afraid she was going to leave."

"Try it again," she says with a smile. "What was happening?"

"She was acting off! Her smile was all lips, no eyes, and she was trying too hard to make memories, as if she was about to leave."

"Tripp, that's your interpretation of how she was acting. Fast forward to the fight at dinner. What was actually, physically happening?"

I wrinkle my forehead in frustration. "I had a headache so she offered to make dinner by herself."

"Good. And what was the thought you had about that?"

My throat is so tight, it hurts to swallow. "I'm just another burden to her. I'm not good enough for her to stay."

"Okay, so how did that make you feel?"

"Horrible. Scared." She waits. "Worthless."

"And when you felt that way, how did you act?"

"Like a jerk. I picked a fight with her."

"And what was the result?"

The answer hits me like a hay bale to the head—something I have personal experience with. "I pushed her away."

"Exactly. Tripp, your limiting belief is that you aren't enough for people to stay. You think your parents treated you like an inconvenience because you weren't enough. They missed your football games and dropped you off with your grandparents rather than change their own plans, but it had nothing to do with you. They were *horrible* parents. Not abusive, not mean, but horrible. Do you see that? Do you *feel* that?"

She sounds clinical, but her eyes and nose are rimmed with red. Seeing her emotion brings on mine. Unshed tears blur my vision.

"Now talk to me about Tag. You said you don't know if you can see him clearly. That's understandable. He died so recently, and there's a lot to unpack there. If he were still alive, what would you want to say to him?"

As much as I've thought about Tag over the last week, I feel more confusion than clarity. All those times he wouldn't let me in the shed with him don't match with the time when he let me build that corral for the animals. I'm trying to reconcile too many different versions of the same man. The Tag Rusty needed, the Tag Duke saw, the Tag I wanted.

The ache of his absence that long weekend comes to mind, but I'm not just upset about him being gone then.

I'm upset that he's gone now.

"I would yell at him," I admit, dashing away tears. "Why wouldn't he give up those stupid cigars and that stupid whiskey? He said he was too old to stop, but he didn't care enough about me. If he'd really loved me, he would have stopped!" I break down into sobs, aching and exposed, and yet it feels so freeing to get it out.

I'm not just angry at Tag for my past. I'm angry at Tag for

cutting short our future. We should have had the chance to reconcile. We almost had the chance …

Millie gives me time to talk my anger out. I can hardly believe how good it feels, but I know I need more. A lot more.

"We could talk about Tag for weeks, but let's shift gears. How do you think this limiting belief impacts your relationship with Jane?"

I nod, the connections finally clear. "I'm so afraid Jane won't think I'm enough to stay that I'm unknowingly pushing her from me." I let the epiphany spread out through my limbs, into my heart and head, everywhere. I try to put into words how I'm feeling. "I think I'm pushing her away to see if she *will* stay. It's my version of a Carville test: something she can't understand, doesn't even know about, and can't possibly pass."

"Is that what those tests were?"

"I don't know."

"But you think there's something more to them now, is that right?"

I both shake my head and shrug at the same time. "Maybe. I don't know."

"And that's okay." Millie's smile is warm and makes me feel strangely proud of myself. "This is a lot to process, and it would be a miracle to have it all figured out in one night. Focus on what you've learned and how far you've come, not where you're still hoping to go. Does that make sense? And use those coping skills I taught you next time Ugly Brain starts acting up, okay." Her smile widens, even if I still can't believe I told her that I called the jerky part of myself my "Ugly Brain." She stifles a yawn, and I immediately do the same thing. I look at the clock and realize it's midnight.

"Shoot, I'm sorry, Millie. I didn't mean to take up so much of your time."

"It's fine. I wouldn't have spoken so long if it didn't matter to me. You're dating my best friend, so I'm more than a little invested in this."

I bow my head in her direction. "Thanks again." I can't believe how much she was able to get out of me so quickly. I think of the way Lottie still hasn't gotten over missing her. I think of how Jane always jokes about her "therapist magic." I was willing and eagerly waiting to talk, so I know it wasn't magic, but it was more than training and expertise, too. She was born to do this.

"I know you have a great job, and I would never dream of poaching my girlfriend's best friend, but we could use you here. I've contracted with that provider you found out of Beaufort for animal therapy, but the offer is permanently available if you want it."

"Thanks, Tripp." Her smile fades rather than deepens, though. "Can I ask ... how's Lottie?"

"A bit better. She asks about you still. You left a big impression on her."

Millie puts her hand to her heart, and her eyes flit from the screen to something on her desk before flitting back. "Give her a hug for me, okay?"

"I will. Thanks again, Millie."

I'm left feeling lighter than I've felt in years. I may not be good enough for Jane, but I can't keep being preoccupied by thoughts of my own worthiness. Instead, I need to thank the heavens that she disagrees and wants to be with me, anyway.

She wants to be with me.

I don't know why she doesn't want to be with me in Chicago. Maybe the city is for her what Sugar Maple is for me: a place of painful memories that she'd gladly leave behind.

And yet, every single memory I have of Jane is here. Our first fight. Our first kiss. The million ways she serves me. The ways I've tried to serve her back. We've worked together and played together. We've held a crying little girl and have shed our own tears.

We'll be able to do all of that somewhere else in the future, if we both want it.

I want it.

It's nearly midnight, but I shoot Jane a text.

TRIPP: Sorry about being a butthead earlier. I missed you tonight.

Her response comes a moment later.

JANE: <3 Missed you too.

I want to say more. I want to tell her all the things I haven't fully processed yet but am working on, but it's late, and some things are better said in person.

Tomorrow.

And this time, I mean it.

CHAPTER TWENTY-FOUR

JANE

*T*RIPP: Emergency at the factory. I'll call you later. <3

I wake up to this text ten minutes before my alarm is set to ring. The pre-dawn sun peeks in the room because the B&B doesn't have the same blackout curtains I installed in Strawberry Fields. I'm staying here while the exterior of all of the cottages gets painted over the next week. As comfortable as my room here is, I didn't fall asleep until after one a.m. I kept waiting for Tripp to text or, better yet, show up and kiss the fear from my heart and tears from my face. I still feel raw over our fight last night. We've bickered a lot before, but this was different. It was so obviously coming from a place deep inside of him, and it scared me how quickly he was willing to write me off and send me packing.

I know he's self-sabotaging, but the way he accused me of making him one of my burdens was so personal, it hurt. The sting of that rejection has dulled with sleep, but not enough. I need an explanation. I need a hug. I need to know that we can make it.

I also need to make good on my promise to his grandfather. But how?

I text Parker to call me when she's up. My phone vibrates seconds later.

"Hey!" I say, shocked to see her awake and putting on mascara.

"Hey girl, what's up?"

She props her phone against the mirror in our bathroom and continues with her mascara.

"What are you doing awake at 5:27 a.m.?"

"Early meeting. What's going on? If you're calling me right now, it must be something big."

"It is." I sit up in bed. "PJ, we had a fight and everything feels wrong and he's going to break up with me and I'm going to have to buy a dozen cats even though I hate cats and I'm going to live alone and they'll probably eat me after I die like what happened to that one lady on the news."

Parker looks down from her reflection. "You had a fight and now you're getting eaten by cats?" She shakes her head. "Rewind and tell me everything."

When I'm done, she isn't having any of it. "Girl, please. You're basically fighting about who loves the other person more."

"Not quite—"

"Yes quite," she says, and I kick myself for texting Parker. Why did I think tough love would help? I should have texted Ash so she could pep talk my face off. "Get your insecurities in check, tell him how you feel, and stop worrying about this promise you made to Mr. Carville. He's not here." Parker never minces words, but she's not being harsh. "Do you really want Tripp to stay on the farm for his grandpa? Or do you want him to stay there for you? You fell in love there, and you've fallen in love with who *you* are there. That's powerful stuff."

"What? I—no. Parker—"

"Protest all you want. If we weren't here, you'd have left Chicago years ago. And if you weren't here, we all would have, too."

I sit up in bed. "Wait, seriously?"

"I got accosted twice yesterday. And yes, one of those times was at Nordstrom Rack, but the other was because I was a human on a sidewalk."

With a sigh, I stand and open the curtains of the second story window. I see so many familiar faces and places. I know where every path and road leads from here. I've kissed Tripp along most of them. This farm is as much my home as Chicago. "I wish you all were here."

"We don't feel like *us* without you," she says. She sets down her eye shadow brush and gives me a cautionary look. "But I mean the old you. If you want to ride off into the sunset with Tripp, you have to get rid of your Clint Eastwood Syndrome."

"Come again?"

"Something bad happened in some corner of the world, and only Clint Eastwood can save the day. We're not your family, though. Tripp doesn't need you to save him anymore than we did. He needs you to love him, and the best way to love him is to ask him what *he* wants. He felt stupid that you made him dinner. I can't imagine why because cooking is the worst. But it sounds like he wanted to help and you wouldn't let him. You treated him like you treated us. If you want this relationship to last, don't make him your sidekick."

"Wow," I whisper.

"I'm not trying to be mean."

"No, you're right. I just never thought about it that way."

"Now, this is going to sound like the exact opposite of what I just said, but could you do me a favor and consider yourself, for once? You've focused so much on what you think other people need that you've ignored what *you* need. What do you need, Jane? What do you want?"

I look out the window again, less sure than ever.

"Sit with that for a bit." She zips up her makeup bag and grabs her blow dryer. "I gotta do my hair, but I'll talk to you later, okay?"

"Okay. Miss you."

"Miss you too."

I'm left with an ache in my chest that expands into a chasm. I don't know what to do. I don't know how to follow my heart when it's tearing me in two different directions. My friends wouldn't begrudge me working from here. Tripp has already said we could be together anywhere. Why do I feel frozen? Why, even after being called out for it, do I feel like the fate of the world rests on this one decision? A decision I don't have all the necessary information to even make yet?

Maybe it's because this decision actually affects *me*. Everyone else *will* be fine regardless of what I choose. But will I?

A phone call distracts me. It's early still, but when I see the name on the screen, I try to keep my heart from hammering right out of my chest. This has to be a good sign, right? That she's calling rather than texting or emailing? Does this mean what I think it means? I pull myself together, switching to competent, friendly business mode. And because you can, in fact, hear it through the phone, I smile.

"This is Jane."

* * *

I've booked the Beauchamps's wedding.

I'm still on cloud nine over the news. No, cloud nine is way too low. I'm on Cloud 999. This is *the* wedding of the year. Eric Beauchamps is South Carolina royalty, and his bride-to-be has 12 million followers. After realizing that a plantation wedding had some seriously problematic elements, she's been looking for a way to "celebrate the South without the ick factor," as she put it. They'd planned to delay till next year, but after seeing the mockup Parker and Ash put together, she's ready for a fall wedding.

This fall.

I've left messages for my friends, but they've only texted back. Lou assured me that she was working on the contracts. Parker said she'd send the routing instructions for the non-refundable deposit any minute. My call went straight to voice-mail when I tried to reach her, so she texted that she was in a meeting and would call me later. It's been a few hours already, but my friends know what they're doing. No need to panic.

And it doesn't even matter that Tripp hasn't called me, either. I didn't want to text him the news because it's too good not to share in person, but I told him to find me ASAP when things are taken care of at the factory.

So in the meantime, I'm working on getting the ball rolling for the wedding, starting with telling Anita. While the wedding is falling under the rebrand, as the caretaker of the farm, Anita could probably decide against using Parker in favor of a different event coordinator, if she wanted to push it. As the former Miss South Carolina, she has plenty of connections and knows her own way around events. I hope she'll use us, though. One more reason to delay staying.

The bride-to-be plans to start posting about the farm next week when she has an open space in her content schedule. I called Ash to talk social media, but she said she's booked all day, so she'll call me tonight.

How are they all unavailable at the exact same time? My friends and I share a calendar, for heaven's sake. They need to add their meetings to it so we all know who's doing what, thank you very much.

Because I'm bursting at the seams, I call Rusty.

"Great news! We got the Beauchamps's wedding!"

"Whoa! No surprise there, but congratulations! That's huge."

"Any chance you'd be interested in helping with social media for your usual rate?"

"You know I'd love to. But hey, Anita needs me to load some things up in the van to take to Columbia. Can we talk later?"

"Of course."

I try Tripp again, but he doesn't answer. How is it possible that on the day that I have the biggest news ever, no one is available to talk?

I head to the main house, planning to wait for him. I run into Anita in the kitchen, talking to the farm worker manager. With a quick smile, she holds a finger up to me, and I wait with superhuman patience as she finishes her conversation about crop rotation. As soon as the man walks away, she throws out her arms and wraps me in a hug as big as Texas (am I even allowed to make comparisons with other Southern states?).

"You are a miracle worker, child! That wedding will put us on the map to shame all other maps!"

I straighten my sundress when she lets go, but I leave my smile as is. "Thanks, Miss Anita."

"You have been a blessing to this place since the moment you set foot here." She holds me at arm length. In her late forties, she's still intimidatingly lovely. "The bride wants a November wedding to take advantage of the red maple?"

"That's right. And my team is ready to continue planning the event—"

"That's a relief. I'm not quite ready to plan a wedding with everything else going on." Her smile is as warm as the summer sun. "Do you need help finding local contacts? I imagine you'll coordinate most of it from Chicago, won't you?"

"Oh." Her question is a kick in the gut. "I, uh, I thought I'd coordinate from here."

She nods slowly. "You know, I assumed with the ads launching next week and the event contracts finally in motion that you'd be returning home soon."

She's already imagining life here without me. And why shouldn't she? It's been over six months, and although I can eke a few more months out of it with the wedding, I don't *need* to. My team could coordinate a lot of this from Chicago and fly out as needed. Tag built leeway into the contract for us to return once everything was in motion.

Which it is.

Processes have been established, necessary people contracted or hired. Events are firmly on the calendar. The rebrand isn't done—we still have a lot of work to do with ads, the factory, and awareness—but everything is set in motion.

My presence is no longer required.

No. I don't want to leave this place. I don't want to leave Tripp. For the first time since Grandpa died, I've felt at home somewhere. I've felt like a contributing partner rather than the lynchpin of the whole operation. And in the last few months, I've felt more. I've felt loved.

You could still have that with him in Chicago.

Tripp and I need to talk. If he insists on returning with me, I can live with that, can't I? I'll miss Sugar Maple, but I'll have my friends *and* Tripp. Win-win!

But if I can convince him to stay, will he want me to stay with him? The ache of missing my friends will subside eventually, won't it? The new bonds I've made here have become precious to me, too. I play back long hours at the B&B with

Anita and Booker. Diner runs where I stop to talk to Tia and others. Joking around with Rusty and Duke. Babysitting Lottie.

And I think of Tripp, of countless hours working, fighting, and laughing together. He's told me through his actions a thousand times that he cares for me. Maybe even that he loves me. But he hasn't told me in word.

We really need to talk.

Anita puts her finger under my chin, lifting my eyes to hers. "I don't think your work here is through after all, is it?"

I scrunch my nose. "I hope not."

"Attagirl. His uncle drove in this morning, and they're in the study. Why don't you go on in and tell them the news?"

"Don't you think they'd mind the interruption?"

Anita smirks. "Child, when it comes to you, I guarantee he'd welcome it."

I make a beeline for the office, where the door is slightly ajar. The blinds on the French doors are closed, but I hear Tripp talking excitedly. I recognize his uncle's voice from our previous phone conversation.

"The events will bring in significant revenue, allowing us to easily pay the loan off on the housing complexes in ten years. If we can roll Halloween into Christmas with Santa's village, it would be even faster." I smile at the excitement in Tripp's voice. He's telling his uncle our plans and accomplishments, and Tripp sounds *proud* of them.

There's a pause, during which time I assume Lawson is looking at projections. I'm about to interrupt when the older man says, "Very nice. Events are good for tourism, which is good for the community, so make sure you push this Food Truck Friday. Maybe take it into town square once a month and get more local businesses involved. Really make Sugar Maple a destination, not just the farm."

I'm impressed by Lawson's insight and approach. While he was pleasant on the phone with me, he was also efficient. I assumed he'd be more cutthroat about it all. But his idea makes my mind whir with possibilities about how to involve the town. Tripp goes back to presenting more of our plans.

I should go in. I should.

Hearing him gush about all we've accomplished, though, is too gratifying when he doesn't know I'm listening. Especially when he invokes my name.

"Jane's work with the local restaurant industry is nothing short of genius. She's secured a handful of contracts with restaurants in Charleston and Savannah to exclusively use Sugar Maple Farms produce and even Booker's goat cheese."

"Excellent. Those are some big names. Chef Raul is a personal friend. I'll call him and thank him for his support."

Huh. Carville Industries doesn't own the farm, so this comment feels a bit out of left field. But maybe he means it more in a proud uncle way?

But if that's the case, why is Lawson telling Tripp, "I'm sold"?

"You've done it, son. The agricultural accomplishments alone are worth bragging about, but you and Jane have managed to turn Sugar Maple Farms from a sleepy brand past its prime into a premier brand *and* destination. I hope you're proud."

"I am, Uncle Lawson. Jane's ideas have been inspired from start to finish, but it's felt good to help bring them to life. The work isn't done, of course. I know you wanted to see updates—"

"I've seen enough," Lawson says, and I hear a sound like the patting of a back. "You've worked hard to prove to me why Sugar Maple Farms should be a flagship enterprise of Carville Industries. My dad always liked the idea of separating the two—making one the family brand and one the global brand—but your presentation is too compelling to ignore. We can and should be both. So I'm prepared to work with the terms of Dad's will to buy you out. I'll have my lawyer draft up the offer next week, and then you'll be free to leave, if that's what you still want. Have you decided what you'll do? Where you're going? You know there's always room at Carville, if you're interested."

Shock courses through me like lightning, one slow, painful zap at a time, and all of them straight to my wounded heart. Tripp is planning to sell Sugar Maple Farms and then just … leave? Was he going to tell me or simply vanish? I know his issues with Tag are tangled up with his emotions about the farm, but I had no idea he wanted out.

He's been so energized for the last few months. It's like he's been jolted into action with each idea we've implemented, offering insight and even improvements. Seeing him work with contractors, seeing him talk to businesses about the possibilities the farm would offer the community, I thought he was inspired. I thought he was finally growing to love this place.

Did he love it all, or did he simply love the idea of making it desirable enough to sell? Was all of this just to sweeten the pot when he sold the farm off?

Was he even going to tell me?

Was he going to tell any of us?

Stop it, I chide myself. By all appearances, he only expected to give updates. He didn't know his uncle was going to offer. Yet. But the subtext was there. That's been his plan all along.

Calm down, Jane. Think.

There's nothing ignoble happening here. This isn't a shameful sale. It will stay in his family. Anita will still be the caretaker, I'm sure. Rusty and his parents will still have their stake in the fruit stands. Nothing about Tripp suggests he'll disappear with no warning.

But still, he's leaving. His uncle said so.

I've failed.

But who have I failed, exactly?

I clearly didn't fail Tripp. This is what he was working toward.

I didn't fail my friends. This account has secured us so much work, our fortunes have changed completely.

I didn't even fail Mr. Carville. Not really. As Parker said, he's not here anymore, and Tripp is proud of the work we've done. If Tag Carville is looking down on his namesake from heaven, I can't imagine him holding a grudge.

So who did I actually fail?

"Wow, Uncle Lawson," Tripp says after a long pause. I know him well enough to hear the emotion in his voice. "Thank you. You know better than anyone how badly I've wanted this."

A sob bubbles in my throat, and I have to rush away from the office to avoid being caught. I run outside and bury my face in my hands, wishing I could undo the last five minutes. What does this mean for Tripp and me? Practically speaking, has anything changed? Our relationship has progressed past Sugar Maple Farms, hasn't it?

You know it has, I tell myself. *He said he wants to make plans with you. Those plans were never limited by geography.*

But then why didn't he tell me about the sale?

I've included him in everything. Everything. *And he didn't tell me about something life-changing he was actively working on.*

For the hundredth time since I moved to South Carolina, I wish my friends were here. Maybe I need a break from this place. Maybe it's time for me to go back to Chicago and regroup. To remember who I am outside of this farm. But for how long? And do I really want to leave Tripp, even if we're not here?

My heart screams a *no* even as I long for the understanding and support of my friends. Being folded into Tripp's life has been wonderful. Magical. But as special as it's been, the people in his life are an addition, not a substitute to the people in mine.

A text from Parker pops up on my phone like an answer to prayer.

. . .

PARKER: Home is where your pals are. Come home, Janie.

She sends a selfie. It's Parker, Millie, Ash, and Lou … in a place I recognize. A grin spreads over my face.

I have to talk to Anita and then hitch a ride to the airport. Home awaits.

CHAPTER TWENTY-FIVE

TRIPP

"Wow, Uncle Lawson." I clear my voice of the emotion growing thick. "Thank you. You know better than anyone how badly I've wanted this."

My uncle runs a hand through his short salt and pepper hair. It's always strange looking at him and seeing glimpses of my dad. Lawson was two years younger than my dad, but light-years older in terms of maturity. He got married just out of college and went to work to provide for his family. He and my aunt have four kids—Kayla, Hunter, Wesley, and Logan—and they found a way to travel the world with all of them. Wesley is my age, but I've always gotten along well with all of them.

More than once over the last several years, I've wondered how different my life would be if Lawson and Jolene had raised me instead of Tag. The thought used to fill me with regret at what I'd missed, but now, it feels me with something different. Nostalgia, maybe. Before I can give it enough thought, Lawson swipes at the tablet.

"Let's talk logistics. I like everything you've done here, but a lot of what can work on a family farm won't work as part of a larger scale operation. We've got a board to answer to. Everything has to be repeatable and scalable across our domestic holdings, at least. The housing complex is a must. Stroke of genius. And having weddings here will help draw enough high-profile attention to make it worth the while, even though I can't see this working anywhere else. Maybe the one in Maine. Hmm. Festivals, maybe." He taps the stylus against his cheek before swiping it across the screen. "But animal therapy is a huge no. Not part of our brand, way too much liability. Same with school visits and the campgrounds. No, *glamp*grounds? Am I reading that right?"

With every cut Lawson announces, I feel like an inch is taken off my height. I'm four feet tall and shrinking. Worse, every cut feels like a memory being excised. The way Lottie's fear faded away when she got to ride the alpaca. Slice. Anita and Booker holding court during movie night. Snip. The first time we had a family come through the Pick What You Pay lot, the mom crying quietly to herself while her kids were so excited for all the fruit. Never happened.

And Jane. Every touch and whisper and kiss, gone, gone, gone.

Lawson it still talking but panic at everything I'm losing swirls around me. Like a gust in a tropical storm, it takes my breath away. I choke on regret, watching everything that matters get whisked away by the swipe of a stylus.

"Okay," Lawson says, putting down the tablet. "I'll send this to the board and we'll start talking details." He leans back in his chair and looks me over. "Tripp, I know you wanted to work with Carville Industries all along, but my dad had other plans. You've mentioned you're eager to get out of here, but how would you feel about coming to work with me? After seeing what you've been able to accomplish, I'm willing to bring you on as the Senior Vice President of Sustainability." He gets to another screen, and I hear the distinct whoosh of a sent message. "And to prove I'm serious, I've sent you the offer. Take a look. It's time to have another Carville on the team."

Another Carville.

I pull up the offer, trying to hide the tremor in my hand. Did I eat something bad this morning? Because I think I'm going to be sick. This is it. The thing I've been begging for and working toward for years. This is my chance to finally attach my work to the family name. My uncle sees enough value in me to bring me into the fold that Tag denied me so long.

The words of his will ring in my ears when he told me Sugar Maple Farms was mine: *I trust you'll know what to do.*

Those are the words he always said. After every Carville test, it was the same thing. For so long, the words felt like a taunt. What would he say about the sale? About Lawson offering to bring me on?

Did I pass his final test or fail completely?

I look up from Lawson's email and my eyes instantly catch on the pictures. So many pictures. Tag with his parents and grandparents. Some of my dad and Lawson, others of my cousins. But more than anyone else—more even than Tag and my grandmother—are pictures of me. Me in football, baseball, and basketball jerseys. Duke, Rusty, and me getting our first (and last) Boy Scout badge. Me at my Eighth Grade Promotion, in spite of the peach cobbler incident. My high school, college, and grad school graduations.

I am everywhere. In the room he spent more time than almost anywhere in the world, he chose to surround himself with pictures of me.

Tag Carville III.

His namesake.

And then I remember the picture next to his bedside. The picture he would have looked at just before he died.

The picture of us picking strawberries.

The memory hits me like a rock. I couldn't recall the conversation Tag and I had when Jane asked me about it—I vaguely remembered that he taught me about strawberries—but it all comes rushing back.

We'd walked through the strawberry fields with the workers. I'd seen plenty of strawberries on the farm. Dad would collect baskets of them when we stayed over. But I'd never thought about anything other than how they tasted.

But now, Papa was showing me the plants, pointing out how they worked, how they had temporary feeder roots meant to absorb nutrients as well as permanent, primary roots meant to transport them. "The thing about strawberries," he told me, "is that all they want to do is eat, grow, and clone themselves."

"Clone themselves?" That sounded so cool to my young mind.

He nodded. We crouched down, our knees resting on the dirt. The mild spring air smelled of soil and strawberries. "But they can't do any of it right until their roots have matured enough to support them. You with me?"

I was. I didn't have a head for ELA, but science had always made sense to me, and this was science. "The roots have to be strong before the plant can grow fruit and clone itself."

"Good," he said. "Establishing the roots is more important than bearing fruit this first year. To help the plant, we have to remove the flowers," he said, popping blossom after blossom from the strawberry plant, "and the runners." He pointed to the horizontal stems shooting out from the plant. Then he handed me a pair of scissors. The metal felt cool and heavy in my hand.

"Why not just cut off the flowers but let the runners grow so you can have more clones sooner?"

"Good question. We cut off the runners because they take energy that could be used to help the roots grow stronger.

Remember, the point of a strawberry plant isn't to take over the farm. The point is to bear fruit."

I looked at the long, skinny stems. All they wanted to do was grow. "Does it hurt the plant?"

"It's a living thing," he said. Which meant yes.

"I don't want to hurt it."

He breathed slowly and stood to his full height. He seemed larger than life to me. I couldn't see his expression, only the outline of his strong frame blocking the sun from my eyes.

"Every strawberry plant is a clone of another plant. You know what the difference is between the ones that thrive and the ones that don't?" I shook my head. "A gardener."

"I don't follow."

"There's two kinds of growth in this life. The kind where you grow however and whenever you want with no struggles. You may get big, but you won't have the roots to become anything but ground cover for other plants. You won't fulfill your purpose. Then there's the other kind. The kind where someone loves you enough to trim your runners and your blossoms while you're young so that you can become strong, so you can be trusted to bear good fruit. That's what the gardener is for."

I looked at the strawberry plant and squeezed my fingers around the garden shears. "I need to be the gardener."

He nodded "Only if you care enough about the plant to let it be what it's meant to be. Nothing can grow how it needs without a little pain. But by trimming the plant now, we can trust it to grow right in the future."

I put the scissors around the runner and snipped.

He squeezed my shoulder, and his words made my heart swell. "Attaboy."

Nothing can grow how it needs to without a little pain.

I think of that photo—of every photo around me—and the weight of doubt and the burden of disappointment fall from my shoulders. I think back to every Carville test, every situation that felt so enigmatic and infuriating at the time.

Tag was removing my flowers.

He was trimming my runners.

He was giving me the chance to let my roots grow until he could trust that I was strong enough to bear fruit. "Uncle Lawson, I've made a huge mistake."

Lawson leans back in his chair. "What do you mean?"

"Tag said in his will that he trusted that I'd know what to do with Sugar Maple Farms. I thought it was some final jab from beyond the grave, but now I think he meant that literally. I think he was trying to tell me that he had faith in me all this time. He believed in me."

"You didn't think he believed in you?"

"No. I felt like he was disappointed in me because he never told me otherwise. I thought each of his Carville tests were a chance to fail."

My mind skips to the summer when I was ten. We went back to that same field and picked strawberries from the plants we'd pruned and prepared. Their harvest was exactly what it should have been. We picked baskets upon baskets of strawberries. We worked for hours. And at the end of the day, Tag put his hands on both my shoulders and told me that I'd done good. The crinkle around his eyes was better than a trophy. He was never big on emotion, but I feel like a fool for having missed it before.

Tag loved me. I *know* Tag loved me.

I choke back emotion. "I was hurt and grieving, and I wished he'd given me more love and affection. But I think he did the best he could."

Lawson smiles and squeezes my shoulder. He's a couple of inches shorter than I am, but he's not a small man by any stretch. When he grips, I feel it. "Tripp, my boy, it's about time. My dad could be a hard man, but he loved you as much as he loved anyone. The 'Carville test' was his way of helping you find yourself, not become a clone of him. He wanted you to discover what it meant for *you* to be a Carville."

"He told you that?"

Lawson barks out a laugh. "Not even remotely. That's fifty-five years of life experience talking. I didn't say my dad made it easy, but he acted rationally from his own perspective. Tag had to struggle and fight for everything he got, and he was a better man for it. I imagine he thought the struggle would make everyone better. The problem was in him assuming that 'the struggle' should be the same for everyone. Your dad and I had each other and our mom to soften and interpret his approach. You didn't. On top of that, the Tag you knew wasn't the bold, risk-taking man who raised us. Your Tag was grieving and terrified. He was so hurt after losing his wife and son that he couldn't handle the thought of something happening to you. And yes, that part, he did tell me."

Tears well in my eyes. I've not thought much about how Tag was grieving all those years, too, only about how much *I* hurt.

"My dad stopped pushing the business and wanted to hold on to what he and Mom had built rather than expanding and innovating. Over the last few years where he took less of an active role in Carville Industries and focused more on the farm itself, we've grown more than we did in the ten years prior to that. But it means that the farm took a step back, too. Dad wanted to hold on to what he'd lost, and, I think, he wanted to get closer to you in his final years."

"And that's when I ran away."

"That's putting it a bit harshly, but yes. The more you retreated, the more he saw his mistake and wanted to be part of your life. He didn't know how, though. The farm was so big and empty without you that he started dating, and we both know what a disaster that was. He was lonely and too old school to know how to express it, even at the end. But he loved you, Tripp. Do you know what he told Jane when he hired her?" I shake my head. "She said he made her promise to turn the farm into the sort of place that *you* would want to grow old. You, Tripp. He loved you the best he knew how."

Our last conversation looks so different to me now. Tag telling me he saw my volunteer work differently, talking about picking strawberries. He was trying to tell me why he'd done the things he'd done. I don't know if he had a sense that that was our final conversation. I don't know if he talked to Jane first and then me or the other way around. But I know that in hiring Jane, he was doing everything he could to show me he loved me.

My chest heaves like I've been sobbing. The feeling of not being enough for my family has hung over me for twenty years. This newfound perspective doesn't erase the pain of my past, but it puts salve on each of those thousand wounds.

A picture of my parents with Tag catches my eye … and for the first time, I feel something different than anger and pain when I look at all three of their faces. Tag wasn't perfect. My parents were even less so. But their stories have shaped mine, whether I wanted them to or not. All I can do is try to take the best of them into myself and hopefully grow into something more. I can try to remember their successes and learn from their mistakes. The way I'm sure they want me to. The way I'll one day want *my* kids to.

I want that. I crave the idea of continuing the Carville name, of seeing my own kids surpass me. I want them to value hard work and stability and the occasional risk, and I want to do that all *here*. The place where Tag wanted me to grow old.

The place where I've fallen in love.

I need to talk to Jane.

Now.

"Uncle Lawson, I know I practically begged you for it, but I was wrong. Sugar Maple Farms isn't for sale."

Instead of disappointment or shock, something like pride

spreads over his lined features. "You're sure that's what you want?"

"I'm sure. I thought the only way I'd ever prove myself was to get as far away from here as possible, to do something huge like change the face of sustainability on a global scale. But I can do that here. I can become the best version of myself here. I don't need to change the world to change *my* world." Jane's tagline has never hit home as hard as it does now.

"And you think you'll be happy as the CEO of Sugar Maple Farms?"

Tears sting my eyes. "I know it. Thanks for coming all this way. I'm sorry to leave so unceremoniously, but I have to go tell someone very special the news."

His grin takes up half his face. "Say hi to Jane for me."

"I will." I grin and run out of the house. I try Jane's cell on the way to my truck.

She doesn't answer. The service on the farm is spotty, especially with storm clouds rolling in, so I tear through the gravel in my truck. I'd get on any harvester for driving so recklessly, the same way Tag used to get on me.

Pulling up to her cottage, I zip up to the front door and knock while the wind whips against me. I feel light. Free. Determined.

I am Tag Carville III, and I am proud of it.

I can be my best self here, and I'll be even better with Jane at my side...an epiphany that would be a lot more powerful if she would answer her door. I rap the door eagerly. "Jane! Open up!"

I try the door, hoping she'll forgive the intrusion, but when I get inside, it's empty.

Not just empty of Jane, empty of her things. I don't see her planner or laptop out. I don't see her keys or an elastic or a pair of earrings. I dart into her bedroom, bathroom, and back into the kitchen.

She's gone. Every trace of her is gone.

I pull up my phone to call Jane and see a few missed texts about calling her, about how she has big news.

And then there's one more. A long one that she sent when I was meeting with Lawson.

It doesn't read like a text; it reads like a letter. Panic writhes in my chest.

JANE: Tripp! Congrats on selling the farm to Carville Industries. We've accomplished a lot here, and I'm glad it's helped you get what you always wanted. I know we've been working on my not taking responsibility for everything, but I can't help but feel a bit responsible for your success. I've never been prouder. XOXO

"What the—" I try to call her again, but again get no answer. I try a third and fourth time, too.

She must have overheard my conversation with my uncle and found out my plan to sell. My guts wriggle like earthworms after the rain. Yet another thing I didn't talk to her about. She's been so patient with my reluctance to open up. What if this was the final straw?

I look around the empty but finished cottage where she left so many touches of herself. From the cheery colors to the fixtures to the flooring, there's not one part of this cottage that Jane didn't leave a mark on.

Yet the biggest mark she left is inside of me.

Is she really ... gone?

Is that why she kept texting me to call her? Was she ...

Was she breaking up with me?

She couldn't have left. She wouldn't.

I call Anita. "Do you know where Jane went? Her truck is here, but—"

"Oh, she asked Rusty to drive her to the airport."

"He *what*? I'm going to kill that traitor."

"Traitor? Tripp, what are you going on about?" Her voice crackles as the service cuts in and out.

"She's gone, Anita."

"I know. I just said he was taking her to the airport."

"No, I mean she's leaving! Her things aren't at Strawberry Fields anymore, and now she's flying back to Chicago? When did they leave?"

"Just a few minutes before you got out of your meeting with Lawson. You must have just missed each other. But Tripp—" Anita's voice cuts in and out. "Tri—"

The call goes silent.

"Anita?" I pull the phone away from my face to look at the screen. "Anita?"

A moment later, my screen shows CALL FAILED.

I slam a hand on the steering wheel then hold on tight as I take too quick a turn on the gravel road. My tires cut through the gravel, sending me to the opposite side of the road before I can crank my wheel and correct course.

Jane was right. It's time to pave *all* the roads.

I try calling Rusty this time, but the call doesn't go through. I can't believe Rusty took her without talking to me. Not like I would want him to outright stop or control her if she's seriously leaving, but a little heads-up couldn't hurt. Some subtle sabotage, like faking car trouble. Or, hey, maybe a warning to his best friend, especially when he knows how I feel about her.

How I love her.

I love Jane Harrington.

And I won't lose her without a fight.

CHAPTER TWENTY-SIX

TRIPP

J'm ripping through Sugar Maple at a dangerous speed, but I don't care. I roll through stop signs, push the bounds of "yield," and peel out on green. A raindrop slaps the center of my windshield followed by another. When a group of tourist takes a crosswalk, I jam on the brakes to keep from running into them. I'm pounding on my steering wheel, as if that will speed them up, when I notice my traitorous friend among a sea of women: one with four-inch stilettos and a high ponytail of jet-black hair. Another has on Kelly green octagonal glasses and a lion's mane of tight brown curls. I spot an ethereal blonde woman and an unnaturally wise redhead. And in the middle of them is the most gorgeous woman I've ever seen, grinning and pointing at the diner across the street.

"Jane?" I yell. She doesn't turn. Of course she doesn't turn. The wind is howling and my window is rolled up. I crank it at warp speed. "Jane! Rusty!"

Heads turn toward me at the same time that a horn honks

behind me. "Get a move on, Carville!" Mrs. Beaty yells from her Oldsmobile. "If I'm late for canasta, you and I will have some words."

I wave and stick my head out the window. "Sorry, Mrs. Beaty." My face feels like I have a sunburn as Jane and her friends smirk. "Wait right there!" I yell at them as I pull into the first available parking spot on Maple Street.

"Right here? In the middle of the road?" Jane sasses, and the urge to kiss her is overwhelming. How can I want to kiss her after that text? It was so cold and impersonal, and it felt more like a breakup than an actual congratulations. I slam my truck door and run across the street to her. In my periphery, I catch more than one man eyeing them, and I get it. Jane is stunning, and her friends aren't too far off. They look like they could be the cast of a movie.

But I only have eyes for Jane. And a mind for punching Rusty.

"What are you doing here?" I ask her before turning to my friend and punching his shoulder much softer than I want to. Another few raindrops fall, hitting my face and arms. "And thanks a lot for the heads up, Benedict Arnold."

Rusty slugs me back. "What did I do?"

"Yeah, what did he do?" Jane asks, getting in between us and sticking her hands on her hips in a way that makes me feel crazy. The more obstinate she is, the more I miss her, and she's not even gone.

Is she?

She had Rusty take her to the airport to pick up her friends, that much is clear. Still, that text wasn't the text of someone staying. Did they come out to help her pack? Did Anita request some sort of exit meeting?

Am I losing her?

No.

I'll do anything, tell her everything, to make her stay.

"Why don't we take this show of manliness somewhere less wet," Millie says. It's only sprinkling, but the dark clouds ahead tell me it won't stay that way for long.

"Hold up. I like seeing hot dudes fight in the rain," Ash says, and I can't help but snort when she winks at me. Millie directs everyone under an awning in front of Nico's thrift store.

Jane looks at me like I'm a puzzle. "Tripp, this is the famous, Parker, and the equally famous Lou, who, you can see, is not a round bald man in a pinstripe suit."

Lou lifts her light eyebrows. "Huh. That ain't the worst compliment I've ever received."

"And I prefer *infamous*," Parker says with a look that I could easily believe hides lasers.

"Sorry, where are my manners?" It takes a Herculean effort for me to calmly shake hands with Parker and Lou and give Ash and Millie hugs when all I want to do is drop to my knees and beg Jane not to leave me. We exchange pleasantries, and I ask them if I can steal Jane for a second. I can't keep the urgency from my face as I take her arm and pull her a few yards away into the alley. The others walk into Nico's to keep cool and dry. The buildings protect us from some of the rain, but the heat would have my shirt sticking to me even if the skies were clear.

"I got your text."

She swallows. "I wish you'd have told me."

"Yeah, and I wish you'd have broken up with me in person instead of text—"

"Excuse me?" Her eyebrows practically jump off her head. "You're the one leaving me!"

I grab her arms. "I would never leave you!"

"Tripp, I overheard you and Lawson. I came by to tell you that I booked the Beauchamps wedding, and I heard Lawson offer to purchase Sugar Maple Farms. Apparently it's everything you've always wanted." The emphasis she puts on it sounds word for word how I put it.

"You don't understand." I see the fire roar in Jane before I realize what I've said. "No, not like that! I mean, you didn't get the whole story." I rub my hand across my face. "Can we sit down? Somewhere with air conditioning?"

"I'm comfortable," she says. Sweat beads on her forehead, mingling with the occasional raindrop, but I know her well enough to know she means it. The weather doesn't bother her. If anything, she seems to enjoy watching me sweat.

"If you're comfortable, I'm comfortable." Her challenging look is a bit too smug after a text that may as well have said *I'm breaking up with you.* "Listen, I was wrong. That's the short of it. I thought I wanted to run as fast and far from the farm as I could, but it turns out that I've just been a hurt idiot who didn't realize that my papa loved me."

She puts a hand over her heart, as if something I said touched her deeply. "You called him Papa instead of Tag."

"Not the point." Her eyes widen. "Sorry! I mean, yes, I'm working through some issues, but I really don't want to talk about that right now!" And now her wide eyes narrow, but I can't stop myself. "Please don't leave, Jane. I love you. I know I've been insecure and all over the place, but I want to be with you. I told Lawson I couldn't sell the farm. You showed me how much I belong here. You made me fall in love with this place again. I don't want to leave it unless you do, in which case I'll go wherever you want to go, but I want to stay, and I want to stay here with you."

"You kind of buried the lede there, pal."

"Pardon?" It's all the manners I can spare.

Her lips spread into a smile that could stop the sun. "You love me?"

Her smile is agony. "You're killing me with the mixed messages here, Jane." I shake my head, flicking rain and sweat all over the place. I'm dying, and she's grinning like a pageant queen. "You disappear, send me some sort of veiled goodbye, yet here you are acting like you won the lottery after hearing me tell you I love you?"

"The lottery? Someone thinks highly of himself."

"Jane!"

"I'm not breaking up with you, you giant goofball. I was processing a lot of emotions and couldn't think of another way to say it, okay? I signed the note XOXO, for heaven's sake. Like I'd do that if I was breaking up with you."

Hope jumps like grasshoppers in my belly. "So when you go back to Chicago we'll do long distance?" It's not enough, but if it's all I can get, I'll take it.

"I haven't talked to my friends yet or anything," she says, her nose scrunching, "but I'm not going anywhere anytime soon."

I reach a tentative hand out to take hers. She threads her fingers through mine, and the grasshoppers become a swarm. "But Strawberry Fields was empty."

"Because Anita is having the exterior painted. Do you ever check your email? I'm staying in the B&B. Ringing any bells?"

"Oh … right. Of course," I say, shaking my head. I tug Jane close and she wraps her arms around my waist. My chest swells at the feeling. I hold her so firmly, I'm not sure I'll ever let go. "Tell me."

"Tell you what?" She bites back a smile.

"That you love me. That you want to stay."

"Oh that?" She rolls her eyes playfully. "Old news."

"Tell me."

"You don't need more external validation. Isn't it enough to know that Tag loved you? Isn't it enough to love yourself?"

"JANE."

She snakes her hands around my neck and pulls my face down toward hers. We're forehead to forehead, nose to nose, and her lips smell like Cherry ChapStick. "I love you and I'm staying as long as you want me."

The rain falls on us, streaming down our faces. "I want you forever," I say before our mouths crash into each other.

"In that case, it's a good thing we have an appointment to look at the office space down the street," a woman's voice says. Our lips break apart, but I tighten my grip on Jane. She doesn't let go, but she does gasp.

"What?"

All of Jane's friends are standing under umbrellas, watching us with knowing looks. Whether they're smirking at us or at the news, I'm not sure. "Nothing's set in stone, but it's the practical choice," Parker says, smoothing her pristine ponytail. I don't know how she hasn't twisted an ankle in those heels in this rain, but she looks as comfortable as Jane does barefoot. "The rent on our space in Chicago is over triple what it would be in Sugar Maple, to say nothing of our loft. The lease would start October first, which would give us plenty of time to figure out details. If it didn't work out after the year, we could reevaluate then. If it did ... " Parker lifts her shoulders, and when Jane shifts, I let go. She runs to her friends and gives them a wet hug that not even Parker seems to mind. There's a lot of laughing and at least a few sniffs. I watch them a bit awestruck.

These women care so much about each other that they would leave their home, move a thousand miles, and set up shop across the country just to support a friend. Or is there more to it? Whatever the reason, I'm happier than ever as Jane gestures me over. When I reach her, she presses her face into my soaking wet chest and laughs while her friends insist that they get out of the rain.

"I'm starving. Diner please?" Ash asks. Her curls are, if possible, getting bigger in the humidity. "You guys coming with us?"

Jane clears her throat in a loud *ahem*. "How many times do I have to tell you? It's either *y'all* or *all y'all* if you're talking to a group, thank you very much." Lou whoops while the others groan, but Jane's voice vibrates deep into my chest.

Suddenly, I want her friends gone. Not forever, just … gone. I catch Jane feeling the muscles in my back, so I flex to make it easier for her to distinguish. When she makes a hungry sound, a fire flares inside me. I want to pick her up, carry her deeper into the alley, and get back to the business of making up.

"Fine. Are *all y'all* coming?" Ash says with a shameless grin that says she knows we're not.

"Not even a little," I say before Jane can reply. I scoop her up and give them a nod. "Good seein' you. Come by the house when y'all are done and we'll show you around. Rusty, I forgive you for not answering when I was panicked that you were taking the love of my life away from me." Rusty nods, the patience of Job on display. "You're a better friend than I deserve."

I kiss Jane's neck, and she leans into me. "Sorry, I love you guys and I am so thankful that you're moving across country for me—"

"Not just for you," Parker says, eyeing Millie. "But no need to send us away twice. We'll catch up with you two later."

Jane and I are already kissing when we wave goodbye.

CHAPTER TWENTY-SEVEN

JANE

"So, if I'm going to stay in Sugar Maple, I'll need a new place to live," I say on the drive back to the farm. I'm plastered to Tripp's side—a little too literally, with how wet we are from making out in the rain. The closeness allows me to kiss his neck, and only fear of him crashing keeps me from nibbling on his ear. My man is ticklish with a capital T.

He side eyes me. "I'll put a ring on that finger soon enough."

I back up enough to take him in. "Did you *want* that to sound like a threat?"

He glares, and I bite back a giggle. I love sparring with him more than I've ever loved getting along with anyone. "You know what I meant."

"Yeah I do. *Or else.*"

He kisses my forehead. "I love you and that sassy mouth of yours. Now can I tell you my proposal ... my *idea*, I mean?"

"I'd rather hear about the proposal."

"Jane," he growls, putting his hand playfully over my mouth.

I bite it just hard enough to appreciate the fact that his muscles extend all the way to his fingers. "Hush that gorgeous mouth for a minute, will you? You should take Tag's house. Not the farmhouse; his actual house on the other side of town, across the river. It has five bedrooms, four bathrooms, a pool. Duke and his ex rented it before his own house got finished. The Janies would have plenty of space, and it may make it easier for you to convince them all to stay after the year."

"I don't think we could afford the rent."

"Oh, stop. Like I'd charge y'all rent."

"My friends won't live anywhere for free."

"Wouldn't dream of it. I'll have them pay the utilities, taxes, fees, and maintenance costs. Duke modernized it a fair amount, but his ex had all the warmth of a copperhead in a snowstorm. It could probably use some personal touches, and the cost of that could be on y'all, if you want."

We're almost at the main house, which I've been itching to personalize since our first kiss. *Give it time*, I tell myself. It's hard not to be overeager, though. With Tripp's arm around me, I feel safer and freer than I've ever felt, even knowing where we're heading, knowing that if all goes according to plan, my responsibilities will only increase, professionally and personally. I have visions of growing Sugar Maple Farms into something unique and world class, of making the town a tourist destination even separate from the farm; I have dreams of filling the farm with kids, little Tripps and Janes who will run around and leave a trail of mayhem the size of a cornfield in their wake.

With Tripp helping me shoulder the load, I'm pretty sure I can do anything.

EPILOGUE
TWO MONTHS LATER

JANE

"*T*ake your places." Parker's voice sounds from my walkie-talkie. I scatter along with her other minions. The Beauchamps wedding is still a week away, and the rehearsal dinner *should* be six days away, but Parker insisted on holding a rehearsal of the rehearsal dinner, catering and stand-in guests included.

Have I mentioned how much my girl loves running events?

While Parker is wearing a black dress that clings to her fabulously, she got the rest of us new dresses for the occasion, so we're running around in these pretty, flouncy, impractical works of art when all I want is to be wearing sneakers or— better yet—to be barefoot. I know for a fact that this grass feels like spongy, dewy heaven on my feet. But I wouldn't dream of upsetting her on a night like this. She's right that the Beauchamps wedding needs to be perfect, so I can forgive some of her neuroticism, even if it's mildly annoying.

And even if I'm just the tiniest bit jealous.

When I see him and his friends dressed in suits on the lawn, that feeling intensifies. In a navy suit tailored perfectly to his body, Tripp makes James Bond look like a kid wearing his dad's tux.

A handful of guests from town are speaking to Tripp, and nearby, rows of tables have been set up for the reception. While sugar maples dot the lawn, the famous sugar maple from the label is picture perfect. Its leaves have turned a deep, rich red. The breeze that rustles through the branches whispers promises of forever.

It's the most romantic setting I've ever seen. I understand now why Tag was so eager to have weddings happen here again. As much as I would hate having to plan something like this, being able to show up for it would be a dream come true.

Ash and Rusty are standing in for the happy couple, and Ash is hamming it up as much as I would expect. She and Rusty have become friends over the last couple of months, and it's been fun to see his shell soften with her. Ash acts as Rusty's translator, interpreting his looks into conversation and including him seamlessly. His parents stand by him as if this were the real thing, though. He has his mother's warm tan skin and long, straight nose, and he has his father's eyes and blond hair, though Rusty's is floppier. His parents are both attractive, but where Rusty's hazel eyes have flecks of green that look like the start of spring, his father's eyes have specks of brown that warn of a dust storm on the horizon.

This isn't a real wedding, though, so they aren't my problem tonight. Or ever, really. I'm working hard on not taking responsibility of every issue I encounter. It's hard, but it's worth it. My sister even called last week to ask me for advice about savings accounts.

"Isn't it magical?" Millie asks as she floats up to me. She's holding her walkie talkie in one hand and a chic white tumbler in the other. She takes a sip through the metal straw.

"Diet Coke?" I ask.

"What else would it be—water?" She fakes a shudder before moving into her place inside.

Peeking into the white barn, I marvel at how it's more beautiful than I even imagined. Sheer curtains are pulled open at the barn doors, and inside, strings of Edison lights dangle from the barn's rafters along with paper lanterns, combining an industrial look with a classic, feminine touch. Anita and Booker preside where the pastor will be, and they peer over the guests. Anita smiles demurely while Booker's teeth are bright against his umber skin.

"Ladies and gentlemen," Booker's deep voice calls, "please gather together in the barn for the main event."

I back up to allow people to walk in. It's my job to make sure that guests are in their seats for the dry run. Tripp's strong hand spreads across my lower back, and he whispers in my ear. "Ready to go in?"

I lean against him, warmth radiating from the center of my chest through my body. Ash and Rusty have disappeared and should be making their entrance any minute. Parker cues everything up but when she calls on Rusty, he doesn't show.

"Rusty? Rusty!" she hisses. Then, "Tripp, go take his place. I need to time this out so it goes flawlessly."

Tripp kisses me and runs around the barn to slip into Rusty's place. Seeing him up there in his suit makes my heart hammer like a runaway train. I'm more than happy with how things are going with us, but I knew months ago that I wanted to be with him forever. Lately, I've felt like I'm waiting for forever to start. I told my friends I'd happily marry him at the courthouse, and they jokingly filled out a wedding license application and told me they'd mail it to Tripp. In truth, I would be relieved to get married in the courthouse. Worrying about managing so many people's emotions and expectations would probably break my brain.

The wedding march starts, but I don't see Ash anywhere, another part of my job. I radio Parker. "I think we've lost Ash."

"Why does the universe hate me?" Parker asks with a growl. "Will you run into the bride's room and figure out what's going on? I have to see if we have clearing for a dress along the aisles, and I want to see just how much dirt and grass it collects. I'm not sure we trimmed the lawn down enough. Fast, please?"

I roll my eyes but do as she asks. I may take on the emotional burdens of the world, but she takes on its to-do list.

The bridal cabin is only a few dozen yards away, so I'm there quickly. But Ash is not. "Ash? Where are you?"

"I'm in the bathroom. I, uh, think I ate something..." She moans, and I call Parker and tell her the news.

"Are you kidding? Jane, get that dress on now and get out here!"

I unzip the bag and pull out the most stunning dress I've ever seen. It's a long-sleeved lace dress that fits tight to the natural waist and then has a slight flare out to the train. It's a bit more rustic than vintage, and it's perfect.

It's my dream dress.

I haven't let myself look at dresses, because once I start planning, I won't rest until Tripp and I are married. But if I'd started looking, I know down to my core that this is the dress I would pick. I put it on and manage to zip it up most of the way when Millie comes in.

"What is taking so long?" she asks before gasping. Her eyes fill up with tears. "Oh Jane!" She runs over and zips me the rest of the way up.

"Don't gush or you'll have me weeping with envy!"

"Right," she says, blinking away her expression. "The dress is too short with those heels. You're going to have to go barefoot. And here," she says, adding a bit of lipstick and putting flowers in my crown braid. The rest of my long hair is down in loose curls. I hold my breath as I watch the effect of those flowers. "May as well show Tripp what he's missing in waiting so long."

I look myself over and am filled with both excitement and longing. In creating this dry run of a dress rehearsal, Parker has unwittingly planned my dream wedding. And Millie's little touches, from my hair down to my bare feet, make my chest ache to be a bride. Tripp's bride.

Today isn't about me, though, and while that thought comes with envy, it also comes with the relief of months or years of planning I didn't have to worry about. So I dutifully make my way out of the bridal cabin and over to the lawn where Parker is waiting. She's changed into a simple, flowy dress like the ones Millie and I were wearing, probably to match some vision she has in her head of the Beauchamps' big day.

"Well, sweetie, here we are," she says in her best impersonation of a doting father. I laugh and link arms with my petite friend. "Stop taking such long strides, you giantess," she teases.

"I thought I was supposed to be rushing down the aisle."

"Not until the music starts, and then walk to the beat. Oh, and here," she says, handing me a bouquet that belongs in a magazine under "rustic wedding chic."

"Wow. You didn't spare a single detail on this, did you?"

"Have you seen the budget they gave us for the rehearsal? I'm embarrassed I only did this much."

The music starts, and she flashes a nervous smile that gives me butterflies. Together, we walk down the aisle. I catch the faces of friends and loved ones, including...

"Is that my sister?" My beautiful sister Meghan is sheepish but smiling as she waves at me.

"She came down for a vacation to surprise you. Just smile." Parker says through her teeth.

Try as I might, I can't smile, though, because this is starting to feel too real. Everything I could have wanted is here, now, and it's not even for me.

But then I see Tripp staring at me with tears in his eyes, and nothing else matters. It doesn't matter if our wedding is tomorrow in the courthouse or next year at a beach house. We're on the right path. And like Millie said, this is clearly showing him what he's missing.

Parker kisses my cheek and stands to the side, and then I see Ash standing with Millie and Parker. And Lou. Lou, who's supposed to be in Nashville in two hours. And they're wearing identical dresses. I look over to Tripp and notice Rusty and all of Tripp's cousins standing next to him in matching suits. And is that Lawson and Jolene? Suspicion takes hold of me and squeezes a fist around my heart. Duke's not here, thanks to his NFL schedule, or I would be even more suspicious.

"Tripp, what's going on?" My hands tremble as he takes them. He's trembling a bit, too.

I wait for Booker to run through the practice lines, but instead, he's looking at Tripp expectantly.

"I didn't know it was possible for me to fall more in love with you, but here I am," he says, still misty-eyed. "I wasn't sure if this would work, but Parker assured me she could pull it off, and she did."

I glance back at Parker with a questioning gaze. She gestures to me to turn around, and when I do, tears spill down my face. Because Tripp is down on one knee, holding a ring in front of him.

"Jane Harrington, since the first moment I laid eyes on you, I was through. I wanted to run away with you before I even knew why you were here. Seeing you closing your eyes, enjoying the hot sun and breeze, I knew you were the sort of woman a man would have to earn the right to be with. And you've proved that a hundred times over. I don't want to go another day without fighting with you, and I don't want to go another night without making up. Will you marry me?"

All the hope, emotion, and love in my heart burst out of me.

"Are you kidding me? Yes! Of course it's a yes!" I bend down and grab his face, kissing those delicious lips of his. But Tripp leans back too quickly. He isn't done.

"I meant will you marry me ... now?"

My eyes jump between his as I try to process what he's saying. He has never looked as handsome as he does with his eyes pooling with vulnerability and emotion. I love him better than ever. "*Now* now? But Duke—"

"Knows and gives us his blessing, even if he's sad to miss. He'll wipe his tears with rolls of hundred-dollar bills." Rusty chuckles behind Tripp. Still on his knees, Tripp's eyes twinkle. "Jane, this could either be an engagement party or a wedding, whatever *you* choose. I'm easy like that."

I'm shaking as I laugh breathily. "Oh, are you?"

"Yeah. I took the liberty of inviting everyone you care about on the off chance that it could actually work."

"Naturally. No big deal. It's just the rest of our lives, and everything."

"Exactly. I knew you'd get it." He grins, like he loves how I'm sassing him. "Parker helped me arrange everything, and the others took care of the dresses and kept track of everything you've sighed at over the last few months." His smile softens into something so open, it takes my breath away. "I hope we did it right."

Tears fall freely down my cheeks. I look at his earnest, strong, loving face and then to the faces of the people I love most in the world, people who knew I could never handle the emotional toll of planning my wedding, so they did it for me. I'm overcome with emotion.

"Tripp, for years, I didn't feel safe to make a mistake. I couldn't relax, couldn't shrug without worrying that I'd drop the load I was carrying. I was too scared about the fallout for everyone else to say what I wanted to say or act how I wanted to act. From the first day, you've let me be my stubborn, ornery, delightful self, and you've shown me how much what I want matters. I will spend my whole life proving to you that *you* matter. You have been enough for me since our first conversation. So this will be the easiest answer I've ever given," I say, crouching down in front of him so we're eye to eye. "I would marry you here or there, I would marry you anywhere. I will marry you, Tripp Carville. I will marry you, yes I will."

Tripp laughs hard enough that he's shaking. "You had to answer me in Dr. Seuss, didn't you?"

"Yes, yes I did."

"Because I hate Sam-I-Am?"

"That is correct."

He chuckles an "I love you," that has me glowing. Then he puts the ring on my finger and springs upward, taking me with him. I whoop and put my arms around his neck as he swings me in a big circle. "We're getting married, y'all! Right now!"

Everyone laughs and cheers, and no one more so than Tripp and me. After we kiss each other's faces off for a sec, we take a minute to hug our friends and family. Then Booker clears his throat. "I didn't get ordained for nothing," he booms. "Everyone, take your seats! The real show starts now."

Tripp and I stand across from each other, holding hands and grinning like the fools in love we are. We already gave our vows, whether we planned to or not, and we've already given our hearts. Next up, the rest of our lives.

And I can't wait.

THE END

BONUS EPILOGUE

MILLIE

I'm not one to kick off my shoes after walking in heels for hours. It's not about suffering for beauty, it's about buying shoes that don't feel like torture instruments, and yes, they do exist, if you have the patience to look and ... okay, if you have the money.

I do not have the money, but thanks to my people-person-personality, I do have a vast network of vintage and luxury consignment store owners who hook me up whenever a size seven finds its way to them. Or a size five, because I'm all about helping Parker, too. She's the only one of my friends who appreciates a good four-inch heel. And boy, does she make them look good.

She's dancing in the barn with one of Tripp's super dreamy cousins. The three men have done their duty and danced with each of us, but the total lack of spark left me wanting a Diet Coke and a chair. I have both now, and I'm content to watch my friends enjoy themselves, especially Tripp and Jane, who look so in love, it actually hurts me.

All right, maybe I'm not so content to watch them, because I want this for myself. I've dreamed of being married and being a mom since I was a kid. Every game I used to play—every last one—ultimately ended in me falling in love and getting married and having babies.

One removed ovary and a ton of radiation later, having babies biologically isn't in the cards, which was a non-starter for my ex. Or non-finisher, I guess. When we got serious and he finally let it sink in that we would become parents through adoption, not biology, he split.

I cursed him out at the time, and I think he's wrong, but I'm grateful he left when he did. It's a personal decision, and it's one I made after graduating with my master's in social work, when my body went to war with me. I've never cared about *how* I became a mom, just that it happened, preferably sooner rather than later and with someone whose heart is as open as mine is.

My biological clock is ticking, even without the biological part.

Which is why it is acutely bittersweet when I see the little girl who stole my heart a few months ago sitting with a beautiful blonde woman. Lottie has darker coloring and features, which makes me think she must have inherited them from her dad. Tripp and even Jane have kept quiet about Lottie's family, but clinically speaking, I'm sure something is going on there. Maybe her parents fight a lot or maybe they're separated, but she has textbook anxiety, specifically separation anxiety. It's one of those buzzwords constantly associated with toddlers and preschoolers. All kids go through that phase, but I'm sure hers is pathological, not merely a stage. Even now with her mom, she's clinging and won't let go. I hope her mom won't mind my coming over.

I tap on the woman's shoulder and say, "Hi, I'm sorry to interrupt. I'm a friend of Jane and Tripp's and met Lottie a couple of months ago. She is the sweetest thing, and I wanted to say hi."

Lottie lets go of her mom's shirt and lunges at me. "Miwwie!"

I rock back a little but hold her firm, rubbing her back as she squeals and clings to me. Her mom's eyes pop. "Oh, so *you're* Miwwie."

"Millie," I correct.

She snorts and speaks in a Southern accent milder than either Tripp's or Lou's. "I've heard your name a couple hundred times in the last couple of months. In fact, she only just stopped asking after you."

With Lottie's arms around me, my chest feels too small for my rapidly growing heart. "I don't know if I should be flattered or apologetic."

She pats the seat next to me and pushes it enough that I can easily drop in with Lottie on my lap. "Apologetic. You were all she talked about for a while. Even more than Peppa Pig or Bluey, and if you don't know what that means, replace it with whatever sport your boyfriend cares most about, and you'll have an inkling."

I laugh and boop Lottie on the nose when she releases my neck for a split second. She giggles and comes back in for another hug.

I breathe deeper than I have in months holding Lottie. Her head presses against my cheek and chin, and I feel complete in a way I can't explain. I know not everyone feels this burning desire for motherhood, but it is as innate as my red hair and freckles. On the other hand, the beautiful woman in front of me looks relieved to have a break. Which I'm sure is also totally innate to motherhood, no matter how deeply you longed for a child. "So you know of me, but I didn't catch your name, sorry."

She reaches her hand out to shake mine. "Reese. Good to

meet you." She looks around. "Would you actually mind holding Lottie just for a minute? I need to pee like a racehorse."

It's official. I adore this woman.

"I'd love to." To Lottie, I say, "Momma's going to run to the restroom. Do you mind staying with me while she goes?"

"Oh, no, I'm her aunt. Her mom is ... *not in the picture*," she mouths, and suddenly it all makes sense.

"Is her dad here?" I whisper.

"Work trip," she whispers back.

I hold Lottie closer. Situations like this are tough. With one absent parent and one having to travel for work, Lottie's dealing with more than any three-year-old is equipped to handle. My heart aches for her.

While I'm playing horsey rides with Lottie, Ash comes and joins me. She and Rusty were planning to take Lou to the airport right after the ceremony, but Lou hired a car and split before she could do more than blow kisses at us. Lou's identity is a closely guarded secret, so no one begrudged her running out. We're pretty used to it by now.

With a Diet Coke, a cute kid in my arms, and a best friend at my side, I know how lucky I am. Even if I want more.

"Come to Aunty Ash," Ash tells Lottie. "I'll put you on my back and we'll go spin circles around all the cute boys out there."

"My daddy is the cutest boy. Aw-most as cute as Uncle Rusty," Lottie says, looking like the physical embodiment of the heart eye emoji. "I'm going to marry him."

"Uncle Rusty is pretty cute," Ash says. She's almost as protective of Rusty as she is of her own brothers. "I approve."

The lights strung around the barn twinkle in Lottie's metallic brown eyes. She puts her hands on my cheeks and squeezes as she peers deep into my soul. "Can you be my new mommy?"

I puff my cheeks out and she pushes them back in. "I don't even know your daddy, sweetheart."

"He's good at footbaw and good at whooshing."

I swap glances with Ash, who snickers. "What's whooshing?"

"Whooshing is whooshing me in the air five or seven times or maybe two times and throwing me onto the beanbag. Sometimes ten times and sometimes he whooshes me with a twist."

Ash laughs uncontrollably behind Lottie's back. "I love a guy who whooshes with a twist."

I kick her under the table, and she only laughs harder. Lottie's aunt returns then and asks what's so funny. "Miwwie is going to marry Daddy so he can give her whooshes. He's going to whoosh her ten times a day."

Ash laughs so hard, she falls out of her chair. Reese smirks. "I think your daddy is done whooshing anyone for a while, honey bun. Now it's time for you to give Uncle Tripp and Aunty Jane a big hug so we can get you to bed."

Reese tries to wrench Lottie from my arms, but Lottie's vice grip won't ease up. "Why don't I walk you and your aunt to the car, sweetie?" Reese mutters thanks and grabs the diaper bag. The *Gucci* diaper bag.

The three of us walk out to the parking lot together, and I almost tear up when I realize Lottie is asleep on my shoulder. The smell of the apples from the orchard fills my senses, reminding me of the apple tree in my backyard growing up. Nostalgia combined with longing is a powerful cocktail of emotion.

"What a relief," Reese says. I put Lottie down carefully into her car seat and Reese buckles her up without so much as a whimper. "Once she's out, she is *out*. She'll wake up in her bed tomorrow, none the wiser of how she got there." She puts the diaper bag at Lottie's feet before closing the door. "Thanks again. You made her night, even if I suspect I'll hear your name about a thousand more times before her dad gets home."

I have so many questions about her dad. He feels more myth than man, like a spy or secret agent, or something. Or maybe he's just a deadbeat who everyone is too embarrassed to acknowledge. No, that doesn't add up. Tripp, Rusty, and their friends are all quality men ... and, fine, I'll say it: they're hot. Lottie is Tripp's goddaughter, which means her dad is probably Tripp's best friend.

The best friend of my best friend's husband is destined to be hot, right?

Stop it, Millie. Don't start fixating on the mystery father of the little girl you've fallen in love with. It's unhealthy. Also weird.

With a final glance at a sleeping Lottie, I say goodbye to Reese and make my way back to the reception. One of Tripp's cousins—Westin? Westley?—asks me to dance, and although I didn't feel a spark the first time he asked, I say yes.

If I want to have everything I've ever dreamed of, I have to be willing to take some chances. Like saying yes to a handsome, interested, available man.

Even if I'm thinking of a man I've never met.

Want more of Millie, Lottie, and Duke? Baby Llama Drama releases Fall of 2023!

Want exclusive bonus content? Stay in the know with all things Sweet as Sugar Maple *by signing up for my newsletter: www.katewatsonbooks.net/newsletter*

ACKNOWLEDGMENTS

Switching from traditional publishing to indie was a leap of faith I could only make thanks to an incredible community of supportive, brilliant authors. Jenny Proctor, thank you for giving me the first nudge and for all the straight talk and advice when I was debating my next move. Melanie Jacobson and Kaylee Baldwin, bless you and that delightful six hour lunch. Melanie, Kaylee, and Ranee, thanks for graciously answering my seven thousand and eleven questions. My fabulous beta readers and dear friends: Sara Larson, Katie Nelson, Gina Denny, Kaylee, and Ranee. You are all amazing, and I'm so thankful to have your eyes on my goods (my *literary* goods. This is a clean and wholesome book, people! Minds out of the gutter!).

Becky Wallace, editor and brain twin (thank you, Vulcan Mind Meld!), thank you for being such a glorious word nerd and delightful friend! You're the McGwire to my Canseco. Except without the snitching. Or steroids.

To my super hot husband whose love language is "not talking about love languages," thanks for your endless love and faith in me. Kids, thank you for putting up with a mom who will never be Bluey's mom but who tries as hard as possible to make sure you know how wholly loved you are.

To my readers, old and new, thank you for coming on this journey with me.

And as always, I thank God for making everything possible.

ABOUT THE AUTHOR

Kate Watson is a fan of cheeky romantic comedies and delightfully witty banter. Originally from Canada, she attended college in the States and holds a BA in Philosophy from Brigham Young University. A lover of travel, speaking in accents, and experiencing new cultures, she has also lived in Israel, Brazil, the American South, and she now calls Arizona home.

She started writing at six years old and sold her first book, "The Heart People," for $0.25 to her parents. It received rave reviews. Since then, she's written many books, including the acclaimed Off Script, a 2020 Junior Library Guild selection. She writes stories full of heart, humor, and happily-ever-afters.

She is currently living her own happily-ever-after with her super cute husband and their four wild and wonderful kids. She runs on caffeine, swoons, and Jesus.

facebook.com/katewatsonauthor
instagram.com/katewatsonbooks

Made in the USA
Las Vegas, NV
15 September 2024